Out and Loud

Songwriters Series Book 3

Ali Spooner

Out and Loud

Songwriters Series
Book 3

Ali Spooner

2023

Out and Loud
Songwriters Series Book Three
© 2023 by Ali Spooner

Affinity E-Book Press NZ LTD
Canterbury, New Zealand

1st Edition

ISBN: 978-1-99-104012-1 (paperback)

Editor: Angela Koenig
Proof Editor: Lisa M
Cover Design: Irish Dragon Design
Production Design: Affinity Publication Services

ACKNOWLEDGMENTS

I thank my fans for following my stories and providing great feedback and encouragement. Writing wouldn't be so much fun without you. I appreciate the frequent reminders to work on the next book in your favorite series and promise to get back to them soon. Thanks to Affinity, Irish Dragon, for the cover art and the great team of editors, readers, and publishers who continue to help me grow as a writer.

DEDICATION

To the three best siblings I could ever ask for. L.A., Lynn, and Bubba. I love you most!

TABLE OF CONTENTS

PROLOGUE

The Bentleys, a new country band formed in Nashville, have completed the final review of their second album, *Midnight in Nashville*, and their second music video. The Covid-19 pandemic has halted all live performances and tour dates, so the group has taken advantage of additional studio time to record the new album. Stone Watson, one of the group's writers, has returned to Florida to spend the Christmas holidays with his wife and daughter, while the rest of the group celebrates at Ma Bentley's boarding house with Hank Tyler, the father of the group's other writer, Cedra.

CHAPTER ONE

Cedra, Juliet, and Hank sat around the kitchen table while Ma taught Keith how to make oatmeal and chocolate chip cookies.

"My mom used this recipe off the Quaker box for years. I could hardly wait until they came out of the oven," Keith told them as he stirred the chocolate chips into the mixture.

"I bet you burned your mouth on them several times," Juliet teased.

"Don't you know it," Keith answered. "Where'd Wayne get off to?"

"I think he may be upstairs working on a song," Cedra replied. "I saw his head bobbing while we ate dinner. That usually means he's got music in his head."

"I think it's great that you all have committed to writing," Hank said. "You did great on your songs for *Midnight*."

Juliet placed her hand on Cedra's shoulder. "I think we all have Cedra to thank for that. She was relentless in insisting we could all write."

"Thankfully so," Ma agreed. "Look what it produced."

Cedra nodded. "I agree. This album is even better than the first."

"You think so?" Juliet asked.

"Maybe not better, but a different sound," Cedra added.

"I think it's the confidence factor," Hank replied. "With the first album done, you all seem much more confident now that you know that you have a great sound together."

"I think that is spot on." Ma watched Keith closely. "You aren't tentative or afraid to try something different. You understand the sound you want to create, and it comes more naturally." Ma nodded to Keith. "You done mixing?"

"Yes ma'am." He grinned. "My arms are aching."

Ma handed him a spoon and pointed to the cookie sheet. "Get to spooning. Three to a row, and we'll put the first batch in to bake." She tore off a sheet of wax paper and spread it on the counter.

"Put them there to cool off?" Keith asked.

Ma nodded. "Yes, sir, that's the plan. Can you keep from burning yourself while they cool?"

3

"I think so, Ma." Keith grinned.

He had just set the timer when Wayne came rushing downstairs. "It's snowing," he cried out.

Keith rushed to the door with him to look outside. "It's sticking, too," Keith hollered. Keith looked at the stove and then at the front door.

"Go ahead," Ma said. "I'll keep the cookies going."

Keith hung his head.

"Go!" Ma repeated. "I've got this."

Keith rushed over and kissed her cheek. "Thanks, Ma." He looked at Juliet and Cedra. "Are you coming?"

Cedra looked at Juliet. "Let's go. We'll be back, Ma."

"You two go ahead. Hank and I'll stay where it's nice and warm," Ma teased.

Cedra handed Juliet her coat. "We'll be back soon."

"Stay warm," Hank called after them. He chuckled and looked at Ma. "What are the chances for a white Christmas?"

Ma cocked her head. "Well, it's Christmas Eve, snowing, and if it sticks, I'd say the odds are good."

"We had a white Christmas once, but Cedra was only two or three. I doubt she even remembers."

They heard the laughter from outside. Ma looked at Hank. "Go ahead and join them. I've got this handled."

"You sure?" Hank asked.

"Go for it. Just don't break anything," Ma teased.

†

Hank pulled his coat on and walked out onto the porch. Cedra was bent over, laughing as Keith tried to scoop enough snow for a snowball. This was the first time since her mother's death that Cedra had seemed so happy. He looked around for Wayne, who was sneaking around the vehicles gathering snow. Juliet and Cedra were so busy watching Keith that they had lost track of Wayne. Hank watched as Wayne molded the snow into a ball and let it fly just as Cedra bent over, hitting Juliet on her arm. The surprise on Juliet's face made Hank laugh.

"You are so in for it now," Juliet yelled and grabbed Cedra's hand as they raced for the cover of her truck. Juliet and Cedra scooped handfuls of snow and formed balls as they stalked Wayne and Keith. They had reached the back of Wayne's truck when Keith and Wayne popped up and launched. Cedra ducked out of the path, but Juliet took both shots before they raced after the boys.

†

Hank remained safely on the porch, leaning against a pillar as the snowball war ensued. It was difficult to determine who was having the most fun, but when Cedra's hands became cold, she stuck them around Juliet's neck.

"Damn, that's cold." Juliet laughed.

"I'm going in to get warmed up and put my gloves on," Cedra stated and dashed through a rain of snowballs as she ran for the porch.

"Duck." She heard Juliet cry out, but it was too late. An errant throw caught Hank in the chest while he watched Cedra.

"Now you've gone and done it," Hank declared as he wiped the snow from his chest and raced out to join Team Juliet.

"Come on, Dad, let's get them," Juliet called as Cedra disappeared into the house.

†

Cedra wiped her feet off on the rug. "It's gotten cold out there," she told Ma as she entered the kitchen.

"Did you abandon Juliet?" Ma asked.

"Naw, Dad teamed up with her. My hands are freezing, but I don't want to ruin my gloves."

Ma nodded toward the foyer. "Look in the bottom drawer of the foyer table. There should be some gloves that will fit you and Juliet. The boys are on their own."

"Thanks, Ma. You okay in here?" Cedra asked.

The timer went off, and Ma pulled one pan out and slipped another into the oven. "I'll put on a fresh pot of coffee, and we can have warm cookies when y'all come inside."

"That sounds good," Cedra said as she slipped her hands inside the thick, warm gloves. "Thanks."

"Be careful," Ma warned as Cedra returned outside.

Cedra rejoined Juliet and Hank, and the added advantage had the boys running for cover. Keith called a truce and started jogging toward the porch when they all tired. When Keith's boot hit the frozen sidewalk, his feet shot out, and he landed in the snow-covered grass.

"Well, damn. At least I had a soft landing." Keith reached up to take Wayne's hand. "I don't reckon I need to tell you to be careful," he said as he wiped himself off.

"That was fun," Hank declared as he pushed the front door open and pulled off his coat.

"Yeah, it was, Dad. You're a great shot."

"I can attest to that," Wayne reported. "He got me in the head twice."

"I probably shouldn't admit I was aiming for his chest then," Hank replied and laughed.

"Does anyone want hot chocolate?" Ma called from the kitchen.

"Sounds great," Keith replied. He pulled off his coat and rushed to the kitchen. "It smells heavenly in here."

"That does sound good," Cedra agreed. "What can I do to help?"

"Grab a bag of marshmallows from the pantry. I've already got the hot chocolate on the stove. There's fresh coffee, Hank."

"Are you ready for a cup?" Hank asked.

"Yeah, that would be great." Ma handed him her mug.

Cedra looked at Juliet. "Coffee or hot chocolate?"

"Hot chocolate," Juliet answered. "The cookies look good."

"Go ahead and plate some, please," Ma told her. "There's more coming out soon."

Wayne took a sip of the hot chocolate. "I had forgotten how good this is from scratch. I'm so used to the packaged type."

"It is delicious, Ma. Thank you," Juliet said.

Ma smiled. "I hope it will help get y'all warmed up after being outside. Is it still snowing?"

"Huge flakes, Ma. They are so beautiful as they come spiraling down," Keith answered.

"Hopefully, it will continue, and we'll have a white Christmas tomorrow." Ma pulled out another sheet of cookies.

"I'll get the next pan ready, Ma. Sit and relax for a minute," Keith told her.

Ma handed him the potholder. "I won't argue with you. Just don't get burned."

Keith smiled. "I'll be careful, Ma." He began working on the next pan of cookies.

Juliet chuckled. "Is it my imagination, or is that pile of presents growing?" She pointed at the tree. "That tree sure looks good with the lights and decorations."

"It is a beautiful tree," Hank replied. "It reminds me of when we'd go out and cut our own when you were growing up," he told Cedra.

"I don't think we ever got one that pretty, though." She chuckled. "I'll admit it was a lot of fun hunting it down. Getting them home and into the house was always a challenge."

Wayne looked at Cedra. "I worked at a Christmas tree farm one summer in high school. I didn't think I would ever finish shaping trees so they would grow to perfection like that."

"We never had a big tree like this one," Juliet replied. "Ours always looked like the Charlie Brown tree."

"I love the smell of a fresh tree," Ma admitted. "Those artificial trees just don't do it for me, and that fake canned smell is horrid."

"I'll agree with you on that," Hank stated. "I mentioned getting an artificial tree one year, and I thought Cedra and her mom were going to toss me out of the house until I promised we'd get a real one."

Cedra smiled at the memory Hank shared. "I remember that, and yes, you almost did get tossed. That was our last real Christmas," Cedra said, then ducked her head to hide the tears suddenly filling her eyes.

"We will always have a real tree then. Next year, maybe two if Ma will let us put one on the front porch," Juliet replied.

"We can get a bunch of lights on sale after Christmas and light up the front porch, too," Keith suggested.

Ma smiled at the thought that the group planned to be with her next Christmas. "Why don't we get one to plant in the front yard this spring?"

"Can we, Ma? I'll dig the hole," Wayne promised. "Maybe if I go home for a visit, I'll stop by the farm and get one already established."

"That would be great," Ma agreed.

Juliet laughed. "Look at us planning for next Christmas; we haven't made it through this one."

Cedra looked at Ma. "I hope this is one of many we spend here."

"Me, too. This house hasn't seen this much joy in years," Ma replied.

"Is there anything we need to prep for tomorrow?" Hank asked.

"Not tonight," Ma replied. "Kitchen Keith will make biscuits, and I'll make some gravy for breakfast. We need to know if we want to eat before or after opening gifts?"

"Let's eat before," Wayne suggested. "Then we can open gifts."

"I've got many of the sides prepped already," Ma said. "You can peel and slice potatoes after the gifts," she told Hank. "Cedra and Juliet already have desserts made, and I can pop the ham into the oven first thing and still have room for biscuits."

Keith pulled out a final pan of cookies, sliding them off the pan to cool.

"You've gotten very handy in the kitchen," Hank praised.

"Ma's a good teacher."

"Yes, she is," Juliet agreed. "I've learned how to make buttermilk pies and caramel cake this week. I hope you like them."

"I'm sure they will be delicious, and no crumb will go uneaten," Cedra stated.

Juliet looked out the window and saw that it was still snowing. "Do y'all want to get another cup of something hot and sit on the porch to watch it snow before it's time to head to bed?"

"That sounds nice," Hank replied. "Will you join us for a bit, Ma?"

"I'd like to. Pour us more coffee while I get my coat and scarf," Ma requested and passed Hank her mug.

"I'm going to wash these pans, and I'll be out," Keith told them.

"I'll get them later," Cedra replied.

"My mess, my cleanup." Keith smiled. "It won't take me long."

"There's enough hot chocolate for three more," Juliet reported as she refilled mugs.

"I'll swap over to coffee," Wayne offered.

Cedra handed Juliet her coat, and the group walked onto the porch and sat in chairs or the swing. Juliet placed her arm around Cedra's shoulder and pulled her close as they began to move.

"It's sticking well," Hank pointed out.

"If it goes like this all night, we could have several inches," Ma suggested.

"It's cold enough," Hank replied, then sipped his coffee. "I'm glad I don't have to drive in this."

Cedra smiled at her dad. "I'm glad none of us have to go anywhere for a few days at least."

"We'll have to make a milk run in a few days," Wayne teased. "I've got four-wheel drive and the most

11

experience driving in snow, so I'll go. Just let me know if there's anything else we'll need, Ma."

"I'll go with you," Hank offered.

Keith stepped onto the porch. "Where are we going?"

Ma rocked in her chair. "Wayne and Hank were discussing a milk run in a day or so."

"Do you think the snow will last long?" Keith asked.

Ma saw the shine of excitement in Keith's eyes. "I hope so. It sure is beautiful."

"I'd love to bundle up tomorrow and build a snowman," Keith told them.

"I've never seen that much snow," Cedra admitted. "It looks like so much fun."

"We'll bundle up after we open gifts and come out to play," Juliet promised.

"That will be fun." Cedra smiled and leaned into Juliet.

"Too bad Stone isn't here," Wayne replied.

"I bet he calls tomorrow," Ma stated.

Cedra smiled. "I'm sure he's having a blast with his family. Destiny is old enough to enjoy Christmas now."

"Speaking of family. I'm going to call it a night and phone home," Wayne said.

"Me, too," Keith added. "I don't want to wait and forget tomorrow. I hope everyone's gifts made it on time."

"Are you going to call home?" Cedra asked Juliet.

Juliet nodded. "I'll wait until the morning. The folks are probably already in bed tonight."

"That's right. Your family is an hour ahead of us," Cedra replied.

"Merry Christmas, guys," Hank called out as Wayne and Keith walked into the house.

"You, too," Keith replied. "Make sure I'm up, please, Ma."

"I will. Sleep well," Ma answered.

Ma stood and collected mugs. "I'll wash these and head to bed, too."

"I'll help you," Hank volunteered and took Juliet and Cedra's mugs. "I'll see y'all in the morning."

"We won't be out much longer," Cedra answered. "Love you."

"I love you, too," Hank replied. He winked at Juliet. "Both of you."

"Love you too, Dad," Juliet replied.

†

"I'm coming, Ma. Hold the door," Hank requested and followed her into the kitchen.

Ma set the empty mugs in the sink and turned for the ones Hank carried. "It warms my heart to see you interact with Juliet the way you do."

"I get the impression her family isn't close," Hank stated.

"Nor are they supportive of her lifestyle," Ma replied. "She doesn't speak of them often."

"Anyone who can make my Baby Girl as happy as she does deserves my love and admiration," Hank replied. "It pains me to think that parents can be so shallow."

"Me, too, but it happens all too often. You couldn't ask for two better young ladies, in my opinion. They are so different but complement each other beautifully." Ma grinned. She opened the door to the dishwasher and began rinsing mugs and handing them to Hank.

Hank loaded them inside the machine and watched Ma start it. "I'm looking forward to biscuits and gravy in the morning."

"That should hold us until lunch."

"I'll see you in the morning for some coffee then," Hank answered and left the kitchen.

"Goodnight." She wiped down the counter and turned off the light.

†

"It's so beautiful out here," Juliet said as she stared into the night.

"There's just enough light to help you see the snow coming down. I'm glad the wind has died down some. It was wicked cold earlier."

Juliet leaned in to kiss her cheek. "Still plenty cold to keep the snow falling. I'm looking forward to making a snowman with you tomorrow."

"Me, too. Another first for us."

"Maybe one year we will go where there are several feet of snow for Christmas," Juliet suggested.

"Snow or no snow, I don't care as long as I'm with you. I love you so much," Cedra replied as she looked into Juliet's eyes.

Juliet closed the distance between them and kissed Cedra passionately. She felt Cedra shiver. "Are you ready to go get warm?"

"I'm ready to be naked in your arms." Cedra grinned.

"That ought to warm us," Juliet replied with a soft laugh. She stood and reached for Cedra.

Juliet's tender caresses turned into passionate strokes as she lay next to Cedra. Her kiss deepened to muffle the moans elicited from Cedra as her climax arrived. Cedra thrust her hips, pressing Juliet's fingers deeper inside her. She could feel her inner muscles squeezing as her world began to spin.

Cedra's body relaxed, and Juliet answered with a softer kiss. "That was intense," Juliet whispered.

"I can attest to that." Cedra was working hard to suppress a giggle. She pulled Juliet's head down for another kiss.

†

Juliet felt Cedra's hand gliding down her body and quickly captured it in hers as she broke the kiss. "I can't be quiet like you, and I don't want to wake up Hank," Juliet replied to Cedra's pout. "I'm good for now. I just wanted to give you an early Christmas present. Merry Christmas, Baby Girl," Juliet whispered. "Our first of many, I hope."

"Me, too." Cedra snuggled into Juliet. "I love you," she whispered.

"I love you, too." Juliet felt the smile grow on her face as she wrapped Cedra in her arms.

CHAPTER TWO

Juliet woke to the movement of Cedra stretching. "Merry Christmas," she said as she rolled over to kiss her lover.

"Merry Christmas to you too." Cedra checked the clock. "It's still early. I thought I'd shower and help Ma with breakfast."

"Wake me before you go down, and I'll get up and shower," Juliet promised as she pulled the covers under her chin.

"I will," Cedra replied. "I love you."

"Love you, too," Juliet replied. "I miss you already."

Cedra leaned down to kiss her. "I'll see you in a few minutes."

†

Juliet dozed while Cedra showered and dressed. She felt the bed compress when Cedra sat next to her. Cedra's warm hand slipped under the covers and caressed Juliet's stomach.

"Hey, sweetie," the angelic voice whispered. "It's time to start waking."

"I had a beautiful dream of your hand on my body," Juliet murmured sleepily.

"It wasn't a dream," Cedra replied as her hand cupped Juliet's right breast and gently squeezed it. Her thumb and index finger captured Juliet's erect nipple with a slow stretch.

"I can't wait to wrap my lips around this tonight," Cedra teased.

Juliet's eyes popped open. "When did you start talking dirty?" Juliet chuckled until Cedra squeezed her nipple. "Damn, that feels good."

Cedra leaned down. "I've had an excellent teacher." She smiled and closed the distance between them. The tip of her tongue trailed across Juliet's lips.

Juliet pulled Cedra's mouth firmly onto hers for an enthusiastic kiss. "I can't wait for more of these." Juliet smiled.

"You will have your fill tonight," Cedra promised.

"We should have gotten your dad earplugs for Christmas," Juliet teased her lover.

"I think I've come up with something to keep you quiet," Cedra replied with a wicked grin.

Juliet's eyebrow shot up. "Care to share your idea?"

Cedra shook her head. "You'll just have to wait until tonight to find out."

"That is so cruel," Juliet complained.

"I promise it will be worth the wait," Cedra replied and stood. "I'll see you when you come down for breakfast."

Juliet smiled. "I need to shave my legs, but I won't be too long. "I'm ready for breakfast."

†

Juliet pulled back the cover and made the bed after Cedra left. She walked into the bathroom and smiled as she thought of a surprise of her own. She waited for the shower to heat and stepped under the warm flow. Juliet shaved her legs but didn't stop at the top of her thighs. "I've got a surprise for you too, Cedra." She chuckled as her hand cupped a cleanly shaved mound. The skin was baby-soft and felt more sensitive to the touch. Juliet finished bathing, dressed, and smiled as the seam of her jeans pressed into her fully exposed lips.

"This may be a long day," Juliet said as she contemplated changing into something looser in the crotch. "I can change later." She grinned and slipped into her shoes.

†

19

Wayne was at the top of the stairs when she exited the bedroom. "Good morning," Juliet called out.

"Merry Christmas, Juliet," he answered.

"Merry Christmas, Wayne," she replied. They descended the stairs together and walked into the kitchen.

"Merry Christmas, everyone," Juliet announced.

"Merry Christmas," Ma replied from the stove, stirring the gravy.

"Those biscuits are almost too pretty to eat, bro," Wayne told Keith.

Keith sat a platter of biscuits on the table and smiled. "Thanks. I am proud of how they turned out this morning."

Cedra had finished setting the table. "Are you two ready for some coffee?"

"I'll get it if you pour the juice," Juliet stated as she watched Ma pour the gravy into a bowl.

Cedra pulled out apple and orange juice. "Does anyone want milk?"

Keith grinned up at her. "I'll save it for dessert later."

"Me, too," Wayne added. "Orange juice and coffee are good."

"Ma, are you ready for a refill?" Juliet asked.

"Yes, please. Hank's ready, too," Ma answered.

Juliet filled everyone's cups and started a fresh pot before sitting beside Cedra.

Ma sat and reached for Keith and Wayne's hands as she prepared to bless the meal. They all held hands as Ma gave thanks for the meal, the birth of Christ, and good health for their friends and family. The group answered with an amen chorus as the platter of biscuits made its way around the table.

Ma looked up. "If you pass me your plates, I'll add the gravy. That bowl's too hot to pass."

Keith split three biscuits open and passed his plate to her. He watched with anticipation as Ma smothered them with gravy. "That looks delicious," Keith announced as he reached for Cedra's plate.

Cedra glanced into the living room at the tree. The lights were on, and she could see that the pile of presents had grown from the previous night. "It looks like Santa paid us a visit last night."

"I thought I heard something up on the roof this morning," Ma teased.

"Crap, which reminds me," Keith replied as he pushed his chair back and walked to the front door.

"Yes, we got almost five inches of snow," Hank reported. "I went out earlier and checked." He winked at Cedra.

"Oh wow, it's beautiful," Keith cried from the hallway. "Are we still making snowmen today?" he asked as he returned.

"Snowwomen, too," Juliet added.

Ma nodded. "After we open gifts."

"As cold as it is, I don't think it's going anywhere," Hank told Keith.

"I want to get some photographs before we start tromping around, too," Cedra said.

Wayne looked at Ma. "Do you have a snow shovel?"

"Yes, it's in the shed," Ma replied.

"I'll clear the front steps and sidewalk once Cedra has her photos," Wayne offered.

"That would be nice. Thank you," Ma replied. "There may even be some rock salt there you can spread on the sidewalk to keep ice from forming."

"No problem. Keith can spread the salt while I shovel." Wayne grinned at Keith.

"No problem, bro," Keith answered and took a sip of juice.

"Make a pile, and that can be a start of a snowman," Juliet suggested.

"Good idea," Wayne replied. "We should have plenty of snow to make a family."

Cedra smiled at the excitement around the table. "This is a great breakfast."

"Keith is doing well on making biscuits," Ma praised. "Eat up, and then after we clear the leftovers and dishes, we can start on the presents."

"That is good with me." Wayne grinned.

Cedra looked over at her dad. "I'm so glad you joined us. We've never spent a Christmas apart."

"Never will as long as I'm able," Hank replied. "I appreciate you having me here, Ma."

"You're one of the family and a great help in the kitchen," Ma pronounced. She smiled at Hank. "It's always good to have you visit, and you're welcome anytime."

"Thanks, Ma." Hank smiled. "May I have more of your gravy?" he asked as he split two more biscuits.

Out and Loud

"You can have all that you want. It will be mid-afternoon before lunch is ready, but we have plenty of things to snack on," Ma informed them.

"I can hardly wait," Wayne stated. "I dreamed of that ham last night."

Ma smiled. "Be careful when you go out the back door. I've got the rolls rising on the freezer, and a loud noise may make them drop."

"We'd better play it safe and go out the front then," Keith suggested. "We aren't good at quiet."

†

Ma, Cedra, and Juliet picked up the kitchen while Wayne took a large garbage bag for the wrapping paper and boxes to the living room. Keith eagerly previewed the gifts under the tree while Hank sat sipping coffee in a recliner.

"Who gets to play Santa?" Keith asked.

"I think you would be a good candidate," Ma answered. "We'll be right there if you want to go ahead and pick out a gift for everyone to open first."

"All right." Keith smiled and rubbed his hands together.

When the ladies came to the living room, Hank looked up at Ma. "I know this is a bit premature, but have you thought about a New Year's Eve meal?"

"Not at all. Do you have something in mind?" Ma asked.

"I thought the boys and I could do a low-country boil and give you ladies a well-deserved break," Hank answered.

"That sounds wonderful. We need to check to see if we can get the shrimp if that's what you're planning," Ma replied.

"I thought shrimp and maybe some crab legs if we can find them," Hank suggested.

"They won't be fresh, but we can get shrimp, crab, and lobster at the wholesale club. I bet we can get fresh shrimp at one of the grocery stores. Sausage and corn won't be a problem," Cedra added.

"Good, we got a meal to plan then, boys," Hank stated.

"You got it," Wayne replied.

"Okay, everyone should have a gift, so start unwrapping," Keith instructed.

†

Ma opened the first gift, and the group thanked one another an hour later. Cedra noted the tears in Ma's eyes when Keith brought the large box forward, and she unwrapped her new television. "I can finally take that old one to an antique store," Ma teased.

"If Wayne or Keith helps me later, we will mount it on the wall for you," Hank offered.

"That will be great. I can watch real television tonight." Ma chuckled.

Everyone seemed pleased with their gifts and was content to play with them for a short while before the snow bug got to the boys.

Wayne looked at Cedra. "Will you come to snap your photographs so Keith and I can shovel and salt the sidewalk and steps?"

"Sure, let me go upstairs for my camera," Cedra replied.

Cedra climbed the stairs, and when she walked into her room, she saw a present lying on her bed. She smiled, knowing it was something personal from Juliet. She picked up her camera and descended the stairs.

Juliet and Hank huddled on the couch as Juliet explained the satellite radio system. "I promise I will hook it up for you and show you how to detach it to take inside before you leave," Juliet promised.

"I'll be right back." Cedra stepped onto the porch and snapped pictures. The air was crisp and refreshing, and the few rays of sunlight that passed through the clouds made the snow shine brighter than Cedra thought possible. Cedra nodded to Wayne and Keith when she finished. They stepped carefully onto the sidewalk to go to the shed for the shovel and salt.

Before Cedra could return inside, Keith hollered for her.

"Cedra, you need to see this."

Cedra walked carefully through the snow to the backyard. Wayne and Keith were gazing into the pecan trees. Icicles had formed on the limbs and glistened like diamonds.

"Wow, that's beautiful," Cedra declared and took several more steps forward. "Is it my imagination, or is the snow deeper back here?"

"I think it is," Wayne agreed. "Room for more snow people."

Cedra grinned. "That's what I was thinking, too. There's more shade back here, so it would take longer for the sun to melt them."

"Should we just scrap the front yard then?" Keith asked.

"No, I think we build a big one there and then return here to build the family," Cedra suggested.

†

Juliet wrapped a scarf around her neck and slipped into her gloves before starting outside. She expected to find Cedra and the boys in the front yard, but it was empty. Juliet spied their footprints in the snow and followed them into the backyard. "Wow," she uttered when she saw the blanket of snow. "It's so beautiful."

Cedra turned at the sound of Juliet's voice. "It's pretty, isn't it?"

Juliet smiled. "Yes, everything looks so clean and pure."

"I think we've decided to build the family back here. There's so much more snow; the shade will help them last longer."

"That makes sense. So, none in the front yard?" Juliet asked.

"We'll make a big one in the front yard." Cedra smiled.

"Let's get the sidewalk and steps cleared," Cedra told Wayne and Keith.

Wayne took the snow shovel from the shed, and Keith grabbed a bag of rock salt and an old coffee can.

"Lead the way," Keith called out after closing the shed door.

"Show us where you want the pile," Wayne requested when they reached the front yard.

"Right in the middle," Juliet suggested. "Is that too far for you to carry the snow?"

Wayne grinned. "I've got this. You and Cedra can start making a base, and I'll bring it over."

Juliet and Cedra used their feet to make a circle and formed a giant ball of snow, packing it tightly to hold it together. Wayne and Keith cleared the sidewalk and steps, then joined Cedra and Juliet to make the center ball.

†

Ma glanced at the front door after checking on the ham in the oven. Hank was peeking out the window, watching the snowman build. "Why don't you join them?"

"What? Leave this lovely warm house? I think I'll stay inside and let the youngins play in the snow." Hank grinned back at Ma. "Is there something you want me to do?"

Ma wiped her hands on her apron. "Not yet. You can peel some potatoes later. I think I'll go ahead and put hot chocolate on. They are going to get cold quickly out there."

Hank poured a cup of coffee. "Should I put another pot on?"

"Yes, please," Ma answered as she pulled out a large pot for the hot chocolate.

Hank started to chuckle when he returned to the door to peer outside. "I wondered how long it would take for the snowballs to start flying," he explained to Ma.

"I reckon it was just too tempting. All that soft, wet snow," Ma answered as she walked to the pantry for marshmallows. "I think everyone has had a good Christmas," Ma stated.

"They did a great job with the presents," Hank agreed. "I love my new radio and the photographs."

"They had fun shopping and wrapping the gifts," Ma replied. "I don't know where they could hide that television, though."

"Under Keith's bed," Hank reported. "Wayne hid the mount in his closet."

"Clever boys." Ma chuckled. "I hope Stone is having a great day with his family. I wouldn't be surprised if he called today."

Hank walked back into the kitchen. "Do you think he's coming back?"

"Who? Stone?" Ma asked. She shrugged her shoulders. "I honestly don't know. It must be hard on him being away from his wife and child."

"I'm not sure the small taste of success they've had is enough to get him back," Hank stated.

"Please don't think poorly of me, but I think the four will be fine if Stone decides to stay home," Ma replied. "Originally, it was to be the four of them. Now that the others have realized they can write and sing, losing a second writer isn't that big of a deal."

Hank smiled. "I'd never think poorly of you, Ma. I agree with your assessment. Stone helped them get a jumpstart, but I don't think his heart is in Nashville. When he learned that Juliet, Wayne, and Keith were writing, I wondered if he felt his value to the group diminished."

"I guess only time will tell," Ma said. "The others may be disappointed initially, but they will bounce back quickly. Would you mind calling them inside to warm up for a few?"

"Sure thing," Hank replied.

Hank opened the front door and called out, "Hot chocolate break time."

"Be right there, Dad," Cedra replied. "Truce," she called out as a snowball whizzed past her.

"That's a good-looking snowman you've started," Hank stated.

"We got a bit sidetracked," Juliet admitted as she stepped carefully onto the steps.

"So, I see." Hank laughed.

†

They settled around the table as Ma added marshmallows to the mugs and poured the hot liquid. Cedra felt her phone vibrate in her pocket and pulled it out. Smiling, she looked at the pictures that Stone had sent of Destiny in her new outfit and ballcap. "What a cutie," she said and shared the photos Stone had sent before reading his text to the group.

She loves her new look and wanted me to send a picture to say thanks. I'm having a great time. I hope all is well and that y'all are having a great Christmas.

Cedra typed in a quick response and then stuffed her phone back into her coat pocket. "This looks and smells great, Ma. Thanks."

"You're welcome. I reckoned it was time for a break to warm y'all up," Ma answered.

"Perfect timing," Wayne said. "We've got the steps and sidewalk cleared. We decided to build a large snowman in the front but the family in the back. The snow is much deeper, and the shade will help it last longer."

"That's a good decision," Hank replied.

"That ham sure smells good, Ma," Juliet stated. "What do you need our help with today?"

"I've got this. Enjoy some time playing in the snow. Hank and I have everything under control here." Ma smiled at Hank. "He's my number one prepper."

"She's right. No telling when you will get snow again, so enjoy, but don't stay out too long and get a chill," Hank replied. "After we eat, I'll need help mounting Ma's new television."

"Do you want to do it now?" Wayne asked.

"No, I think it'll go better once you're tuckered out," Hank teased.

"How much longer until we eat?" Keith asked.

"About four hours," Ma answered. "Do you need a snack to hold you over?"

"No, ma'am. I'm just trying to determine how much time we have to build the family," Keith answered.

Ma nodded. "Try to come back inside in no more than two hours for something to warm you up. We don't need anyone getting sick."

Cedra finished her drink. "We will, Ma. If you need something before then, give us a holler."

"We've got most of it prepped already. I'll put the casseroles into the oven and whip up the mashed potatoes and gravy closer to eating time."

Cedra stood and rinsed her mug before placing it in the dishwasher, then reached for Juliet's. "After we eat, I want to try my new keyboard while you guys work on the television."

"Mind if I join you with my harmonica? I can't wait to hear what a nice one will sound like," Juliet said.

"You didn't do too bad with the old one," Ma reminded her.

Juliet smiled. "No worries. It will always be my first."

Hank looked at Ma. "Will it be safe to hang some of your pictures while the ham is cooking? I don't want to cause the rolls to fall." He grinned.

"I think they will be safe," Ma replied. "That reminds me. I need to pull out some butter to soften."

Wayne and Keith handed Cedra their mugs. "We'll be back in a bit," Wayne told Ma.

†

Working together, they had two snowmen and two snowwomen formed and decorated with twigs and stones. Hank could hear them laughing from the back porch, especially about the snowwomen with large snow boobs. "I think the kids are channeling their inner Dolly," he told Ma when he walked back into the kitchen.

"What?" Ma asked.

"The snowwomen are anatomically correct," Hank replied, cupping his hands against his chest.

"Oh, my goodness. I bet that was Keith's idea." Ma chuckled. "Should I start another batch of hot chocolate while you hang that last photograph?"

"I think they are about ready. The kids' cheeks are getting a bit flushed," Hank replied. "Where do you want this one hung?"

Ma looked at the photograph taken in the kitchen and pointed to a space on the wall. "How about there?"

Hank nodded. "I think that will look nice there." He picked up the framed photograph. "Y'all are very photogenic. I love the prints the girls gave me."

They were very excited to be able to give you the prints. I didn't realize they had copies for me, but I'm glad they did." Ma turned on the burner. "They are a good bunch."

"I couldn't agree more," Hank said.

†

"I need a break," Juliet replied after finishing the second snowwoman. "Let's let the guys start the next."

"That's fine with me. I expect Dad to come after us for a break anytime now. He's been peeking out the back porch watching us."

Juliet pulled Cedra into her arms. "Are you staying warm enough?"

Cedra laughed. "Probably not, but I'm having so much fun."

"I hope Ma has more hot chocolate ready for us. That hit the spot."

"Yes, it did." She reached up to brush the snow from Juliet's hair. "I love you."

Juliet cocked her head at Cedra. "I love you, too." She leaned in and kissed her sweetly. "I can't wait until tonight to show you how much."

"Hey, lovebirds, are y'all ready for a break?" Keith asked.

Cedra nodded. "We all need to warm up for a while. We've done well so far. I love the twin Dollies."

"Not twins. One is Dolly, and the other is Reba. This one is Hank, and the other is Johnny," Wayne called out.

"Our Music City legends." Keith smiled. "I think we've got enough snow piled up for a shorter Garth." He laughed.

Juliet shook her head. "Let's see if we can talk Ma into more hot chocolate."

Hank was coming around the corner of the house. "Ma is sending me out to collect y'all. Well, look at those snow people."

Cedra grinned. "Hank, Johnny, Dolly, and Reba."

"I can definitely tell which one is Dolly." Hank chuckled.

"Go big or go home," Keith replied with a smirk.

"Ma has created a tasty snack for y'all. She sprinkled the potato peels with salt and Parmesan cheese and baked them until they were crispy."

"I take it you've already sampled?" Cedra asked.

"We had to make sure they were edible," Hank replied and winked.

"Let's go try these out. They sound delicious," Juliet told them.

CHAPTER THREE

"I will die if I eat another bite," Juliet groaned. "It was a delicious meal, Ma. Thanks."

Ma smiled at Juliet's praise. "I'm happy you all enjoyed the meal. I thought it turned out pretty well."

"One of the best meals I've had in a long time," Hank admitted. "Since Thanksgiving."

Cedra grinned at her dad. "It was delicious, but I'm afraid we won't be good for anything for a couple of hours."

"I was thinking the same thing," Ma replied. "It wouldn't hurt us to nap after a meal like that."

"I won't argue with that," Hank agreed. "I think even Keith is looking a bit sluggish."

Keith sopped up the last bit of gravy on his plate. "I could do a nap," he admitted. "Do you think the snow will last, Ma?"

"I think it will stick around a few more days according to the forecast. We may even get a bit more."

"More snow?" Keith sat up in his chair.

"It's a possibility. A large winter storm sweeping in from Canada may dip this low," Ma informed them.

"I won't feel guilty about napping then." Keith grinned and popped the gravy-soaked roll in his mouth.

"Why don't you and Dad start on your naps while we take care of the kitchen?" Cedra asked. "We'll do the dishes, and the boys can put the leftovers away."

"As your dad said, I won't argue with that. We can warm up some leftovers for supper around seven if that's good with everyone," Ma suggested.

"I can't even think about eating again right now," Juliet moaned.

"Seven will be fine, Ma," Hank replied. "I'll see you all then."

Ma stood and followed Hank out of the kitchen.

"Let's get to it." Cedra began rinsing the dishes and handed them to Juliet to go in the dishwasher. Wayne and Keith started putting away the leftovers.

"Man, we didn't even think about saving room for your buttermilk pie," Keith complained as he placed containers in the refrigerator.

"It only gets better," Cedra promised. "We can eat a lighter meal at supper and save room for dessert."

Wayne stored the ham slices. "Should I wrap this ham bone in some foil so Ma can use it in some beans?"

"I think she would appreciate that," Cedra replied. "Wrap it tight and put it in the freezer. Keith, will you take the garbage out?"

Juliet dumped used coffee grounds in the garbage and set up the pot for supper. Cedra wiped down the table, counters, and stove. "I think we're good to start the dishwasher," she told Juliet.

"On it, boss."

"Do you need anything else?" Wayne asked. "I think I'll call home before I lay down."

"That's a good idea," Keith agreed.

"Nope. We're good to go," Cedra answered. "I want to snap a few photos of our handiwork today before losing the light. I'll be right back," she told Juliet. "I'll see you boys tonight."

†

Cedra pulled on her coat and picked up her camera. She stepped outside the front door and snapped several pictures before walking around the house. The snow was still a pristine white, and she took photos of the Music City snow stars they had built in the backyard. When she turned back toward the house, Juliet was sitting on the back steps waiting for her. She lifted her camera and shot several frames of the woman who had become her world.

"Damn, you look great," Cedra told Juliet as she walked toward her.

Juliet's face filled with a smile. "I do believe you are biased but thank you."

"Biased because I love you, but you are very photogenic," Cedra replied. She sat beside Juliet. "It's still beautiful out here."

"Yes, it is. I hope Ma's right, and we get more snow. I want to move the tree to the back room and have a nice fire," Juliet stated.

"I bet that we could arrange that. We can't take it down before New Year's, though. We don't want any bad luck." Cedra smiled and reached into her pocket. "Look what I found." She held a tiny bit of mistletoe and lifted it above her head.

Juliet leaned in and kissed her. "You never need mistletoe for a kiss."

"I know, but I couldn't resist picking it out of the snow," Cedra said. "It's not as cold out here since the wind has died down."

Juliet nodded. "That probably won't last if there's a front coming in. Maybe we'll get another nice day tomorrow before it arrives."

Cedra laid her head on Juliet's shoulder. "Maybe, but any day I get to spend with you is perfect."

"Today was nice, and I think everyone enjoyed their gifts, don't you?" Juliet asked.

"I think so, too. I know I love mine. You and Dad are so sneaky," Cedra replied.

Juliet shrugged. "I knew I couldn't keep it hidden if I bought it, and he was looking for ideas. I say it worked out pretty well."

Cedra raised her head and looked into Juliet's eyes. "I noticed a gift on the bed when I went upstairs to get my camera."

Juliet's smile widened. "A gift for both of us to enjoy, but not until later tonight."

"Do I have to wait until tonight to open it?"

"Hmm," Juliet considered. "If you open it now, you may want to use it sooner, so I'll leave it up to you."

"Now I'm dying to see what it is," Cedra admitted and bit her lower lip.

"Open it then. Just don't forget I warned you," Juliet teased. She stood and reached for Cedra's hand.

They climbed the stairs after hanging up their jackets. Cedra picked up the wrapped gift and gave it a shake. She frowned when she didn't hear any sound. She sat the present on the desk with a sigh and started to undress. "I'm thinking of a T-shirt and sweats. What do you think?"

"That will be comfortable, especially after that huge meal," Juliet responded. She unfastened her jeans and pulled the shirt over her head before kicking off her boots. "I've had a great Christmas so far with you. Thank you for loving me," Juliet said with tears in her eyes. "The best Christmas yet."

Cedra pulled Juliet into her arms. "The first of many to come, my love. Thank you for loving me so much and getting me nice gifts. I would have been content just being with you and our family."

"Me, too, but I always want you to know how much I cherish you and our love," Juliet replied. She kissed Cedra deeply.

"More of those, and we won't be napping." Cedra grinned.

"We've got all night for kisses," Juliet promised as she bent to pull back the covers. She climbed into the bed and took Cedra in her arms. Cedra pressed a leg between Juliet's and snuggled close.

†

The location of Cedra's leg between her thighs tugged on the fabric of her sweatpants, and Juliet moved slightly to ease the pressure on her bare mound. She could already feel her wetness growing. It had been years since she had shaved clean, and the sensation was more potent than she remembered. *Probably because, for the first time, I'm in love.*

"Are you okay?" Cedra asked. "Am I hurting you?"

"Heaven's no, I just needed to reposition a hair." Juliet laughed. "I am very comfortable."

"Good. I am too," Cedra agreed and buried her face in Juliet's neck. She slipped her hand beneath Juliet's shirt to feel the warmth of her skin and sighed.

Juliet kissed the top of Cedra's head and closed her eyes.

†

Hank was stretched out on Juliet's bed and smiled when he heard Cedra and Juliet arrive. He loved how Cedra's eyes lit up when she was near or talking about Juliet. Selfishly Hank had hope for a grandchild but seeing his daughter so in love with another woman warmed his heart. He knew a grandchild wasn't totally out of the question. They were both still young and had many years of childbearing opportunities ahead. He felt his smile grow at the thought. He couldn't imagine Juliet carrying a baby, but he knew she would be a great parent, as would Cedra. He remembered when his wife Melinda was pregnant with Cedra, and how she glowed with the prospect of being a mother. She had doted over Cedra all her life, and Hank suspected Cedra would do no less.

"Don't rush, old man. Let them enjoy being young and in love." Hank chuckled and snuggled into a pillow before drifting off to sleep.

†

Cedra listened as Juliet's breaths slowed as she fell asleep. Her skin could feel the strong beat of her heart against her chin. She breathed in deeply. Cedra loved the warm earthy smell of Juliet. *Home. It smells like home.* She matched Juliet's breathing and allowed the slow beating of her heart to lull her to sleep.

†

"Hey, that was a great shot," Keith hollered at Wayne in the front yard. He wiped away the snow from his head and ducked just in time to dodge another snowball from Wayne.

Ma heard him and walked out onto the front porch. "What are you two doing up?"

"Couldn't sleep, Ma," Wayne replied. "The snow was calling us."

"Well, keep it down so the rest can finish their naps," Ma said.

"Sorry, Ma. I didn't realize I was loud," Keith apologized.

"The cold carries any noise farther," Ma informed him.

Keith grinned. "I'll be quiet," he promised and let a snowball fly toward Wayne, who was still looking at Ma.

"Why don't you take it into the backyard?" Ma suggested. "You can be as loud as you want back there."

"Great idea, Ma. Come on, bone head," Wayne called to Keith.

"Are y'all getting hungry yet?" Ma asked.

"Not yet, Ma," Wayne answered. "We can wait for everyone else."

"Remind me to save room for dessert this time," Keith requested as he walked past Ma. "I forgot about Cedra's pies."

"It's so unlike you to forget about sweets," Ma teased.

"I must have been in a ham daze." Keith chuckled. "We saved the bone for you. Figured it would go well with some beans."

"Great idea. I'm glad you didn't toss it. Ham and beans do sound good with cornbread and some onion slices."

"Come on, Wayne, she's making me hungry talking about food."

"We'll be inside in a little while. I don't know how much more of a beatdown Keith can stand," Wayne teased as he slung his arm around Keith.

"Just wait, and I'll show you a beatdown," Keith warned.

"Don't hurt yourselves," Ma said. She shook her head at their antics and walked back inside. Hank was standing at the coffee pot. "Did those knuckleheads wake you?"

Hank turned to look at her. "No, I was already awake when they went out, but I watched them from upstairs. Wayne's got a wicked arm."

"They can be like teenagers sometimes." Ma grinned. "They are having so much fun with this snow."

"Let them play like kids as long as they can. There's so much serious time, it will do them good to laugh and play."

Ma walked into the kitchen. "That is all too true. I'll take a cup when it's ready, please."

"I've already got your mug loaded with sugar and creamer," Hank replied. "Do you know where you want your new television mounted?"

"I do, but it doesn't have to happen today."

"I need to feel like I've done something productive," Hank replied.

"You've helped me with the meals and hung my pictures," Ma reminded him.

"It won't take long. I may get the boys to help me while you warm up leftovers to keep us out of your way." Hank smiled.

Ma smiled back at him. "There is that. After everyone is up and about, I'll take you upstairs and show you the spot."

"I'll get them to help me install the mount and leave them to program the television. It would take me all night to do what they can accomplish in minutes," Hank stated.

"I know that feeling. I'm still trying to learn my smartphone," Ma replied and sat at the table.

†

Cedra woke to the sound of laughter. She looked up to see Juliet awake. "Did you nap at all?"

"Yes, but I love watching you sleep," Juliet answered. "I haven't been awake all that long. Wayne and Keith were whooping it up in the front yard."

They heard the front door open, and the laughter died down. "I think Ma just arrived to tell them to hold it down." Cedra chuckled.

"It did get quiet rather quickly." Juliet caressed Cedra's bare arm. "Are you in a hurry to get up?"

"No, I'm enjoying laying here with you."

"Great answer," Juliet said. "We don't get time often to just laze in bed together."

"You are so deliciously warm," Cedra stated. "I hate to think of moving."

"You're just fine right where you are. We don't need to be up for at least half an hour," Juliet replied.

"Maybe longer," Cedra answered and then laughed.

"What?"

"Listen. Ma moved the boys to the backyard, but you can still hear them," Cedra answered.

"They can have all the fun out in the cold they want. The snow is pretty, but it doesn't hold a candle to snuggling in with you."

"Amen to that, sister," Cedra replied. "The snow will still be there tomorrow."

"You've got two more days off, right?"

Cedra looked up at Juliet. "Yes, ma'am. Is there something you want to do?"

"Would you be interested in taking a ride to the Shoals? I bet it looks even more beautiful covered in snow," Juliet suggested. "We could toss a few logs in the back of your truck, and I can get a fire started while you take some pictures."

"I can make a thermos of hot chocolate to take with us," Cedra suggested.

"Do you mind a couple of hours away from Hank?" Juliet asked.

"I think we can send him and the boys on a shopping trip to get ready for their low-country boil. I'll give them my wholesale club card. They can scout out fresh shrimp, too," Cedra replied.

"I like your plan." Juliet smiled.

Cedra's hand stroked across Juliet's stomach. "Do you still want to play some music tonight?"

"I'd like to for a little bit. I bet we can talk the others into jamming with us after supper. Then a shower and a night of snuggling with you."

Cedra wiggled her eyebrows. "I have a bit more than snuggling in mind."

"I do, too, but I need a shower before climbing into bed. I got a bit sweaty this morning playing in the snow."

"You can come up and shower while I clean up the kitchen, and I'll shower when we come upstairs," Cedra suggested.

"That sounds like a perfect plan." Juliet rolled onto her side to face Cedra and pulled her in for a kiss. "I want a bunch more of your kisses tonight."

Cedra smiled. "I promise to kiss you breathless."

Juliet grinned. "That would make a great song title."

"I am so glad your writer's brain has kicked into gear. That would be a great title. Why don't we work on that while enjoying a nice fire tomorrow?" Cedra suggested.

"Works for me," Juliet replied and reached up to shut her alarm off before it began to chime. "Just one more kiss, and I'll be good for a while."

Cedra ran her fingers through Juliet's hair and pulled her head down for a deep kiss. She could feel the moan escaping Juliet's body and held the kiss a moment longer.

"Maybe that will give you something to look forward to," Cedra stated as she released Juliet's hair.

"Ah, yes, most definitely." Juliet smiled. "Let's go so we can get this party started."

Cedra slipped into her shoes and reached for Juliet's hand.

CHAPTER FOUR

The supper meal was much lighter, and everyone remembered to save room for dessert. Cedra made coffee while Ma cut slices of the pie. "Do you need Juliet and me tomorrow morning?"

"Not that I know of," Ma answered. "What do you have planned?"

"I want to go down to the Shoals for some pictures while we still have snow. I thought Dad and the guys could hit the wholesale club and start picking up supplies for our low-country boil." She looked at her dad. "If that's okay with you, Dad."

"That sounds like a good plan. We got Ma's television mounted today. We need a propane cooker and a large pot with a basket. I know we already have propane for the grill. We can look at seafood and other supplies there, too."

"I'll give you my club card," Cedra offered.

"No need. I got one when I gave that one to you. Do you think we should try grocery stores for fresh shrimp?" Hank asked.

"If they don't have them, maybe you can order them to be picked up later in the week," Cedra suggested.

"Would you join us, Ma?" Hank asked.

"I think I will," Ma answered.

"Can I make a thermos of hot chocolate to take with us?" Cedra asked.

"I'll make it for you after we all have a hearty breakfast. We have a bunch of ham left. We can freeze some, but ham and eggs would be good in the morning."

"I'll grate some potatoes if you make your hashbrowns," Hank offered.

Juliet chuckled. "I think you have him hooked."

"They are great, especially with some onion cooked in them," Wayne suggested. "I'll chop some onion tonight."

Ma shook her head. "I think the girls want to jam a bit tonight, so I'll prepare the onions while y'all play. Thanks for putting my television up for me."

"Hank did most of the work. We just supplied the muscle," Wayne answered.

"We got her done. That's what matters," Hank replied with a grin. "You did an excellent job on this pie, honey," he told Cedra.

"It is great. I'm glad you made two," Keith said.

"I agree that the extra day of refrigeration has only made it better. It has almost crystalized," Juliet replied, examining her next bite.

"The good thing here is that I know there won't be any wasted," Cedra said.

Keith swallowed. "Not with Wayne and me around."

Juliet finished her pie and coffee. "If y'all don't mind, I'm going to shower before we jam. I'm beginning to feel a bit funky."

"Go ahead. I'll get the kitchen cleaned, and we can jam," Cedra suggested.

"You know it feels weird that we haven't played any music for a few days," Wayne admitted. "We all needed a short break, but I'm ready. I even have some music bouncing around my head."

"For a new song?" Hank asked.

"I think so. I don't have lyrics yet, but the music is coming to me," Wayne answered.

"Whatever works for you," Cedra replied. "I'd like us to start thinking about some new songs. We're far ahead of Bud's schedule, but I'd like to be ready to cut *Out and Loud* whenever we get the nod. That gives us plenty of time to create."

"Any idea of when you'll be able to begin performing live again?" Hank asked.

"Not yet, but we will be ready when we do," Cedra answered. "We can play any gig offered with two albums cut and a ton of covers."

"That's going to be so exciting," Hank stated.

"I know we're all looking forward to the opportunity to play live," Cedra answered.

"Keep me posted on any live shows, and maybe I can come to see you perform," Hank told Cedra.

"You will be my first call," Cedra promised and smiled at him. "Why don't you two set up your guitars in the living room? Tomorrow, could you put the Christmas tree in the back by the freezer so we can have a nice fire in the fireplace?"

"Do you want us to remove the decorations?" Wayne asked.

"Absolutely not," Ma warned. "We don't need bad luck under this roof. We can take it down after New Year's."

"I guess I should have asked if it was okay to move it, Ma. I'm sorry," Cedra replied.

"No, thanks, it's wonderful, and it would be nice to have a toasty fire," Ma quickly answered. "I've been thinking about it for days."

"We've got plenty of wood stored outback. We can move the tree and lay a fire once we get back from town," Keith replied as he handed his glass and utensils to Cedra.

"Any thoughts for supper tomorrow night?" Ma asked. "I'm sure we have had enough ham for a bit."

Cedra grinned at Ma. "How about some fried chicken, rice, and gravy?"

"That meal is always delicious," Wayne said. "Maybe we can even find some okra." He winked at Cedra.

"Now we're talking," Cedra declared and began rinsing dishes to place in the dishwasher.

†

Wayne and Keith returned downstairs with their guitars and took seats in the living room. "Are you going to use your new keyboard?" Hank asked.

"I sure am," Cedra replied. "Do you mind setting it up for me while I finish here?"

"I'd love to," Hank answered and walked into the living room.

"What time do you girls plan to leave in the morning?" Ma asked as she dried a pot Cedra had washed.

"Not at the crack of dawn, that's for sure," Cedra answered. "I've only got two days before returning to work. I would guess we would leave between eight and nine."

"That gives Hank and me plenty of time to drink coffee before breakfast."

"For sure," Cedra replied. "Knowing my luck, I'll be up early anyhow, but I'm going to try to sleep in."

Ma placed the pot on a hook. "Good luck with that."

Juliet came bouncing downstairs with her guitar and her harmonica. "You almost done?"

"I'll be right there," Cedra answered.

Juliet sat beside Cedra's keyboard where Hank had set it up and placed her guitar beside her. She lifted the harmonica to her mouth and played the beginning of "Midnight in Nashville." "Wow, the sound is so much better." She grinned at Cedra as she entered the living room.

"That did sound nice," Cedra agreed as she sat beside Juliet. "Wayne, do you want to play the music in your head for us?"

"Sure," Wayne answered and began a simple tune.

Cedra picked up on the rhythm, and she and Keith were the first to join. Juliet joined them within a few seconds on her guitar.

"It's got a nice cadence," Juliet said. "Have the lyrics started coming to you yet?"

"Not yet," Wayne answered.

"What do you think of when you play the music?" Cedra asked.

"Living here with all of you," Wayne answered. "How we all pitch in to make the work and words flow."

"That sounds like an interesting story," Hank said.

"It will be by the time he's finished." Cedra smiled. "You remember the exercises to start creating the bones, right?"

"I sure do," Wayne answered. "I think I may work on them sometime tomorrow."

"That sounds great. Tomorrow might be a good writing day for all of us," Juliet replied. "We can get our planned stuff done and wait to see what the weather brings. I feel snow is coming."

"My old bones tend to agree with you," Ma answered.

†

They jammed for an hour before deciding to call it a night. "I'll get the bed warm while you shower," Juliet said as they entered Cedra's room.

"I won't be long."

Juliet lit one of the new candles she had given Cedra for Christmas, undressed, and climbed into the bed to wait for her lover. She watched the flicker of the candle as she listened for the water to stop. She was sure the night would be filled with epic lovemaking. The smile grew as her eyes landed on the remaining unopened gift on the bedside table.

†

The warm water pelting against her skin felt wonderful to Cedra. She had been thinking about being intimate with Juliet all day. She didn't wish the beautiful day to go quickly, but she longed to be in Juliet's embrace. A warmth that had nothing to do with the shower flowed through her as she turned off the water and began drying off. There was no need for clothing, so Cedra wrapped a robe around her body and quickly dried her hair. It would be a hornet's nest by morning, but she wanted to look presentable for Juliet. Her heart raced as she brushed her teeth and left the bathroom.

Juliet was stretched out under the covers and watched her approach. Cedra loved how Juliet's dark eyes burned with passion when she looked at her. She sat on the edge of the bed and reached for the gift. "Now is it safe to open this?"

54

"Now is a perfect time," Juliet replied.

Cedra carefully unwrapped the paper, and she couldn't help but smile at the thought of wondering who wrapped this gift since Juliet had confessed that she couldn't wrap presents. "Nice wrapping job," she whispered.

"Thanks. I did it myself. I took my time and remembered how careful you were to tuck the edges. I will admit to starting over twice because I cut the paper wrong, but you hold an original Juliet Tucker wrapping job in your hands."

Cedra leaned down and kissed her. The fact that Juliet had wrapped the gift made it more perfect. "You did a fantastic job." Cedra peeled back the paper to find a sample box of four types of Kama Sutra massage oils. "These look enticing. Do you have a favorite?"

"The cherry almond, but all of them are nice," Juliet replied.

Cedra pulled out the cardboard canister and lifted the top. She pulled out the glass bottle with a small cork lid and examined the red-tinted oil after placing the box on the table.

"Would you allow me?" Juliet asked as she reached for the bottle.

Cedra smiled. "Of course." She handed Juliet the bottle and removed the robe, placing it over her chair before slipping into the bed.

†

Juliet's heart raced as she took the bottle in her hands and loosened the cork from the bottle's neck. She turned it upside down to coat the tip of the cork as she rolled toward Cedra. "Close your eyes," she whispered. Juliet traced the cork tenderly across Cedra's lips when her eyes were closed.

"That's warm and sweet," Cedra replied. A soft moan escaped her as her tongue encountered her lips.

"A mouth or tongue activates the warm sensation." She pulled back the sheet, exposing Cedra's chest. "It takes the slightest amount in the right spots to heighten the experience." Cedra's nipples reacted to the sultry sound of Juliet's voice. Juliet circled a nipple with the oil-dampened cork. She leaned down to blow a soft breath against the nipple. Juliet repeated the action with the other nipple, then smiled at Cedra. "Does this feel good?"

"It's an incredible sensation," Cedra admitted.

Juliet coated Cedra's lips again and placed the cork in the bottle resting on the table. Her tongue circled her lips to enjoy the flavor as she leaned down to kiss Cedra to share the taste. Juliet noted how the oil warmed and deepened the kiss as her hand cupped Cedra's breast, gently squeezing the soft flesh.

"That tastes good," Juliet whispered against her lips as she broke the kiss. "I can't wait to taste this on the rest of you."

†

Cedra watched as Juliet poured drops of the oil into the palm of her hand. Her body whirled with excitement as she anticipated the feel of the oil against her clit and lower lips. She watched Juliet's head move down to her breast, and her hand cupped her mound. "Oh, hell, yes." She moaned as Juliet massaged the oil into her, as her mouth covered her breast. The heat of Juliet's mouth set her nipple on fire as her tongue and teeth teased the sensitive flesh. Cedra's body rippled with excitement as Juliet's oil-coated fingers teased her opening. Cedra's hand moved beneath the sheet and floated down Juliet's side to reach between her legs. Her hand stopped when she reached the cleanly shaven mound, and the wetness against her palm confirmed she had not missed her mark.

"This feels nice," she whispered as her fingers stroked across Juliet's opening. "Juliet?"

"Yes, Baby Girl?"

"I want this right here," Cedra answered as she cupped Juliet's mound and pointed to her mouth.

Juliet sat up and smiled as Cedra poured oil into her hand.

Cedra reached between Juliet's legs and coated the sensitive skin with the warming oil. "This is a great Christmas gift."

†

Juliet reversed her position and straddled Cedra's head. Cedra's fingers reached up to tease her opening with soft fingertips and then placed her hands on Juliet's hips to urge her to lower her body. When the tip of Cedra's tongue touched her bare skin, Juliet gasped. The sensation of her hot tongue felt glorious, and Juliet fought to control her excitement. She realized Cedra had devised a great plan to stifle their lovemaking as her head lowered between her open thighs. Juliet covered Cedra with tender kisses until she felt Cedra's tongue slide between her lips into her molten center. Juliet moaned and entered Cedra to keep from crying out as Cedra feasted on her wetness. Cedra's hands reached between them to roll Juliet's nipples, adding another layer of sensation.

†

Cedra's tongue lapped at Juliet, and the cleanly shaved skin was entirely new to her. Juliet's wetness spread across the smooth skin, and her tongue happily licked and probed Juliet's entrance. The mixture of the oil and Juliet's wetness exploded in Cedra's mouth, and the movement of Juliet's tongue deep inside her made restraint difficult for her. She feared Juliet was having a similar struggle. Her moans were muffled into Cedra's body, but they created delicious vibrations deep inside her. Cedra's right hand pressed against Juliet's lower back to bring Juliet's mound within Cedra's mouth. Her thumb stroked across Juliet's clit as her tongue swirled deeply inside her. Cedra raised her hips, urging Juliet's tongue deeper into her body. Juliet's tongue stroked across an area uncontrollably sensitive for Cedra, and she felt her body erupt in climax.

†

Juliet felt the contractions of Cedra's body surge through her, and she released, coating Cedra's face with moisture. She continued to lap at Cedra's lips as her body trembled uncontrollably. Juliet feared for Cedra's safety as her body neared exhaustion and reversed her position to lay next to Cedra. "Holy shit, that was intense," she said between gasps for breath.

Cedra wiped her hand across her mouth. "You can say that again. That felt fantastic." Juliet placed a leg between Cedra's knees and leaned in to kiss her. Her bare mound contacted Cedra's thigh, leaving a trail of wetness, but damn, it sure felt good.

†

The moisture pouring from Juliet's body made her mound glide up Cedra's thigh. Cedra raised her thigh, placing more pressure against Juliet's body, and she felt Juliet moan in her mouth. Cedra used her hands to prompt Juliet to move between her legs, and when their mounds touched, Cedra's hands dug into Juliet's ass, pulling them close, and their bodies ground together. Cedra broke the kiss.

"This is too good to waste," she whispered as she reached into the drawer to remove the Feeldoe and remote. "Fuck me, Juliet. Neither of us needs any lubrication."

†

Grinding into Cedra was bringing Juliet close to a second orgasm. When Cedra broke the kiss, reached for the sex toy, and asked to be fucked, Juliet thought her heart would explode. The toy slipped into their bodies easily, and when Cedra turned on the vibration, Juliet began slowly withdrawing from Cedra. She wasn't sure how much more stimulation her body could take, but she was determined to leave Cedra completely satisfied. Cedra's ankles locked around Juliet as she thrust deeply into her.

†

Cedra locked eyes with Juliet. Her dark eyes burned with passion as she pleasured her. Tiny beads of sweat rolled down Juliet's jaw from the continued exertion, and Cedra could tell she was tiring. A press of a button changed the vibration setting to maximum, and with the next deep thrust, Cedra held Juliet deep inside her as her body exploded. She could feel Juliet's climax arrive as her body convulsed with pleasure, and then she dropped exhausted into Cedra's arms. Cedra turned off the vibration, and her hand stroked Juliet's face.

"I promise to keep you supplied with razors if you keep us supplied with oil," Cedra said.

Cedra could feel Juliet's body move as she laughed at her lover's statement. When Juliet raised her face, it was filled with a smile.

"I will buy it by the gallon," Juliet teased. She lifted her hips to withdraw the toy slowly and then collapsed beside Cedra. "That was fucking amazing."

"Yes, it was." Cedra turned on her side, placing her head on Juliet's chest as her left hand covered Juliet's mound. "I may even have to try this," she said with a squeeze. "That was an incredible surprise."

"Merry Christmas, Baby Girl," Juliet whispered.

"That was the best present of the day," Cedra replied. "I love you."

"I love you, too."

CHAPTER FIVE

After breakfast the following day, Ma handed Cedra a large thermos of hot chocolate and a bag of marshmallows. "Wayne and Keith have already loaded firewood into the back of your truck. Have fun, and we'll see you later today."

"Thanks, Ma." Cedra pulled on her coat and picked up her camera bag and the thermos. She looked at Juliet. "Are you ready?"

"Yes, ma'am. Do you want me to drive since I've had a little more experience in snow?"

"That's not a bad idea." Cedra tossed her the keys.

"We'll get everything we need for New Year's," Hank promised.

"Do you need some money?" Juliet asked.

"We've got this," Hank assured her. "You two go have some fun."

"We'll have a fire tonight and a hot meal for supper," Ma said. "Now scoot."

Juliet looked at Cedra. "I think we're being kicked out."

Ma shook her head. "Be careful and have a wonderful time."

"I put a bucket in the back so you can make sure the fire is out before you leave. Don't stay out too long and get chilled." Keith smiled at them. "Have fun."

Cedra followed Juliet out to the truck and climbed inside. "I'm glad you offered to drive."

"No problem. We'll take it slow and careful. No need to hurry."

†

Cedra was scared when they hit a patch of black ice, and the back of the truck fishtailed. She was proud of how proficiently Juliet steered, maneuvering back into the road. "I would have surely hit my brakes," Cedra admitted.

"Unless it's a dire emergency, never use your brakes on ice. I'm sorry that patch snuck up on me. Are you okay?"

"I think I saw my life pass before my eyes," Cedra teased.

"It wasn't that bad." Juliet had both hands on the wheel. "We're almost to the turnoff, so we've passed the worst of the ice. We need to watch the time and ensure we leave plenty of time to make it home before dark."

"It will be harder to see the ice in the dark, won't it?"

"Yes, and much more dangerous. Especially if it is actively snowing, I wouldn't be surprised if we got more today." Juliet turned on her turn signal and pointed at the low-hanging clouds. "Snow clouds, for sure."

"Do you regret coming out this morning?"

"Not for a second." As they climbed the last hill on the trail, the Shoals came into view. "Damn," Juliet said and pulled to a stop. She looked at Cedra. "Do you want to get some distance shots before we move closer?"

"This would be the perfect spot. I'll be right back." Cedra pulled her camera out and stepped out of the truck.

Juliet watched as Cedra took various shots, and the flush on her cheeks rose from the cool breeze. She hoped they would be protected from the cold wind once they descended the hill. When Cedra returned, Juliet drove closer to the icy water. Icicles hung from the rock faces and sparkled in the sunlight.

"This spot is lovely. I'll get a fire started while you take your photos."

"That sounds good, and then we can have some hot chocolate."

Juliet cleared a spot they had used for a bench in the past to make a fire. It wasn't hard to find the ring of stones under the layer of snow or the log they would sit on. Within minutes, she had a fire started in the pit and turned to find

Cedra taking photos of her. She smiled and walked back to the truck for the thermos.

†

Cedra was amazed at how bright the snow-covered rocks appeared along the water. The ice dangling from the rock face looked like large teeth as they stretched toward the water. Cedra was surprised to find the water hadn't frozen over, even though there were sections along the bank where ice had begun to form. When she turned away from the water, she watched Juliet build and light the fire. She snapped off several shots and smiled when Juliet looked up and saw her. Cedra took dozens of pictures and returned her camera to the truck. She smiled when she found one of the new songbooks on the back seat, and pulled it and a blanket out to carry to the fire.

"You've got the fire burning well," she said as she placed the blanket and book on the log. "It feels good."

"I used to make campfires all the time growing up. My family had a small fish camp we would go to often, and I'd sit around a fire and stare at the stars for hours."

Cedra saw the smile of a pleasant memory grow on Juliet's face. She didn't talk about her family or childhood often, but she was glad Juliet had memories that would make her smile. "That sounds like fun." Cedra spread the folded blanket along the log to sit on as Juliet poured the hot drink.

"It is so beautiful here. I'm glad we got to see it covered in snow." She handed Cedra a mug and sat beside her.

"It is gorgeous, and I'm glad we are here together. This was a great idea. I hope some of my photographs will be suitable for framing."

"I'm sure they will be." Juliet smiled. "Are you warm enough?"

"Yes, that fire feels great." She looked at Juliet. "I wanted to thank you for such a wonderful time with you last night. It was incredible."

"It was enjoyable for me as well. I didn't believe things could be more intense between us, but last night was special."

Cedra stuck her hand between Juliet's arm and body. "Life with you keeps getting better by the day."

Juliet leaned down to plant a soft kiss on Cedra's lips. "Yes, it does. Some days I still feel like I'm dreaming. Then you look at me or say something, and I realize it's not a dream."

Cedra couldn't hold back a soft chuckle.

Juliet cocked her head to the side. "What?"

"Not that I had any doubt that you love me, but so much of what you tell me sounds like lyrics. It may just be my crazy writer's brain kicking in, but you have become a romantic whether you admit it or not."

Juliet looked at her with eyes shining with excitement. "You have my heart, so full the feelings and words spill out of my mouth." Juliet laughed at the look on Cedra's face. "I did it again, didn't I?"

Cedra nodded with a smile. "I'm loving it, though."

"Do you want to try to write?"

"Yes, but right now, I want to share this beautiful fire with you. We can always write later, but this spot won't look like this for long." Cedra sighed. "Everything looks brilliant in the snow, even with low light."

"It looks like a postcard setting, doesn't it?"

"Yes, so pure and clean. I hope my photos capture that."

"Can we turn around on the log and snap a selfie with the fire burning behind us? I'm not sure how long it will burn like this."

"Sure, but you'll have to take it. My arms aren't long enough for good selfies."

Juliet laughed. "I can't guarantee I won't cut heads off, but we can do it until we get it right."

It only took four attempts to get a great shot. Then Cedra leaned over to kiss Juliet's cheek. "I love that one," Juliet said and made it her background on her phone. "I'll send them to you as well."

"Thanks," Cedra replied as they returned to face the fire. Cedra snuggled in close to Juliet and laid her head on her shoulder. "Perfect."

"What, Baby Girl?"

"I said this is perfect. Beautiful scenery, a great fire, and snuggled into the woman I love. I don't know how it could get more perfect."

"I do," Juliet replied and pointed toward the north. "We have snow moving in. If you want to stay longer, I suggest putting your songbook back in the truck. We can't have that gold mine damaged."

"Do you mind staying?"

"Not as long as you are here." Juliet's eyes were sparkling as she reached for the book. "I'll be right back. Pour more hot chocolate, please."

Cedra refilled their mugs with the steamy liquid and handed one to Juliet when she returned. "Should we pull the blanket around us?"

"That's probably a good idea." Juliet lifted the blanket, leaving a small section to sit on, draping it across their shoulders as they sat. "Are you warm enough?"

"As long as I'm snuggled into you."

Five minutes later, the snow reached them. "I love it when the flakes are large and seem to swirl down from the sky." Juliet reached out her palm, and a flake landed and began melting.

"I guess you're too hot for it, baby," Cedra teased.

A log shifted in the fire, drawing their attention. When Juliet looked back at Cedra, she whispered, "I love you."

Cedra threw her head back, and at the top of her lungs, she yelled, "I love you, Juliet Tucker."

"Wow."

"I've wanted to shout that for ages." Cedra smiled. "This seemed like the perfect spot."

Juliet smiled. "You never cease to amaze me." Her head started to bob with imaginary music.

"Tell me what you're thinking right now."

"Since the first day we met, I couldn't imagine my life without you in it," Juliet replied.

"Keep going."

"You make me wanna, wanna, kiss you breathless. Uh-huh, oh yeah, breathless," Juliet continued. "Your smile makes my heart skip a beat."

"That's a good start. Can you remember that, or do I need to grab my book?"

"I think we can remember it between us," Juliet teased. "Just in case, though," Juliet said and leaned in to kiss Cedra. "I wanna kiss you breathless."

Cedra wiped a strand of hair from Juliet's face. "Bring it."

Juliet dropped the blanket from her shoulder and turned to face Cedra. She took Cedra's face in her hands, and a gentle kiss turned passionate within seconds. Juliet laughed. "Uh-huh, oh yeah, breathless."

"I am so proud of how you have embraced writing."

"Our love inspires me. It's a matter of putting the feeling into words."

Cedra's smile filled her face, and Juliet grabbed her chest.

"There you go again, making my heart skip a beat."

Cedra reached for Juliet's hand. "I can see we will have fun writing and singing this one."

"We can work on this and 'Out and Loud' before you need to go back to work," Juliet suggested.

"I think that's highly possible." Cedra drank the last of her hot chocolate and turned to face Juliet. A movement to her right caught her attention. She placed a finger over her lips and pointed behind Juliet.

Juliet turned toward the water, where a small deer had arrived for a drink of the cold water. She watched the women for a few seconds and then lowered her head to drink.

"Isn't she beautiful?" Cedra asked.

"Yeah, she is. Do you think you can get a picture with your phone?"

"I can try," Cedra replied and quietly removed her phone and snapped a photo of the deer. The deer sensed movement and lifted her head long enough for Cedra to capture another shot before she bolted back into the woods.

The snow was quickly covering the ground and steadily falling. The wind had picked up, and the temperature was dropping. Juliet looked at Cedra. "I hate to cut our trip short, but it's getting colder, and the snow is falling fast."

"Let's go home. If Ma and the guys aren't back yet, we can light a fire in the fireplace," Cedra suggested.

"I'll put the fire out if you take our mugs and the blanket and get the truck warming," Juliet offered. "I'll drive us home."

"Thanks," Cedra replied.

Juliet dowsed the fire and joined Cedra in the truck. "You've got it toasty in here."

Cedra smiled at her lover. "It's so beautiful. I hate we must leave, but I don't want us stranded out here either."

"The boys would never let us live it down. One thing before we leave." Juliet leaned across the truck and pulled Cedra into a kiss.

"That's certain to steam up the windows," Cedra replied when the kiss ended.

"Would you care to test out your theory?" Juliet wiggled her eyebrows.

"I'm afraid we won't make it back up the hill to the highway if we wait much longer," Cedra answered. "We could go to the bluff to test it out. That's much closer to home and an easier drive."

"Your wish is my command." Juliet put the truck in gear and reached for Cedra's hand.

"Sorry, love, both hands on the wheel until we're home safe."

"Spoilsport." Juliet turned on the radio, and they sang along.

They were treated to an announcement from the station DJ. "Happy holidays, everyone, and to celebrate, I want to share a brand new song from one of my favorite new groups, The Bentleys."

Cedra smiled at Juliet when she heard the opening of "Midnight," the melancholy sound of Juliet's harmonica flowing through the speakers. They listened without singing along, their heads bobbing to the music.

Juliet looked over at Cedra. "Hearing us on the radio will never get old."

"Every time I hear that song, I see you walking down Lower Broadway when we shot the video. It was cold, but you were smoking hot that night."

Juliet shot her a pouty face. "Just that night?"

"No, babe. You are hot all the time to me."

"You are so good for my ego."

†

When they reached the bluffs, Juliet stopped and cut the engine. The snow was falling rapidly, and the view out the windshield was a beautiful white vista. Juliet nodded toward the city. "It looks like a beautiful black and white postcard."

Cedra's gaze followed Juliet beyond the windshield. "It's so pristine. I love our town."

"Now about that theory," Juliet teased.

It didn't take long for their kisses to grow heated, and while they did manage to fog up the windows, the truck cooled off quickly.

"Theory evaluated and proved." Cedra giggled as she drew a heart on her window and traced Juliet's initials in the center. "I love you, Juliet Tucker."

"I love you, too." Juliet turned the key and fired up the engine. She laughed when she turned on the defrost to clear the windows. "Let's go home. I hear a fireplace calling our names."

†

Juliet parked the truck. "I'm surprised Ma and the boys aren't back yet. I don't know if we should be excited or worried."

Cedra pulled her phone out. "No missed calls or texts. They are probably just having fun. Do you want me to call and check on them?"

"No, let's get a fire started. Maybe we'll hear from someone soon."

Cedra rinsed out the mugs and thermos while Juliet started a fire. "Would you like more hot chocolate?"

"Nope. I want to snuggle up on the couch and enjoy the fire."

"That works for me," Cedra replied. Her phone pinged with a text as she entered the living room. "Ma is warning us that the snow is getting heavier, and she hopes we are heading home soon."

"I guess you better tell her we're already home and snuggling by the fire so that she won't worry about that." Juliet arranged pillows and stretched out on the couch. She motioned for Cedra to join her after she finished texting.

They could see the large flakes spiraling from the sky out the front window and could feel the warmth of the fire filling the room. "This is the best. We still have snow falling, and you've built a nice fire."

"All I need now is you." Juliet opened her arms to Cedra, who moved close to her and snuggled against Juliet's warm body. "Now, this is what I call heaven."

"Well, I'll be dipped in shit," Keith groaned as the truck came to an abrupt stop after spinning in several circles.

Wayne had a firm grip on the dash as they landed in a ditch.

"Is everyone okay?" Keith asked. "I'm embarrassed to say I hit a patch of black ice, and now we're in a ditch." He turned in his seat to find Ma wrapped in Hank's arms.

"Yes, we're good back here. Do I need to call for a tow truck?"

"Not yet, Ma. I think I may be able to winch our way out. If worse comes to worst, I'll call Cedra for a rescue." Keith looked at Wayne. "Will you help me?"

"Yep," Wayne answered. "The girls will get a kick out of us getting stuck."

"Well, if we can winch our way out, they will never know." Keith grinned. "Let's get to it before it gets any colder."

"You need my help?" Hank asked from the back seat.

"Sit tight. We've got this under control."

"There's no way you could have known there was black ice on the road. It's a good thing you were going slow," Wayne told Keith.

"I know. I hate scaring Ma and Hank."

"It looked like Hank had everything under control in the back seat." Wayne snickered.

Keith looked at the position of the truck. "This isn't too bad. We should be good if we can hook the line to that solid oak and pull ourselves out of the ditch."

"I'll pull out the line and get it secured, but you need to straighten your wheels if we're going to clear that ditch." Wayne grabbed the winch line by the hook and started walking to the tree.

Keith climbed back into the truck and straightened his wheels.

"Do you need me to steer while you operate the winch?" Hank asked.

"Yeah, that is a good idea," Keith replied.

Hank climbed in behind the wheel.

"Once you feel like we're back on solid ground, give it a bit of gas to get us back on the side of the road. Hit my emergency flashers if you would, please."

"Got it." Hank turned on the flashers.

Wayne gave Keith a thumb's up sign when he secured the cable. Keith picked up the control box, moved away from the truck, and began pulling the slack on the line.

"Cross your fingers," Hank told Ma as he felt the tension of the winch strain against the truck's weight. "Come on, baby. You can do this." When he felt forward movement, he pressed the gas pedal until he could feel the tire on solid ground.

"Yeah, that's it," Keith cried out. He hollered to Wayne to release the line and returned the cable to the case. "Good job."

"Let's go home. It's colder than a witch's tit," Wayne grumbled.

Hank returned to the back seat, and Keith got them home safely.

†

Ma stepped onto the porch with arms filled with groceries. She glanced through the front window and turned to Hank and the boys. "Try your best to be quiet. The girls are sleeping on the couch."

Hank pushed the door open slowly, and they entered the kitchen. Even Keith, usually the loudest of the bunch, crept quietly. A burning log split and crashed to the fireplace floor with a loud crack. Cedra sat up quickly at the sound and glanced around the room.

"So much for not waking them." Wayne laughed.

Ma looked over the top of a box of supplies. "At least we didn't wake them."

Cedra turned at the sound of their voices. "I didn't hear you come home. Do you need help?"

"No, we've got this. Keith, Wayne, and I will grab the last load." Hank opened the door and followed them outside.

Juliet stirred on the couch. "We fell asleep, didn't we?"

"Yes, we did. A log splitting in the fireplace woke me to find a bunch of elves working in the kitchen," Cedra teased. She nodded as Juliet sat up. "They were so quiet, too."

"It was just a matter of time before one of us dropped something to make a noise to wake you." Ma waved them over. "You can help me store the supplies."

Cedra leaned over to kiss Juliet. "Let's go." She reached for Juliet's hand and pulled her to her feet. "No wonder you were gone so long. Did you buy out the store?"

"We tried. We didn't want to make another run to town for supplies until after New Year's."

Hank pushed through the door carrying another box. "The boys are setting the keg up on the porch. I promised them we'd tap it after we've eaten later tonight."

Another log shifted in the fireplace. "I'll add more wood if you want to help Ma get started."

"I've got the wood," Hank told Juliet.

"Did you find everything you needed?" Juliet asked Ma.

"And then some." Ma emptied a box onto the table.

Juliet looked at another box. "Is this frozen goods for the freezer?"

"Yes, will you empty it into the chest freezer?"

"Sure thing, Ma." Juliet lifted the box and started toward the back porch.

Hank held the door open and then carried an armful of firewood into the living room.

When everyone returned to the kitchen, Ma asked, "Is building a burrito okay with y'all for supper?"

"That sounds great to me," Juliet answered, and the rest nodded in agreement.

Cedra pulled out a small crockpot. "If I can have a pound of that hamburger, I'll make a queso dip to go with these chips."

"Oh, heck yeah. I love your dip," Wayne said. "Do you want me to start browning some hamburger for you?"

Keith looked at Hank. "Where do you want me to store this cooker for now?"

"You can put it next to the freezer unless it will be in the way." Hank looked at Ma for confirmation.

"That will be good." Ma nodded.

"What can I do?" Hank asked.

"Chop lettuce and tomatoes. I'll get Keith to grate some cheeses."

"What do you need, Ma?" Keith said when he heard his name.

"Grated cheese. You up for it?"

"Cheddar and pepper jack?"

"Works for me." Wayne grinned.

Cedra handed Juliet cans of chili beans and Rotel. "Will you open these for me?'

†

After gorging themselves with Mexican food, they all pitched in for the cleanup.

"I think it's time for you boys to tap that keg," Hank suggested. "It should be settled and icy cold by now."

"Would you mind us listening to the new CD, Ma?" Juliet asked.

"I was hoping you'd pop it into the player. We could play poker, drink cold beer, and listen to good music."

"Poker?" Hank rubbed his hands together.

"No real money, so don't get your hopes up, Dad." Cedra leaned over and kissed his cheek.

"Do we have chips?"

"I thought we'd break out matchsticks or a penny jar," Ma teased. She watched the smile leave Hank's face. "Yes, I have chips."

Hank and the boys carried chilled pilsner glasses out to the keg and filled them after sampling a taste each. "That's what I'm talking about," Keith said and refilled his glass.

Ma looked at Cedra. "I'm going to text Patsy that we'll come to pick her up at three tomorrow. Would you send Lisa Marie a text to remind her as well?"

"I'm on it, Ma." Cedra sent the text as Juliet placed the poker chip rack and cards on the table. Cedra's phone pinged. *I'll see you at three.*

"What time do you want to plan on dinner tomorrow night?" Hank asked Ma as he began shuffling the cards.

"Do you think six is too early?"

"I think six would give our food time to settle while we wait to ring in the new year," Hank answered and began dealing the hand.

Juliet looked at Cedra. "Did you forget to inform us that Hank is a card shark?"

"Nope. He taught me everything I needed to know to play Go Fish." Cedra shot a wink at her dad.

It didn't take Hank and Ma long to accumulate large piles of chips. Wayne and Keith kept the glasses filled with beer.

"It's a good thing we aren't playing with real money," Wayne groaned as he folded his hand. "I'd be dead broke."

"I'm right there with you, bro." Keith laughed as he drank a sip of beer. "Maybe we should have stuck to Go Fish."

"I'm done," Juliet said and tossed her hand into the pile.

"We should all call it a night. We have a long day ahead of us," Ma reminded them.

Hank and Ma loaded the glasses in the dishwasher after everyone else headed upstairs. "Tonight was fun. I'm looking forward to ringing in the New Year with our family," Ma said.

"Me, too. I'm sure it will be a smashing success. Goodnight, Ma."

"Goodnight, Hank. I'll see you for coffee in the morning."

"Yes, you will." Hank smiled and climbed the stairs as Ma locked up and turned out the lights.

CHAPTER SIX

Juliet handed Cedra a towel as she stepped from the shower. "Last night was fun. I'm glad we weren't playing for money, though."

"Dad has always been great at cards, but Ma gave him a run for his money."

"She was holding her own for sure."

When they entered the bedroom, Juliet looked out of the window. "The snow is fading fast, but it still looks as cold as a well digger's ass out there."

Cedra wrapped her arms around Juliet's waist. "That's pretty darn cold."

Juliet pulled her close. "Don't worry; I'll keep you warm. Is there anything special we need to do this morning?"

"Not that I'm aware of. Dad and the boys will have the cooker ready late this afternoon. I think they'll be glued to the television watching football. We can see if Ma needs our help. Is there something you'd like to do?"

"I'd like to do some writing."

Cedra smiled. "That sounds like a good plan. Let's have some breakfast and make a writing plan. It's too cold for the porch."

"I promise to be on my best behavior if we come back upstairs."

Cedra stepped out of Juliet's arms. "What if I don't want you on good behavior?"

Juliet leaned forward to kiss her forehead. "I will be anything you want me to be."

"You are perfect, just as you are. I wouldn't change a thing." She reached for Juliet's hand. "Let's go get some coffee."

†

Ma and Hank were sitting in the living room drinking coffee. There was a fire burning in the fireplace. "Grab some coffee and join us," Ma called out to them.

Juliet turned to Cedra. "Go ahead and join them, and I'll bring our coffee. Does either of you need a refill?"

"No, I just poured us a fresh cup," Hank replied.

Cedra bent down to kiss his cheek. "Good morning. I hope you slept well."

"I always sleep like a rock here."

"It looks like a beautiful morning. Have you been outside?"

Hank nodded. "The sun is melting the snow quickly, but it's still bitterly cold out."

"Is there anything you need our help with today?" Cedra looked up to take the coffee from Juliet.

"No, I think it will be a restful day. Most of the prep work for the boil is done. I'll go pick up Patsy around three. Is there something you wanted to do?"

"We thought we might get some writing done today," Juliet said.

"I think that's an excellent idea. I know you both must be anxious to return to writing," Ma replied.

Juliet looked at Ma. "I'm afraid I'll lose my newfound ability if I don't keep in practice."

"I don't think you have to worry. Do you want to use the kitchen table?"

"No, we'll head back upstairs. Football games will start soon, and we don't need the distraction."

"Let's enjoy some coffee, and I'll make a simple breakfast. Then you can get busy. I was thinking of fried egg sandwiches. Enough to hold you over until a light lunch."

"That sounds perfect, Ma. Have you heard any movement from the boys?"

"No, Cedra, I thought I'd let them sleep in. I'll cook for them when they arrive."

"Do you mind if we write today, Dad? I don't want you to feel we are abandoning you."

"I think I'll survive with football, snacks, and good company. I know you have been itching to write for a few days."

"Yes, I've got a few lyrics bouncing around my head."

"Is there anything we need from town, Ma, or are we all set?"

"I believe we are good, Hank. Was there something you wanted?"

"No, I just didn't want anyone to have to make a run if we needed something."

†

The group was drinking coffee when they heard boots on the stairs. Cedra looked up to see Wayne enter. "Good morning."

"Good morning, everyone," he answered.

"We wondered if you would sleep in this morning," Cedra teased.

Wayne shook his head. "My body is used to waking up early for work."

A log shifted in the fireplace, drawing their attention. Hank looked at Wayne.

"Why don't you help me carry some wood inside? Ma will be cooking fried egg sandwiches for breakfast."

"That sounds great," Wayne replied.

Ma looked at the girls. "Ready to eat?"

Juliet stood. "I'm always ready for your cooking." She offered Ma a hand to help her out of her chair.

"Let's get to cracking then."

†

They were nearly finished eating when Keith finally ventured downstairs, rubbing his eyes. "The aroma of cooking food finally reached my subconscious. What smells so good?"

"Fried egg sandwiches. Pour yourself a drink, and I'll start cooking," Ma told him. "Does anyone else need another?"

"Heavens no. I'm already about to pop." Hank chuckled. "I don't know how you make something so simple, taste so good."

"It's because it's made with love," Cedra said as she loaded dishes into the dishwasher. She winked at Ma. "We're going to head upstairs. Holler if you need anything."

"Good luck," Ma said. "I'll try to hold down the noise from the living room to a mild roar."

"Uh yeah, good luck with that, Ma," Juliet said as she reached for Cedra's hand.

†

"What do you plan to work on?" Cedra asked.

"I want to see if I can knock out a draft of 'Out and Loud' today." Juliet flipped open the laptop on the desk and turned to Cedra. "What about you?"

"I've got some new words bouncing through my brain." Cedra picked up her songbook and propped herself against pillows on the bed. She opened the book to a blank page and jotted down "Still My Hero." Spending time with her dad over the holidays brought back many memories for Cedra. She still considered him her first hero and wanted to write about their love. She glanced over her book to find Juliet tapping away at the keyboard. The glow from the screen illuminated the smile on her face. There was no doubt about how much she loved Juliet, and Hank's acceptance of them as a couple made her heart swell with joy. Hank had never once questioned their commitment to each other, and he treated Juliet with more love and kindness than her family. Cedra jotted down more notes and then flipped back to read over what they had started on "Kiss You Breathless." She looked up to find Juliet watching her.

"I need something cold to drink. Do you want something?"

"A glass of tea would be nice."

"Do you need a break, or should I bring it here?"

Cedra looked at the time. "I'd like to get at least another hour of writing done. Would you mind bringing it upstairs, so I don't lose my rhythm?"

"Not at all. Do you need a snack?"

"I'm good." Cedra leaned over to kiss Juliet.

Juliet could hear cheering from the living room as she descended the stairs. Hank, Wayne, and Keith were glued to the television and looked up when she entered.

"Good game?"

"The Dawgs are giving them a beat down." Keith gave Wayne a high five.

"I hope we aren't being too loud."

"Naw, Dad, we've barely heard a peep out of y'all. Where's Ma?"

Hank smiled. "She decided to get a nap in while she could. Ma set up meat and cheese trays with fruit in case we got hungry."

"Not hungry, but thirsty," Juliet replied as she turned to enter the kitchen. "Y'all need anything while I'm up?"

"Touchdown," Wayne cried out.

Hank smiled at her. "I think we're all good. How's the writing coming?"

"We both have a good flow going. Cedra wants to write for another hour or so."

"There's no hurry. I told Ma that I'd ride with her to pick up Patsy, so write as long as you can."

"That sounds good." Juliet poured two glasses of tea and returned upstairs.

"Welcome back." Cedra took the glass Juliet offered. "What's going on downstairs?"

"The boys are watching football, and Ma is taking a nap. She and Hank will pick up Patsy, so he said to write for as long as we want. There are snacks in the fridge if we get the munchies before dinner."

Cedra took a long drink. "That hits the spot."

"Drink up, and if you need more, I'll get more." Juliet leaned down to kiss Cedra and then sat at the desk.

†

Cedra had reached a stopping point and was about to stand to stretch when her phone started ringing. She looked at the screen. "Stone," Cedra answered the call and hit the speaker. "Happy New Year's Eve, Stone."

"You, too, Cedra. I hope you had a great Christmas."

"We did, thanks. I loved the pictures of Destiny you sent."

"She had a great Christmas. Do you have time to talk?"

"I sure do. Juliet and I are upstairs getting some writing done. Is everything okay?"

"Hey," Juliet called to him.

"Yes, and no," he answered. "I've had to make a difficult decision, and I wanted to talk with you first. You've done so much for me and helped me realize my dream."

"You've worked hard for it," Cedra reminded him.

Stone sighed deeply. "I'm not coming back. Dad has not recovered from his illness and only has the stamina to work about two hours daily. Sarah and Mom have been working hard to keep the ranch running, but it's more than they can manage. I need to step up for my family and stay home."

"I don't think anyone could blame you for making that decision. Family should always be the top priority." Cedra looked up at Juliet, who nodded in agreement with her.

"Cedra's right, family always comes first. Is there anything we can do to help?"

"No, but your offer means the world to me. I can see the physical toll exhaustion has taken on Mom and Sarah. Mom rarely smiles any more, she's so worried about Dad. I hate to leave Lisa Marie and the band so suddenly."

"We will all survive. I understand, but I know how disappointed you must feel."

"I know I'm good enough, thanks to y'all and the boys. I've never had so much fun, but the need for me at home outweighs my return to Nashville. Please let me know if I need to return part of the advance check."

"As far as we're concerned, you've earned every penny of it. We will talk with Carrie, but I think she'll agree and advise us on how to move forward. If situations change and you can come back, you'll be welcome to join us again."

Stone cleared his throat, and Cedra could hear the emotion in his voice. "I am sorry it's come to this."

"It's not your fault, so don't feel bad. You're doing what any of us would do for our family," Juliet assured him.

"Do you want us to tell Ma, Lisa Marie, and the guys?"

"Please, if you would, Cedra. Tell them I'll call them in the next day or two. This has been a hard decision, and I need time to come up with the right words to relay my thanks to them."

"Trust that everyone will support this decision," Cedra replied. "We will miss you, but you never know when circumstances change. Don't stop writing; we'll review anything you send us."

"You know you could also send your stories to Carrie," Juliet suggested. "You have great skills; I'm sure she could help you market them."

"That's a great idea and could generate some additional income," Cedra agreed.

"I will ask her about that this week when I call her. I won't keep you all any longer. I'm betting you have big plans for tonight."

"Dad and the boys are doing a low-country boil. Lisa Marie and Patsy are joining us."

"That sounds like fun. Enjoy, and I hope we can talk again soon."

"Call anytime and keep us posted. We love you like a brother, Stone. Never forget that," Cedra told him.

"Y'all are the best extended family I could have ever asked for. Good luck with the new album. I'll be waiting to hear it on the radio."

"Thanks, Stone. We'll talk again soon." Cedra tapped the button to end the call and slumped back against her pillows.

"I'm not surprised with Stone's decision. Are you?" Juliet asked a frowning Cedra.

"Not really. I think we all could see this coming, but the reality of it has hit home."

"Are you worried more about the band or the café?"

"We started as an idea of four for the band, and since you all have begun writing, I'm not concerned about the loss there."

"So, what if I talk to Lisa Marie about coming to work with you until we can begin to play gigs? Hopefully, by then, the restrictions on the café will be lifted." Juliet watched the smile grow on Cedra's face, and her eyes sparkled with excitement.

"You would do that?"

"Of course, I would. More time with you, a little jingle in my pocket, and I get to help Lisa Marie in the process."

Cedra laid her book on the bed. "I love you so much." She stood and took Juliet in her arms. "Let's go break the news. My creativity is shot for the day."

Juliet hugged her close. "We've got this, so don't worry."

Cedra looked into Juliet's face. "As long as I have you, there's nothing we can't do."

"That's right. Don't you forget that." Juliet kissed her sweetly. "Let's go gather the crew and break the news."

†

"I don't think this is a surprise to any of us," Ma said as she looked around the table. "Stone has family responsibilities the rest of you don't, and I'm proud of his decision."

"Do you think it will affect the band?" Keith asked.

"Not really. We started the idea of the band with just the four of us. We will be fine if you, Wayne, and I continue to write. The only instrument Stone played that we haven't tried is the fiddle. I'm sure one of us can learn how to play it if necessary."

"I've played around with a fiddle for years. I'm sure I can play well with some practice," Keith said. "Maybe I can borrow one from the studio and practice during the day while you all are at work. I'd love to learn to play 'The Devil Went down to Georgia.'" He grinned.

"That's a good idea." Cedra looked at Juliet. "Juliet plans on talking with Lisa Marie about working with us temporarily."

"I can help out, too, if needed," Ma added.

"Thanks, Ma. So, I think, given the circumstances, we are in good shape. Just keep writing."

Wayne grinned at Keith. "We will. We've already talked about a few ideas."

"That's good to hear. Fortunately, we are at a point where we have the luxury of time to develop 'Out and Loud,' so there's no need to rush." Cedra looked around the table. "I'll schedule a meeting with Carrie to discuss the changes and to start plans moving forward. Do you all want to be a part of that?"

"You and Juliet represent us well. You can always call in Ma if you need big guns," Wayne teased.

"Ha! I've got your big guns. Help this old lady bring out some snacks. I've got the munchies," Ma called to Wayne.

†

Lisa Marie called to see if there was anything needed or if she should go by to pick up Patsy.

"Ma and Hank left to get her a few minutes ago. We are all set for supplies, so come out when you can," Juliet told her.

"I'm on my way. I'll see you soon."

"Drive safe."

Wayne and Keith entered the house. "We've got the cooker set up and the pot filled with water, so we're good to start cooking in a few hours," Wayne said.

"We're going to have a cold one. Will you two join us?"

"Sure, Keith," Juliet answered.

"I'll toss a few more logs on the fire and join you in a minute," Wayne said. "It's still wicked cold out."

Keith carried a tray of solo cups and placed them on the table. He picked up the remaining cup and lifted it to his friends. "To our first New Year's together. May we all stay healthy and our band successful."

"I'll drink to that," Juliet said. "To an exciting new year ahead of us."

93

"While it's just the four of us, does anyone have a concern about moving forward without Stone?"

"Not a one, Cedra. We lost a good songwriter, but Keith, Juliet, and I will work hard to fill the gap."

"Stone offered to send a portion of his advance back, but we told him to keep it. He earned it, and we will get Carrie's advice about future royalties. We can discuss royalties if we use more of his music in the future. If we all make a concerted effort to write, we won't need any songs, but we'll look at anything he sends."

Juliet nodded. "He's also going to talk to Carrie about promoting some of his songs for extra income."

Wayne grinned at Juliet. "Are you prepared to get up with the chickens?"

"I've been practicing. I think it will be fun to work with y'all."

"I'll remind you of that statement after the first few days." Cedra laughed softly. "It's not hard work, but getting up early and being on your feet for hours requires adjustment."

"We can put a stool at the side door, so she can take a break when not making or delivering coffees," Wayne suggested.

"Perfect," Juliet said and took a drink of beer.

When they heard a car door slam, they watched the front door for Hank, Patsy, and Ma to arrive. Keith stood and retrieved three more cups. He rushed to hold the door open. "Are you three ready for a cold one?"

94

Hank returned his smile. "It's five o'clock somewhere. Bring it on."

†

Dinner turned out well, and everyone had their fill of the delicious meal. The group drank beer and played cards while waiting for the Midnight Music Note to drop to ring in the new year. Juliet had talked with Lisa Marie and agreed to start work when the café reopened in two days. Cedra was not used to drinking that often and was experiencing a buzz while they talked and played cards. Keith, Wayne, and Juliet were scattered around the living room watching football, and Cedra felt her attention drawn to the musical sound of Juliet's laughter. Unable to concentrate on the game, she excused herself and joined her friends in the living room. She sat on the couch next to Juliet, snuggling into her warm embrace. "I missed you."

Juliet turned to her and kissed her. "I love you."

"I love you, too."

"Hey, should we turn to the local channel to watch the drop?" Keith asked. "It's only fifteen minutes away."

"Do it, bro, and I'll pour us fresh beer. Anyone else?"

Cedra shook her head. "None for me. I'm already buzzed."

"I'll take a half," Juliet said. "That will be plenty for us to toast in the New Year."

A reporter was broadcasting live from downtown. The camera was fixed on the Music Note perched on a tall building, lit and ready to perform. The camera panned through the crowd, which was dismal compared to normal, pre-pandemic times. Since most local venues were closed or at minimal capacity, many attendees opted to party at home or in smaller venues to limit exposure.

Ma, Hank, Patsy, and Lisa Marie joined them in the living room. "I hope this pandemic ends soon," Lisa Marie said. "Downtown is normally wall to wall with partiers for this event."

"As more people get vaccinated, the slower the virus will get. Especially if people use common sense and mask up as directed," Hank said. "I've got my second dose scheduled for a week after I go home."

"We all need to get started," Ma said. "There's no need to tempt fate."

"A sore arm and a headache were all I experienced from the first shot. The next day I was back to normal."

"I will call and get us all scheduled if we want to go together," Ma offered.

"I'll volunteer to hold your hand, Keith," Juliet teased.

"Really, guys, it wasn't bad at all. I've had worse reactions from a flu shot," Hank told them.

"Go ahead then, Ma." Cedra looked at Juliet. "We will go with you."

"Us too," Wayne said.

Lisa Marie looked at Patsy. "Count us in, too. We can't miss a party."

"I'll call Tuesday when y'all go back to work and see what I can get scheduled."

"Here we go with the countdown," Keith called out as the Music Note descended. Fireworks were let off in the background, filling the sky with bright lights as the countdown to midnight arrived, and they called out "Happy New Year" and raised their glasses in a toast.

Juliet kissed Cedra and Hank gave chaste kisses to Ma, Patsy, and Lisa Marie, and high-fives to the boys. "Thanks to everyone for a great celebration," Hank said.

"You and the boys made us a great meal, and the company couldn't have been better," Ma replied. "I know you youngins may want to stay up longer, but this old gal is toast. Happy New Year, everyone."

"I'm coming right along with you," Patsy said.

"I'll get Lisa Marie set up in the downstairs room," Juliet offered. "Then I think we'll call it a night too."

"Hank, will you stay up with us a bit longer?" Keith asked.

"I do believe I can handle one more beer. I'll lock up before we head upstairs, Ma."

"Don't be in a rush to wake up in the morning. Our last day to sleep in before we go back to work," Ma replied.

"I'm right behind ya, Ma," Cedra said.

Juliet smiled when she saw a slight glaze in Cedra's eyes. She planned to get Lisa Marie settled in and then return for ice water and Tylenol for Cedra. Juliet feared Cedra would have a hangover in the morning, so taking something tonight might minimize the aftereffects.

†

Cedra kissed her dad on the cheek. "Don't stay up too late with these two."

"I won't. Happy New Year, Baby Girl."

"You, too, I love you, Dad."

"I love you, too. See you in the morning."

Cedra climbed the stairs and undressed, then pulled a T-shirt over her head to sleep in. She pulled back the covers and relaxed between the cool sheets. As soon as she closed her eyes, the room started to spin. Cedra sat up in the bed, holding the sides of her head. She was still there when Juliet entered the room.

"Are you okay?"

"No, the room starts spinning when I lay down," Cedra groaned.

"Oh my. Here take these and a sip of water." Juliet handed her the Tylenol and glass of water. "Just a sip. Then brush your teeth to get the beer taste out of your mouth."

Juliet joined her at the sink to brush her teeth and then undressed. Cedra started to climb into bed, and Juliet stopped her. "Tonight, I think you should sleep on the side closest to the bathroom. You may have to relieve your bladder or, worse, your stomach," Juliet said as she moved onto the bed.

"I pray it doesn't come to that," Cedra said.

"Take another sip of water and stretch out on your back. Kick your left foot from under the covers. I've found that helps to stop the room from spinning."

"I'm not much of a drinker if you couldn't tell," Cedra apologized.

"We started too early." Juliet snuggled into Cedra. "I've got you, so just try to fall asleep." She added pillows under Cedra's head.

Cedra moved her left leg off the side of the bed and closed her eyes. "That is better," she slurred against Juliet's cheek.

"I hope you won't need to but wake me if you need anything."

"I will, my love."

Juliet listened as Cedra's breathing slowed, and she began to purr softly. "Sleep well," she whispered and closed her eyes.

CHAPTER SEVEN

Juliet was propped on her side when Cedra's eyes began to flutter. Cedra's eyes opened briefly, then slammed shut. "Did you get the train number that ran over me?"

"Good morning, darling," Juliet whispered. "That bad, huh?"

"The sunlight coming through the window feels like icicles piercing my brain."

"Why don't you hit the bathroom, and I'll shut the blinds? I'd recommend you try to sleep a bit longer unless you feel you could manage some dry toast."

"Dear God, no," Cedra groaned as she sat up slowly in the bed. "Just thinking about eating is making me nauseous."

"Toast or a biscuit might help later to soak up the acid in your stomach."

"Not now." Cedra waved her hand and walked to the bathroom. She rinsed her mouth with cool water after washing her hands. Her mouth felt like it was filled with cotton. Cedra took a sip of the water beside the bed when she returned.

"Cottonmouth?" Juliet asked.

"Yeah. I feel like I swallowed a few bales last night."

"Is the water okay, or do you want to try apple juice? I'll get more Tylenol and juice if you want."

"Tylenol, but I'll pass on the juice for now."

"Climb back in bed, and I'll be right back." Juliet slipped into sweatpants and a T-shirt before leaving the room.

†

The house was quiet. She was surprised to find only Ma and Patsy awake, sitting at the table, sipping coffee. "Good morning."

"Good morning. I didn't expect you awake so early," Ma said.

"I've come down for more Tylenol for Cedra."

"Does she have a hangover?" Ma asked.

"You could say that." Juliet smiled. "I've convinced her to go back to sleep if she can. She's not ready for toast or anything else on her stomach yet."

"Are you staying up?"

"Yes, I'll be back after she takes these. You can go ahead and pour me a cup if you would. I'm surprised Hank isn't up with you."

"I think he was up later with the boys than he had planned." Ma chuckled. "I bet he joins us soon if he heard you up and about."

"Probably. I'll see you in a few."

†

Juliet sat on the bed beside Cedra and handed her the pills and water. "Take these and sleep for a few hours. Ma and Patsy are the only ones awake."

"Dad isn't even up yet?" Cedra asked.

"Nope. He had a good time with the boys last night."

"Just don't let me sleep all day."

"I won't. I promise." Juliet brushed her lips against Cedra's. "I'll check in on you later."

"I love you."

"I love you, too."

†

Juliet joined Patsy and Ma at the kitchen table. She took a sip of the coffee. "This hits the spot."

"I'm sorry Cedra isn't feeling well this morning," Ma said.

"She's not much of a drinker, and I think we started too early for her. I don't think we'll see her drinking again anytime soon."

"I can't remember ever seeing her drink more than one or two beers. I believe it's easy to lose count when it's fresh on tap. Keith kept them coming regularly after we ate."

Juliet grinned. "That he did. I was feeling buzzed for a while." Her finger traced the rim of the mug. "I think she'll be okay after she sleeps a few more hours. What's the plan for today?"

"Sipping coffee until the others begin to stir. We can eat biscuits, meat, and gravy for breakfast, and I'll start an early dinner."

"Black-eyed peas and greens?" Patsy asked.

Ma nodded. "For starters, to continue the tradition of a good luck meal. I thought I'd fry some pork chops and okra, then top it off with cornbread."

"I know Cedra will get out of bed for your okra. What can I help with?"

"Nothing yet. I've got the peas soaking. After breakfast, I'll get them and the greens cooking."

"Would you mind two other requests?"

"What would you like, Juliet?"

"Some white rice and sliced onion for the peas, and some gravy from the pork chops to go with the rice, too, if you wouldn't mind. I love your gravy."

Ma smiled and nodded at Juliet's suggestions. "Those are easy requests," Ma said.

"Do you have a dessert planned?" Patsy asked.

"Not really. Do you have something in mind?"

"I thought I'd make a couple of buttermilk pies if you have the ingredients."

"That's a perfect idea, Patsy. I do believe I have everything you will need."

"My contribution to our New Year's Day meal."

"Do you want me to start a fire?" Juliet asked.

Ma smiled. "Let's leave that chore for Hank once he arrives and gets some coffee."

"I don't think he'll be long. I heard him stirring when I came back down."

They all turned toward the stairs when they heard footsteps on the treads. Hank saw three smiles welcoming him. "I'll grab a cup. Do y'all need a refill?"

"I'm almost ready," Ma replied.

Patsy shook her head. "I think I'm good for a bit."

"Did you sleep okay?" Juliet asked.

Hank poured his coffee and turned toward them with the pot. "Once we finally went to bed around two. I haven't been up that late in years."

"I'm surprised you're up this early then," Ma said.

"My old bladder got the best of me, and then I smelled coffee." He poured Ma a fresh cup and topped off Juliet. "Is Cedra sleeping in?"

Juliet shot him a grin. "Uh, yeah. She's a bit hungover this morning. She doesn't drink often and has a thumping headache. I gave her a dose of Tylenol and pulled the blinds closed."

"That's probably what she needs right now. Her mama wasn't much of a drinker, either. Maybe she can stomach some toast later."

"I told her I'd give her a few more hours to sleep and bring her some toast." Juliet stirred creamer into her coffee. "She'll be tickled to hear Ma is making fried okra with supper."

Hank smiled. "I hope you have plenty."

"I don't think anyone will go hungry with everything we have planned."

"Last night's supper was a delight," Patsy said. "I haven't eaten that well since the last time I was here."

"I thought I heard voices," Lisa Marie said as she wiped her hair back from her face. "Good morning, everyone."

"Coffee?" Hank asked.

Lisa Marie sat beside Juliet and held out her arm. "Can you run an IV line?" She smiled at Hank. "Last night was a blast, but I'm glad it only comes around once a year."

"Do you need some Tylenol?" Juliet teased.

"I took some before I left the room. I'm unsure if the coffee will settle my stomach, but it smells terrific."

"Do you need some toast on your stomach first?"

"Not a bad idea, Juliet."

"Anyone else?" Juliet stood to make some toast.

Patsy shook her head. "I'm holding out for Ma's biscuits and gravy."

Hank rubbed his hands together. "That does sound good. What can I do to help?"

"Finish your coffee, and then you can start a fire," Ma said.

"Also known as stay out of the kitchen." Juliet shot him a wink.

"I kinda got that," Hank replied. "You can help me carry some wood inside."

†

Ma was pulling a pan of biscuits from the oven when Wayne and Keith came downstairs. "Happy New Year," Wayne said.

"You, too, boys. As usual, you have great timing." Ma transferred the biscuits onto a platter. "Why don't you lightly butter one and see if Cedra dares put anything in her stomach yet."

Keith looked at Juliet. "Is Cedra not feeling good this morning?"

"She's suffering a bit of a hangover," Juliet said as she buttered a biscuit.

Ma poured the gravy into a serving dish. "Take her a small glass of apple juice. That should be easy on her stomach."

Keith shot a wink. "Baby sister isn't much of a drinker."

"I can remember my first hangover. I felt like a Mack truck ran over me a few times," Wayne replied.

"Go easy on her. She tried her best to keep up with us last night," Juliet warned them. "I'll be back."

†

Cedra's arm was draped over her eyes when Juliet crept into the room and sat on the edge of the bed. "Hey, sweetie," she whispered.

Cedra moved her arm and opened her eyes. "I'm not sure I can handle that."

Juliet waited until she sat up in bed. "At least try. The sooner you get something into your system, the better you'll feel. I promise."

"Have you eaten yet?"

"Nope, I got you the first biscuit out of the batch. I'll eat in a few."

"Are the boys up yet?"

"Just barely. You know they arrive when the food is ready."

"There may not be much left if you wait too long."

"Trust me. I won't starve. You're going to love what Ma has planned for supper."

Cedra winced. "Wait until I can get this down first." She took a small bite of biscuit. She chewed and smiled at Juliet. "Ma's biscuits are magical."

"I'll let her know you approve."

"Go eat. I'll finish and then take a shower. Maybe food and some hot water will get me moving."

"Take your time. There's no rush. It's going to be a chill day. Hank has a fire going, and I bet there will be more football today."

"I'm not sure my head can handle football. They get loud." Cedra grinned.

"We can come back here."

Cedra shook her head. "No, I need to spend time with Dad. I know he'll be leaving in a day or two."

"Why don't you two go for a ride? You can share the bluff with him."

"That's not a bad idea."

"Dress warmly. It's sunny but still cold out."

"I will. Thanks for the food. I love you."

"Love you, too."

†

"I think she'll live. She's going to shower and then ask you to go for a ride," Juliet told Hank.

Hank frowned. "Everything okay?"

"Cedra wants to spend some time with you before you head home." Juliet split two biscuits and passed her plate to Ma for gravy. "Oh, she said to tell you that your biscuits are magical."

Ma smiled. "Did you tell her our supper plans?"

"Only that you had something great planned. I don't think Cedra was ready to talk about food just yet."

CHAPTER EIGHT

"Is everything okay, Cedra?" Hank asked when he climbed into her truck.

"Yeah, Dad. I don't feel like I've spent quality time with you on this trip."

"Baby Girl, I've enjoyed every minute here. I don't require one hundred percent of your time when I visit. I enjoy my time spent with the rest of the crew."

"Thanks, Dad. Your time here always passes so quickly. It seems like you just got here."

"I'll be back, and I hope you and Juliet will visit once it warms a bit."

"The first chance we get. I promised her a day trip to the beach."

"You two are welcome anytime you can sneak away. I hope Stone's decision doesn't complicate things for you."

"I don't think it will be harmful to us. We'll surely miss Stone, but it won't stop us from pushing forward. I'll know more after Juliet and I meet with Carrie."

"Please keep me posted."

"You're usually my first call." Cedra pulled into the bluffs and parked.

Hank looked out the windshield. "I can see why you two like this place so much. It's beautiful and peaceful."

"Most of our important decisions have been made right here."

Hank smiled and reached over to hold Cedra's hand. "She makes you happy. That's all that matters to me. I like having a second daughter."

"Thank you for being such a great dad."

"You make it easy. You've always been the daughter I hoped for, and you make me and your mom so proud."

"I feel her watching over me often. Sometimes when I write, I hear her humming along or get a whiff of her perfume."

"She would be so proud of you for making your dreams come true. She would love Juliet just like I do."

Cedra felt tears filling her eyes. "I wish we hadn't lost her so young."

"I do too, Baby Girl. I miss her every day." Hank wiped his eyes. "You done got my eyes leaking."

"I'm sorry, Daddy," Cedra said. She placed her hand on his shoulder.

"Forever wouldn't have been long enough. We had a great love. I will go to my grave knowing I've experienced love if I never have another."

Cedra cocked her head. "You know she would approve if you found love again. She wouldn't want you to be alone."

"She always said I needed a good woman to care for me. First, I had your mom and then you."

"I hardly took care of you, Dad."

"You helped me through my darkest times," Hank said. "It would have been easier to get lost in my grief, but your love pulled me through."

"That works both ways. It was a challenging time for both of us."

Hank brushed a tear away. "Look at you now. All grown up and with a love of your own."

"Some days, I feel like I'm living in a fairy tale. I have to pinch myself to make sure I'm not dreaming. I know we've worked hard, but most new artists struggle much longer on their path to success."

"The cards fell in place perfectly for y'all. Don't question fate. Just continue to work hard and love what you do and each other."

"I don't think we have any issues with commitment. We all realize the opportunity we've been given."

Hank pointed out of the windshield. "I'm surprised there's snow left. It was nice to have a white Christmas. It was a great visit."

"Yeah, it was. Being surrounded by family was great."

"They love you almost as much as I do. Did Ma tell you she was cooking fried okra for you?"

"No, but I think she was worried about my stomach handling the thought of food. She cooks it just like Mom used to. The boys are always good about letting me finish the dish."

"With everything she has planned for tonight, I don't think anyone will go hungry."

"If they do, it's their fault. I did hear Patsy was making buttermilk pie."

"That's quickly becoming my favorite dessert. My mouth's watering just thinking about a slice."

"Mine too. Are you ready to head back home? Ma's probably chomping at the bit to start cooking."

"Thanks for sharing this with me."

Cedra gazed out of the windshield, then turned to look at her dad. "It's my favorite spot. I always leave here smiling."

†

"I swear his biscuit isn't cooked in the middle," Patsy declared.

"Not the sharpest tool in the shed or the brightest Crayola in the box?" Ma chuckled.

"No, but Rudy's a good provider for his family. I have to give him points for that."

"What on earth did we walk into?" Hank asked Ma.

"Just a bit of southern gossip. Chatting about my son-in-law."

"I haven't heard about this for a month of Sundays," Hank teased.

"Are we really going there?" Juliet asked.

"Where?" Cedra asked, confused.

"A Southernism competition." Juliet winked.

"Like?"

"You better sweep around your own back porch." Juliet laughed.

Lisa Marie laughed. "My favorite is, you and I are about to have a come to Jesus moment. I always ran for the hills when my mom said that."

"I've got one: it looks like it's going to be a toad strangler," Cedra said, proud she could contribute.

"That dog don't hunt," Hank said.

"He looks like he fell out of the ugly tree and hit every limb on the way down," Ma chimed in. "I'm hangin' in there like a hair on a biscuit."

"What in tarnation?" Wayne said when he entered the kitchen.

Keith raised his hand. "Run with the big dogs or stay on the porch."

"That girl ain't wrapped tight." Juliet smiled. "We got this. What started this conversation anyhow?"

Ma pointed at Patsy. "She was talking about her son-in-law being as dumb as a box of rocks." She shook her head. "Bless your hearts. We could probably do this for hours, but you all need to get out of my kitchen if you want supper before midnight."

"Can we help?" Lisa Marie asked.

"You, Patsy, and Cedra can stay. The rest of you go watch football or something." Ma shooed them out of the kitchen.

"You heard the lady," Hank said.

†

"That meal was a wonderful start to a new year, Ma," Lisa Marie said. "The café opens in the morning, so I'm calling it a night. Patsy, can I offer you a ride?"

"That would be great and save Hank a trip," Patsy agreed. "Let me go up and get my bag."

"I'll run up and get it for you," Keith offered and left the table.

"Thank you for including us in your celebration. I had a wonderful time. I'm going out to warm up my truck."

"Go ahead, and I'll bring your bag, boss," Wayne said.

"I'll see you all in the morning," Lisa Marie said and hugged Ma's neck. "Stop in before you leave if you can, Hank."

"I will," he promised.

†

114

Cedra and Hank were drinking coffee in the living room. "I can't believe it's time for you to go home already."

"Elvis and Elvira probably think I've abandoned them."

"I'm sure they are just fine. You should consider bringing the cats with you next time."

"Ha. Six hours in a truck with two squalling cats does not even remotely sound like a fun time."

"That's a good point. Will you drop by for some coffee before you leave?"

"Of course, I will. Is Juliet excited about her first day?"

"Everything except getting up at the butt crack of dawn."

"I hope you will enjoy working together. Just don't forget to take some 'you' time. No matter how great you are together, every couple needs a bit of breathing space from time to time. Now that you're working together, you'll be around each other even more."

"I'm looking forward to it, but I know what you're saying, and I agree. I promise we won't burn each other out."

"I love how happy she makes you."

"That she does. I couldn't imagine a better partner."

Ma stopped at the door. "I've locked up. I'll see you both in the morning."

"Goodnight, Ma," Hank answered.

"We probably need some jet-fuel coffee in the morning. I know I've gotten lazy, and Juliet will need a wake-up boost."

115

Ma smiled. "I've already got it loaded in the pot."

"I guess we should head up, too. You've got a long drive ahead of you." Cedra reached for his coffee cup. "I'll place these in the dishwasher and get it started. See you in the morning, Dad. Love you."

"I love you, too, Baby Girl."

†

Cedra snuck into the room and smiled to find Juliet already fast asleep. She changed into sleep clothes and went to the bathroom when she heard Hank exit. She brushed her teeth and turned off the lamp before climbing into the bed. Juliet mumbled in her sleep and turned on her side, facing the wall. Cedra wrapped her body around Juliet's and quickly fell asleep.

CHAPTER NINE

Hank and Ma were drinking coffee when Cedra led Juliet down the stairs. Ma looked up to see them enter the kitchen. "Is she awake yet?"

"I'm not sure. Juliet's moving and talking, but her eyes don't want to open yet."

"Am I sleepwalking and having a dream?" Juliet asked.

Ma handed them both a travel mug full of coffee. "This should help. Jet fuel, as you requested. Wayne is already out warming the truck."

Cedra looked at Hank. "I forgot to ask you if you wanted help loading your truck."

"Keith took out everything last night except my bag. I believe I can still handle that on my own." Hank reached for Cedra.

"I'll be fine. Ma is making us breakfast, and I'll drop into the café for coffee on my way out of town. Drive safe, and I'll see you soon." Hank hugged Juliet. "Enjoy your first day at the café."

"Thanks, Dad," Juliet replied and hugged him close.

"Let's go, sleepy head." Cedra reached for her hand. "We'll see you tonight, Ma. Call if you need anything."

"I will. Stay warm."

Juliet followed Cedra out the door. "Damn, it's cold and still very dark out."

"It will take a few days to adjust. I'll slide into the middle, and you can have the window seat." Cedra opened the door to Wayne's truck and slid across the bench seat. "Thanks for driving this morning and getting the truck toasty warm."

"I figured you'd have your hands full with sleeping beauty," Wayne said with a nod toward Juliet.

"This is an insane hour to be up and moving," Juliet groaned.

"Trust me, people will be milling about waiting for us to open, so we're not the only ones awake at this hour." Cedra took a sip of coffee. "Drink up. It will help to get some caffeine running through your veins."

†

Cedra was sad to see her dad drive away. Hank had stopped off at the Redbird Café for coffee as he promised, and Lisa Marie couldn't talk him into breakfast after Ma had fed him well. She did send a large slice of caramel cake and coconut cream pie with him to snack on later. She watched his truck disappear and returned inside. Cedra observed Juliet serving coffee to customers from the half door and smiled.

"She's doing good. A natural people person," Lisa Marie said.

"Yes, she is. I don't think Juliet ever meets a stranger."

Juliet turned to find them watching and smiled.

"Are you two about ready for some breakfast? Our main rush is over."

"Yeah, that sounds good. I'll put an order in for us. Do you want something?"

Lisa Marie smiled. "I've already put my order in with Teddy."

"Great. Do you mind if I send a text to Carrie quickly?"

"No need." Lisa Marie pointed toward the door. "Dippers, bacon, and toast?"

Cedra nodded. "A bowl of grits on the side for both of us, please."

"Here's Carrie's order. Go outside to chat if you need to."

"Thanks, boss."

"Hey, Carrie. Happy New Year. Do you mind if I walk out to your car with you?"

"Sure thing, Cedra. Is everything okay?"

Cedra handed her the bag. "Basically, yes. There have been some developments that Juliet and I would like to discuss with you. Tomorrow after work if you have time."

"At the studio or my office?"

"Whichever is better for you."

"Let me check my schedule to see where I'll be after lunch tomorrow. I will text you later this morning. Everyone is well, right? You know the curiosity will kill me."

Cedra opened the car door for Carrie. "Stone is not coming back. He is needed at home to run the family business while his dad recuperates from a severe illness. We want to discuss our options."

"I'm sorry to hear that. Let's plan on meeting at the studio then, so we can pull Mark in if needed."

"Thanks. We should be there by three-thirty at the latest."

"I will start thinking about the issue. Royalties and other things?"

"Mostly royalties and if it will affect the band negatively, too."

"That is easy. I like Stone, but I don't think his absence will make much difference. Most of the music you have recorded were songs written by you or the others. It might cause a minor speed bump to work through future royalties, but not the future of The Bentleys."

Cedra let out a sigh. "That's a big relief."

"I believe Felecia will have some good news for you, too. I'll see you tomorrow. Relax, we've got this."

Cedra smiled, closed the car door, and walked back to the café.

Teddy called out, "Order up."

"Keith's good timing must be rubbing off on you," Juliet said as Cedra walked up to the counter. "Everything good?"

"We have a meeting with Carrie and possibly Mark tomorrow afternoon."

"That's good to hear."

"Did you tell her about Stone?" Wayne asked.

"Yes, I did. Carrie does not seem worried about the news."

"That's a relief."

"Exactly what I said," Cedra answered. "I think Felecia has some news on the Bentley Break schedule, too."

"That would be awesome." Wayne grinned at Juliet and cut into his French toast. "How are you feeling?"

"Now that I'm awake, not bad. I can't imagine how y'all feel after being on your feet all day. I'm not walking near as much as you normally would, but I can feel it in my legs."

"It takes some getting used to for sure. I believe it will be a while before we can offer sit-down service again." Lisa Marie topped off their coffee cups.

"People were glad to see us open this morning," Cedra told them. "I think they missed us."

†

Juliet climbed into Wayne's truck and closed the door. "I have a new appreciation for what you two do at work now. I am ready for a nap."

"It takes some getting used to." Wayne backed the truck from the parking spot. "Will you ask Carrie about recording time when you meet with her tomorrow?"

"Are you anxious about getting back into the studio?"

Wayne nodded. "It seems like forever since we've been there."

Cedra bumped his shoulder. "It's been less than two weeks."

"See what I mean. Forever." He grinned and put the truck in gear.

"We will see what we can get arranged. We need to be sure we have some new music ready. I don't want to waste Bud's time or resources."

"I've got a new song, and I think Keith is close, too."

Juliet looked at Cedra. "Looks like we've got catching up to do. I'm close on one."

"I have gotten one done and another close. Let's meet to discuss the songs tonight, so we have a game plan when we meet with Carrie tomorrow."

"Should we do it when we get home?" Wayne asked.

Cedra turned to Juliet. "Do you need a nap?"

"I think I'll survive. Besides, I think Keith works tonight. We can meet early, have supper, write a bit, and call it an early night."

"That works for me," Wayne said. "I think I've got the lyrics down, but I'd like your opinion on the music."

"Good deal." Cedra turned on the radio, and they sang along until "Midnight in Nashville" began playing.

"That harmonica always gives me the chills," Wayne said as he turned on his blinker.

"I see the video in my head every time I hear the song. It is rather haunting."

"Are you implying I'm scary?"

"No, my love, but you do have to admit the harmonica sound is a bit melancholy."

"I'll have to write something that will be more upbeat then," Juliet teased.

Cedra placed her hand on Juliet's thigh. "I think that would be great. I want to hear more of your harmonica."

Juliet leaned over and kissed Cedra. "Then you shall."

†

"Ma, will it bother you if we work at the kitchen table this afternoon?"

"Not at all, Juliet. What are y'all planning?"

"Cedra and I have a meeting with Carrie tomorrow after work, and we wanted to compare notes on new songs to see if we are ready to spend some time in the studio. We've all been working on some new lyrics."

"I've got dinner in the crock pot. All I'll need to do is bake some fresh biscuits."

"To go with what?" Keith asked.

"Chicken and dumplings, corn and green beans."

Cedra poured a glass of tea. "Sounds delicious, Ma. Let's get our songbooks. We can work on adding music after supper for a bit."

†

"Oh, hell yeah," Keith said as Juliet finished singing the song "Out and Loud" for the group. "I can see that being a summer Pride event anthem. It's got a catchy tune and is upbeat."

Juliet's face beamed with pride at her bandmate's praise.

"The perfect title track of the new album, too," Wayne agreed.

"Who wants to go next?" Cedra asked.

"Ladies before gentlemen." Keith smiled at her. "I know you're going to knock our socks off."

"I love your confidence. Okay, here goes. This is one Juliet and I started." Cedra sang the lyrics to "Kiss you Breathless."

"That came out freakin' awesome," Keith raved.

Ma stirred the food in the crockpot. "I really like that one, too."

"This next one I wrote with Hank in mind. It's called 'Hero.'" Cedra took a slow breath and began singing. Three sets of eyes were glued to her as she sang, and she saw Ma remove a tissue from her apron to wipe her eyes.

"That is beautiful. Hank will love that song. It captures the love you two share so beautifully. It's a shame he didn't hear it before he left."

"I wanted it to be a surprise, Ma." Cedra's phone rang, and she saw it was her dad. "Speak of the devil. Hey, Dad," Cedra said as she placed the call on speaker. "Did you make it home?"

"Just a few minutes ago. Elvis and Elvira haven't left my lap since I sat down."

"Aww, they missed you."

"It appears so. How did Juliet's first day go?"

Cedra nodded to Juliet.

"My dogs are barking, but I survived with a greater appreciation for the Redbird workers."

"You'll adjust, and you have some great teachers. What are y'all doing?"

"We're sitting at the kitchen table going over some new songs. Juliet and I have a meeting with Carrie tomorrow after work, and we wanted to see if we have enough new material before we request studio time with Bud."

"We should also get a schedule of when the Bentley Break shows are set to begin," Juliet added.

"Call me and let me know so I can listen to them. What fantastic concoction is Ma working on for supper?"

Ma leaned in closer to the phone. "Chicken and dumplings, biscuits, corn, and green beans."

"That sounds delicious, Ma. Y'all think of me as you enjoy that meal. I won't keep you from your songs. I just wanted to let you know I arrived home safely. Love y'all."

125

"We love you, too, Dad. Miss you already," Cedra replied. "I'll call tomorrow night."

"Get Juliet to bed early," Hank said with a chuckle.

"No doubt, Dad. Love you," Juliet told him.

Cedra ended the call and looked at Keith. "You're up."

Keith surprised them with a song celebrating many of the older country stars that had performed at the Ryman and Grand Ole Opry in their heyday.

"I wasn't expecting that from you, but I like it," Juliet said.

"I had a chance to study some old black and white photographs at the Ryman one day, and I came home and started making notes."

"It's perfect."

Keith smiled at Cedra. "What you got, bro?"

"Nothing near that good, but here goes." Wayne stared at his notebook, and his hand began drumming a beat on the table. When he finished, everyone was smiling at him.

"You all are getting good at writing songs," Ma said. She slid a pan of biscuits into the oven. "It won't be long until supper if y'all want to clear and set the table. Are you going to work on music tonight?"

"Yes, at least for a little while," Juliet said.

"Go ahead and set your instruments up in the living room. By the time you're done, supper should be ready."

"Finally. That smell has been killing me for the last hour," Keith said.

"Go," Ma said and shooed him from the kitchen.

"If you'll bring our guitars down, I'll clear the table and set it," Cedra offered.

"You have yourself a deal. I'll be back." Juliet placed their songbooks in the living room before disappearing upstairs.

Ma checked the vegetables. "Do you think you have enough new material to start recording again?"

"It depends on how quickly we can develop the music. Five songs are enough, but we may need more practice since they are all brand new. We have plenty of time, so there's no need to rush."

"It's refreshing to see how far the others have come with their songwriting. I couldn't help but tear up during your song about Hank. I feel you'll have him bawling like a baby when he hears the song."

"I wouldn't be surprised either." Cedra set the table and began pouring drinks. "Do we have dessert?"

"Indeed, we do. Kitchen Keith made a sizable batch of brownies today."

"That sounds good. Do we have milk?"

"I just opened a fresh gallon today."

†

Two hours later, they had the music down for "Out and Loud" and "Hero."

"Those two were easy. The rest will take more time," Wayne projected.

"What if we take the next few days to fine-tune them, and we can request studio time next week? I want to ensure we are prepared to record each one," Cedra said.

Juliet placed her guitar in the case. "Yeah, I agree that's a good idea. I never want to disappoint Bud as we did with Stone's songs."

"That sounds like a good plan. Take a break and come have some brownies."

"I think we should call it a night after that. I need a shower and a soft bed."

"We'll be up early again in the morning," Cedra teased.

"Did I hit my head before I agreed to this?"

"Nope, you were of sound mind and body," Wayne reported.

†

"I haven't been this tired in a long time." Juliet plopped down on the bed.

Cedra ran her fingertips down Juliet's cheek. "You'll get used to the schedule in a few days." She stood and began undressing. "I'm going to take a quick shower. I'll snuggle in if you're already asleep." She leaned down to kiss Juliet. "I'm proud of you."

"What for?"

"Your hard work today at the café and finishing your song."

"The words are coming easier. Thanks for your suggestions and support."

"You just needed to believe you could write."

"I've gotten over that hump, and I think the boys have, too."

"It's so nice to see the excitement in their eyes. Yours, too, when you share a new song."

"I believe The Bentleys will be just fine moving forward."

"Me, too. I'll be right back."

†

Juliet fought to keep her eyes open, but they closed minutes after she heard the water in the shower. She felt Cedra's weight on the mattress as she entered the bed and turned to snuggle with her lover.

CHAPTER TEN

"I'm not surprised by Stone's decision," Mark said. "We knew he had a family and more risk, but I'm not concerned about the band's future success. At all."

"I agree. Stone is a decent writer, but his family needs come first." Carrie handed Cedra a folder. "Are you ready to get to work?"

"Always, boss," Cedra said.

"Inside the folder are several items we need to discuss. The first is the schedule of dates and times for the Bentley Break streaming show. I don't need to remind you how excited Felecia is about kicking this off." Carrie smiled. "Next are your access codes to a new account we've set up for the band on various social media platforms."

"We have an email address, Twitter, and Instagram handles?" Juliet asked.

"I was busy over the holidays, and you all have some catching up to do," Carrie teased and placed a box on the table. You have comments on social media to respond to, and this is snail mail for the band." She pointed to the box of cards and letters.

"We've also begun receiving requests for performances at live venues in several college towns, just like you hoped," Mark added. "When the guys come in with you, we can look at some schedules and start bookings."

"When do you want us?" Juliet said. "I'm sure we can all be here tomorrow."

"The sooner, the better, so we can nail down some commitments." Carrie turned the page. "I've included a list of venues and potential dates for y'all to review before we meet. We don't expect you to accept them all right away."

"Wow." Cedra was surprised by the list. "This is a lot of potential shows."

"This starts in February," Juliet pointed out. "Will we be ready?"

"We think you are more than ready. The shows would be forty-five-minute sets for one to two nights at the same venue. You have more than enough original material and covers to handle that, so start coming up with two set lists." Mark smiled at them. "We will also make travel arrangements and secure the necessary equipment. They are intimate venues, so you won't need huge speakers or massive sound equipment."

"Will we receive training on setting up and using the equipment?" Cedra asked.

"All you need to provide is some muscle to set up the speakers, amps, and your instruments. Bud has come up with an option for the sound equipment he thinks will work well. He wasn't available today, but if the guys can join us tomorrow, we'll let him make his proposal," Mark said as he rocked in his chair. "This is very exciting."

Juliet looked at Cedra. "Yes, it's almost unbelievable. Things are moving so fast."

Carrie nodded. "You all have worked hard, and your efforts are being rewarded. Every song we've released has done well, and 'Six Strings' is holding strong on the charts."

Cedra flipped back through the pages in the folder. "How do you recommend responding to our fans?"

"I'd recommend you all decide on assignments about who will do what. I think it's important that your fans understand you are reading their feedback, but you don't have to go to great lengths or detail in correspondence," Carrie suggested.

"We will get started on that tonight." Juliet peeked inside the box. "I think you or I should handle this assignment. Let the boys post on social media to start."

Carrie laughed softly. "You might want to recruit Ma's assistance, too. I'm sure she'd be delighted to help. There are hundreds of social media messages, and they grow every day."

Juliet looked at Cedra and shrugged. "That would give Ma something to do during the day."

"I don't have a problem with that," Cedra answered.

"I think Ma would feel honored that you asked for her help," Mark added.

Cedra smiled at him. "I think we're convinced that we need her help."

"We've been busy, too, and have five new songs that will be ready to record soon. Is there a chance of getting some studio time next week?"

"Like you even have to ask, Juliet," Carrie teased. "Bud has been chomping at the bit."

"This pandemic has many of our artists off-kilter, and not much is getting produced, but you all seem to be thriving in this environment," Mark informed them.

"It's been great to have Juliet and the guys to write with. Everyone is excited to share new projects, but we need practice time to prepare them."

"I'm sure Bud would love to help you with the music," Mark replied. "He's getting anxious about keeping up the recording sessions."

Cedra winked at Mark. "We can't have that. We will fine-tune the new songs and get Bud to help with the final products."

"We've got work to do." Juliet stood and offered her hand to Cedra. "Same time tomorrow?" She picked up the box.

"That will be fine. Mark and I will be here all day."

"Thanks, Carrie," Cedra replied. "We'll see you tomorrow then."

Cedra slid in behind the wheel and looked at Juliet. "I wasn't expecting all this."

"Me either. I thought we'd chat about Stone's exit and maybe some studio time."

"Great surprises, however. Open one of the envelopes and read it while I drive us home."

Juliet read several pieces of mail to Cedra. "These are some sweet messages."

"I'm sure we will have some that are not quite as pleasant," Cedra warned.

"Those will go into the trash. We need to discuss what messages we want to send our fans with Ma and the boys."

"True. We don't need to respond negatively to threats or nasty comments, especially on social media."

"It may be hard to bite our tongues or sit on our hands," Juliet said with a chuckle. "I am confident that the positive messages will far outweigh the negative."

Cedra parked the truck and turned off the engine. "Are you ready to get to work?"

"You know, we may need to consider buying an extra laptop or two. It may be easier and faster to respond on a laptop instead of our phones."

"It would certainly be faster for me. I hunt and peck on my phone's tiny little keyboard."

Juliet picked up the box of mail. "Let's go share the news and get to work. Don't forget to send Hank a copy of the Bentley Break schedule. I know he's looking forward to listening to them."

"I'll do that later tonight. Let's check in with the group to see where we want to start."

†

"You have got to be kidding," Wayne said and blew a low whistle. "Over three hundred messages on Instagram alone."

"Facebook and Twitter are about the same." Keith grinned. "This is incredible."

"There's probably a hundred or more envelopes in that box, too," Ma said.

"Would you be willing to help us with responses, Ma?" Cedra asked.

Ma's face lit up with a smile. "I'd love to help."

Cedra began removing stacks of cards and letters. "I have an idea."

"Let her rip, potato chip," Keith teased.

"Why don't we create postcards with a photo on one side and a message of thanks to our fans on the other? We could all sign them, and they would cost less postage."

"That's a brilliant idea, Cedra." Ma looked at Juliet. "You're the laptop queen. Can you order them?"

"I'm all over it. Let me grab my laptop, and I'll be back."

"We could probably have stamps of our signatures made, too," Wayne suggested.

"I think, for now, our fans deserve the individualized touch of an authentic signature. If the snail mail continues to grow, we may reconsider," Cedra replied.

Ma nodded. "I agree with Cedra. It would mean so much more."

Juliet returned with the laptop. "A cover photo or group photo?"

"Why not several group photos and a cover photo?" Wayne grinned. "Variety is the spice of life."

"Okay, and our message?"

Everyone looked at Cedra. "Thanks for your kind words of support and encouragement. We hope to see you in an audience soon."

"Short and sweet, just like me." Ma chuckled.

"Well, we are limited on space, and we have to include four signatures," Juliet replied as she typed. "How about these?" She turned the laptop around to face the group.

"I like having four options, so they don't get stale," Keith said. "Let me know how much, and I'll kick in some money."

"I still have some wardrobe money left that should cover this round," Juliet told them. "You can pick up some nice pens to sign with."

†

Ma frowned, mumbled, "Asshat," and tossed a letter in the trash.

"What was that Ma?" Juliet looked up from a card she'd been reading.

"Just some idiot is showing their ignorance. If you write something hateful, you should at least know how to spell the words. I guess anything over four letters can be a challenge."

Juliet reached toward the letter Ma had dropped in the garbage.

"Don't," Ma said and blocked her hand. "You don't need to read that trash. I'd rather you focus on the good stuff."

"You realize I'll probably open one or more just like it." Juliet pulled her hand away.

"I know I can't get them all, but I hope I do. That's just such bullshit."

Keith looked at Ma. "Do you think we need to track the address of any hate-filled letters?"

"We can, but I doubt they will post a return address. They are at least smart enough to do that."

"Or cowardly," Cedra replied.

"I would lean toward the cowardly. The writing looked like an eight-year-old's handwriting."

"Ma, I know it is not pleasant, but we do have to expect that we won't be welcomed with flowers and praise by everyone. We are drawing attention with our music. Both good and bad." Cedra placed her hand on Ma's.

"I know. The good will far outweigh the bad, but it irritates me just the same."

"Really, Ma? I couldn't tell." Juliet smiled at Ma.

137

†

"I haven't made it halfway through Facebook." Wayne ran his hand through his hair.

"We can't expect to catch up in one night. I think it's time we all call it a night. We have a big day again tomorrow," Cedra reminded them.

"I'll start creating a mailing list tomorrow," Ma volunteered.

"I can keep working on the social media responses too." Keith shut down the laptop. "I've got a new song I'm working on, but I can dedicate several hours to the project."

Cedra raised an eyebrow. "Another new song. That's excellent."

"Hold off on judgment until I finish," Keith answered. "It may be total crap."

"I seriously doubt that. All three of you are doing an excellent job of writing."

"It feels good that the words are starting to flow. Is it okay to leave everything on the table, Ma?"

"Sure, Keith. It's just you and me, remember?"

†

"This has been an exciting day, but I'm ready for a hot shower with you and our comfy bed." Juliet grinned. "Wanna conserve some water with me?"

"I'd love to. Let's go." Cedra reached for Juliet's hand. She massaged the lather into Juliet's hair.

"I'm glad the water in the shower hides my drooling," Juliet purred. "That feels so nice."

"Have I told you lately how proud of you I am?"

Juliet turned to face Cedra. "For what?"

"Many things. For starters, your songwriting and working long hours at the café without complaining."

"I'll admit I enjoy spending my days at the Redbird with you and the others. It's nice to turn around and see you smile as you interact with a customer or hear your laughter at one of Wayne's jokes."

"Since we are making confessions, I enjoy turning toward the window to glimpse your cute ass as you're delivering coffee. How those jeans fit you perfectly fills my stomach with butterflies."

"How is your stomach now?"

"Fluttering with excitement being so close to you."

"Why don't we see what we can do about that?" Juliet rinsed her hair. "Finish, and I'll start drying off."

Cedra leaned in to kiss her. "I won't be far behind you."

Minutes later, Cedra entered the bedroom.

Juliet welcomed Cedra into her arms. "It's toasty now that you're here." She rolled Cedra onto her back and moved on top as their mouths met in a long, slow kiss. "I know we should get some sleep, but I'm so excited about today's meeting I won't sleep. Just yet."

Cedra could feel the pressure of Juliet's hips and lifted her body to match the rhythm that was building between them. The smoothness of Juliet's clean, shaved skin was too tempting for Cedra's fingers to pass. She slipped a hand between them and entered Juliet with two fingers. Juliet's moan of pleasure vibrated in their kiss, and her hips thrust onto Cedra's fingers.

Juliet's fingertips slipped into Cedra, and they moved together to the brink of climax. "Come with me, baby," Juliet breathed against Cedra's cheek.

The sound of Juliet's voice was all Cedra needed to push her over the edge. She could feel her muscles contracting around Juliet's fingers, and Juliet's body shivered with pleasure as her orgasm filled Cedra's palm with a burst of wetness.

"Damn, that felt good," Juliet whispered as Cedra slowly withdrew her fingers. "I can hardly wait until we have a day off together so we can take the time to love each other properly. That was amazing, but I know we need some sleep. I can't be dragging around tomorrow." Juliet kissed Cedra and rolled onto her side.

"I know how you feel. There doesn't ever seem to be enough time for us. We've always got something going on."

"As long as I'm with you, that's what is important to me right now. I am glad that I took Stone's place at the Café."

"Even when you have to get up at the butt crack of the day?"

"Especially then because I wake up next to you."

"That is so sweet."

"I get all mushy when I'm near you. I love you."

"I love you, too."

Juliet buried her face in Cedra's hair and listened as her breathing slowed. Her life was fantastic with Cedra, and the lonesome memories of trying to make it on her own were fading away. She couldn't help but smile as Cedra's hand draped over her hip. Juliet loved the way Cedra always slept, touching her in some way. Hell, she had to admit she loved everything about the woman in her arms.

CHAPTER ELEVEN

Keith was waiting for them at the studio. He sat in his truck listening to the radio and smiled when he saw Cedra pull up beside him.

"Why are you waiting out here?" Cedra asked.

"Just listening to some music. This great new band called The Bentleys was on the radio."

"I hear they are good," Juliet said with a wink.

"Good? They are the bomb." Keith stepped out of his truck and walked inside with his friends. "Oh, heck yeah." He pointed to a box of cookies next to bottles of cold water.

"Go ahead and help yourselves. You'd better let Keith go first, though. He's got that look in his eyes," Carrie teased. "Mark, Felecia, and Bud will join us soon."

Mark and Felecia walked into the conference room. "Hey guys," Mark said. "I hope you had a great holiday."

"It was fantastic, but we're ready to get back to work," Wayne said.

"That's what we love to hear."

The door opened, and Bud walked in with a young woman. Keith dropped the cookie and jumped to his feet to hold the chair next to him for her.

Startled by his actions, Cedra looked up to see what had caught Keith's attention so drastically. She met Juliet's eyes and smiled.

Bud sat next to Wayne. "Hey, everyone, I'd like to introduce you to Riley Cooper."

"Bud has decided to take on an apprentice," Mark explained. "Riley will be working with Bud in the studio, and we have an idea we'd like to discuss with you."

"I'm Juliet." She placed a hand on Cedra's arm. "This gorgeous woman is Cedra." She nodded to Wayne. "This is Wayne, and the sugar hound is Keith. He's a great guy. Just don't get between him and anything sweet," Juliet teased.

Cedra saw Keith's face grow red. "He does like his sugar, but we love him."

"It's nice to meet you all," Riley said. She looked at Keith and smiled. "Would it be okay if I have a cookie?"

Keith nearly dumped his chair, rushing to get Riley a plate of cookies and a water bottle. "Bud, would you like something?"

Bud chuckled. "Water for me. I'm trying to watch my boyish figure."

Keith placed the cookies and a bottle of water in front of Riley and handed Bud a bottle.

Cedra didn't miss the sparkle in her warm brown eyes as Riley thanked Keith.

"So, where were we?" Carrie asked. "I hope Cedra and Juliet shared the schedule for the Bentley Break with you last night and all the correspondence you guys have been receiving."

"They did. Juliet has already ordered postcards for us to sign and send to the fans who wrote to us," Wayne said. "We started on social media responses last night, too. Ma is going to start a mailing list for us."

"That's a great idea," Mark said. "Send me the invoice, and I'll reimburse you for the expenses. Bring the postcards, too, and we'll have them mailed from here."

"I heard Juliet is working at the Redbird, too, since Stone isn't returning," Felecia said. "I hope you will all be able to listen to the show launch next Monday at one."

"You can bet we'll have it cranked up loud," Juliet promised.

"We will post the launch on all the social media sites, too," Wayne added.

"That's perfect. I know it will go well. I've had many requests for information on the show."

"Speaking of requests," Mark added. "We've gotten quite a few requests for small venue performances. Do you think you all are ready to venture out? If you are worried about the pandemic, declining is certainly okay."

Juliet looked at her bandmates. "I think the risk is worth it for us. Our only concern would be infecting Ma."

"We would do everything possible to limit exposure," Carrie said. "The last thing we'd want is for any of you to get sick."

Cedra smiled at Carrie. "If you give us a list of venues and potential dates, we can review it and let you know. If they are close, we could do a Friday and Saturday night show."

Bud cleared his throat. "Carrie tells me you have new music and want some studio time."

"We've got at least five new songs written with a possible sixth," Cedra replied and winked at Keith.

"Everyone is still writing then?" Bud asked.

"Doing a fabulous job, too," Cedra answered. "We thought we'd practice playing them this week and ask for your help fine-tuning the music if you have time next week."

Bud looked at Riley. "I told you they would be eager to get back into the studio."

"Nothing wrong with that," Riley said. "It will allow me to work with them and get some recording practice."

"Our schedule is wide open next week, so let us know when you will be ready," Bud suggested.

"Is after work Monday too soon?" Cedra teased.

"I'll book you for several days next week," Bud answered.

"You also mentioned training us on some equipment for doing small shows," Juliet said.

"We have an even better idea if you will entertain one," Mark said. "Bud suggested that Riley travel with you to run the soundboards and help with equipment set up and sound checks."

"That should not be a problem. We will have to take two vehicles to accommodate everyone and the equipment," Cedra replied.

"That brings us to idea number two. The studio has access to a small motor home that will sleep five comfortably and a small trailer for equipment. It's no tour bus, but I think it will work well to meet your initial needs."

"Are you freaking kidding? That's awesome," Keith said a bit loudly. "I can finally use the CDL license I got."

Mark nodded. "It's not necessary for the size of this unit, but I'd recommend someone else get some practice to help split the driving duties."

Wayne raised his hand. "I can handle that."

"I'll email you the additional proposed venue and schedules tomorrow," Mark told Cedra. "I'll see you next week, if not before."

"Thanks for everything, Mark," Cedra told him.

"We'll leave you with Bud and Riley to get acquainted and discuss your new music." Mark, Carrie, and Felecia left the room.

"I am so excited to be working with you," Riley said. "With Bud, too."

"You should know, Bud doesn't let just anyone in his sound booth, so he must see great potential in you," Cedra told Riley.

"That doesn't mean he won't work you hard and expect your best at all times," Juliet added.

"I graduated top of my class at Vanderbilt, but I'm sure I'll learn much more from Bud than my instructors could ever teach me."

"He's the best," Juliet said.

"So, tell me about this new music," Bud said.

"I've written the title song for *Out and Loud*."

"Cedra has written two songs. The one called 'Hero' is about Hank and is very tender," Juliet said.

"That's secret code for making you cry," Bud informed Riley.

"You're too funny," Cedra teased. "There's also a new love song. It's called 'Kiss You Breathless.'"

"I like the sound of that," Bud said. "What have you two added?" he asked Wayne and Keith.

"We both have some rockabilly tunes," Wayne said.

"Keith is working on a love song, too," Cedra said.

Keith's head whipped around to look at Cedra. "But it's not done yet."

"It will be by next week," Cedra replied and elbowed him.

"Yes, boss," he teased.

Riley noticed Keith had a chocolate smear on his cheek and picked up her napkin to wipe it off for him. Cedra heard Keith's sharp intake of breath when Riley caressed his face.

"We will have several ready," Cedra promised Bud.

"Y'all have been busy. We can also work on some playlists once you decide which venues to play. You'll need at least an hour and a half of music, maybe more."

"Thanks, Bud. Mostly originals with a few covers mixed in?"

"Yeah, Juliet. I think that would be a good plan. I'd stay sharp on a few extra covers if you need them to liven up the crowd."

Keith tapped on the table. "That shouldn't be a problem. We've got some great covers, and I'm working on learning the fiddle to replace Stone."

"That's a great idea, Keith. I'd like to see you and Wayne add your voices to more of the lyrics too."

Wayne smiled at Keith. "We don't have any problem with that, Bud. We've been practicing."

"Which songs do you want to start with?"

"Juliet's and Cedra's first to give us a bit more time," Keith requested.

"We realize we have plenty of time before we're expected to have the next album out, and we want to make it the best yet," Juliet told Bud.

"I have no doubt it will be. Don't worry. We'll get the music perfect. Y'all keep writing," Bud told them.

"I don't think that will be a problem," Cedra answered. "We've all gotten the bug."

"I look forward to hearing the new songs. We'll start on Juliet's song Monday, and work on others if we get it down quickly. If not, we'll take whatever time it needs. How close to settled are you with the music?"

"We've got a good idea of where we want to go but would appreciate your blessing and suggestions for any changes," Juliet said.

"You know I won't just settle. We've got plenty of time to dedicate to your music right now," Bud promised.

"Thanks," Cedra said. "I guess we'd better get busy. It was nice to meet you, Riley, and we look forward to working with you."

"We sure do." Keith stood.

"We'll see you next week," Juliet told Bud and Riley.

†

"I think I'd better ride with Keith," Wayne whispered to Cedra. "He may end up in a ditch."

"That's probably a good idea."

Juliet climbed inside beside Cedra. "That was an exciting meeting. Did you see Keith's reaction to Riley?"

"It was kind of hard to miss it." Cedra smiled. "From the moment she walked through the door, you could almost hear his heart pounding."

"I've never seen Keith drop a cookie for anyone before. You must admit they would make a cute couple."

"Whoa, slow down a bit. They just met. Don't rush them."

Juliet turned up the radio. "I don't think we'll have to worry based on Keith's initial reaction."

"It will make traveling together in an RV exciting. We may be sick of one another after the first road trip."

"Cedra, do you really think that could happen?"

"Stranger things have happened. Five people in one RV can get cramped quickly. I think we get along well enough to prevent that from happening. One of the boys will be doing all the driving."

"That doesn't break my heart at all." Juliet reached for Cedra's hand. "That's much bigger than my Toyota. At least y'all are used to driving trucks."

"I bet you'd learn quickly, but we'd have to get them out of the driver's seat first."

"I don't think Keith will be a problem," Juliet said with a chuckle.

"I wonder how many more letters ended up in Ma's trash today."

"Hopefully not many. I thought it was kind of cute how upset Ma got last night. I think she loves us just a bit."

"You certainly don't see Ma irritated like that often. A first for me, I think."

Juliet lifted Cedra's hand to her mouth and kissed it. "Not that you could, but I wouldn't want to be on Ma's bad side. Did you remember to call Hank last night?"

"Dang. I knew there was something I had forgotten to do. I'll call him as soon as we get home. Thanks for the reminder."

"Do you want to work on social media until after supper? Then maybe we can work on some music?"

"That sounds like a good plan. Start with yours first since that will be the first recorded?"

"Then your two, next. I think Keith works tonight, so it will just be the three of us and Ma."

"Somehow, I don't think Keith's brain will be on music tonight."

"Probably not. It's nice to see him excited, however. I think Wayne's still holding out for a woman back home."

"When someone takes your heart, you pray they are worth the wait. I hope she's worth the wait. Are they still talking?"

"On occasion, I think. Maybe we should give him a nudge."

"Hell to the no. Love must be genuine. If it's meant for them to be together, it will happen. We don't need to be meddling with his love life."

"I know. I'd like the guys to be as happy as we are." Cedra parked the truck. "Ready?"

†

"That was another fine meal, Ma," Keith said. "I've got an hour before I need to leave for work." Keith looked at Juliet. "Would you mind if I borrow Cedra for a bit?"

Juliet nodded. "We can knock out more social media responses."

"Cool." Keith reached for Cedra's hand. "I promise I won't keep her for long."

Cedra followed Keith upstairs to his room. He pulled out his chair for her and then sat on his bed.

"What's up?"

"I wanted to talk to you about the lyrics for the song I'm writing."

"Sure. What's it called and about?"

"I'm calling it restless. It's about a heart that is missing love. I watch you and Juliet interact and want that in my life. Someone I can share everything with."

Cedra smiled at his compliment. "Thank you. I couldn't help but notice how you responded to Riley today."

"Isn't she cute? She must love music, too, which is a big plus in my opinion. Did I mention she was cute?"

"I do believe you did." Cedra smiled at him.

"Those soft brown eyes just make me melt."

"Maybe you should think of Riley when creating your lyrics," Cedra suggested. "Show me what you have so far."

Keith handed over his songbook and turned to the page. He waited for Cedra to read through the lines he had written.

"I like this. A lot," Cedra said. "You should concentrate on how meeting Riley makes you feel. I love that her soft brown eyes make you melt."

"You don't think that's cheesy?"

"Not at all. I think it's an honest feeling you have when Riley looks at you. Romantic, too."

Keith began writing on the page and looked up to find Cedra smiling. "What?"

"I was just thinking of how much of a sugar hound you are, but when she stepped into the room, you dropped your cookie."

Keith cocked his head. "I can't compare her to a chocolate chip cookie."

"How did she make you feel to forget you were munching on your favorite cookie? Or that sharp intake of breath when she wiped the chocolate from your face."

"You caught that, huh?" Keith's face flushed.

"It was hard to miss since I was sitting beside you. There was nothing wrong with it, though."

"I'm not sure I can describe how she makes me feel. I never believed in love at first sight, but damn, she could make me a believer."

"Think about it tonight, between shows, and write down anything that comes into your head. You need to focus on work, so push Riley back from your mind, or you'll end up slinging hash with the rest of us." Cedra punched him on the arm.

"That alone is a scary thought. I'd be worse than a bull in a china shop."

"Stay focused. The words will come. I love what you've done so far. Do you work tomorrow night?"

"Nope, it's my night off. Why?"

"Work on your song tomorrow while we are at work. Then you and I can review what you've accomplished."

"We need to practice our songs, too," Keith reminded her.

"We will. After dinner. After a jam session tonight, we'll be closer to having the music down."

"Thank you, Cedra."

"For what?"

"Listening to the ravings of a mad man. I feel like she's turned my world upside down." Keith smiled. "Not in a bad way, though."

†

"Whoa, did you take a look at this schedule?" Wayne asked as he pushed the paper toward Juliet.

"Not closely. Why?"

"The first date on this list is barely three weeks away in Knoxville."

"That seems a bit rushed," Ma said and frowned.

"Mark and Carrie told us we could choose the ones we wanted and not feel pressured into anything we aren't comfortable with."

Juliet looked up when she heard footsteps on the stairs. Cedra smiled. "Why do you look nervous?"

"Wayne just pointed out that the first show on the list is in three weeks." Juliet handed her the list.

"Are you worried it's too soon?" Cedra took a seat. "We can always pass on the date."

"Do you think we are ready?" Wayne asked.

"There is only one way to find out. We've worked hard and have plenty of covers, so why not?"

Keith rushed down the stairs.

"Hey, bro, do you think we are ready to play a gig in three weeks?" Wayne asked.

"Hell yeah. We've been waiting on this forever. Where?"

"Knoxville."

"Just a few hours' ride from here. I say let's go for it."

"Okay then, you've got another assignment for tomorrow," Cedra said to Keith.

"What's that?"

"Hit the internet and look up these venues and find out what information you can on them. Once we know more, we can make better decisions."

Wayne smiled at Juliet. "I'm glad one of us has some business sense."

"Right. I'm just in it for the sexy lead singer role," Juliet answered.

"Damn, what does that leave us?" Wayne asked.

"The best musicians and male vocals on the band," Juliet teased.

Keith looked at Wayne. "You asked for that. Just don't forget we're the only two male singers in the band."

The smile faded from Wayne's face. "Aw man, did you have to go there?"

"I think I can speak for Juliet when I say we wouldn't want anyone else for bandmates," Cedra informed them.

"Damn straight. What she said." Juliet bumped shoulders with Cedra. "After all, we are The Bentleys."

"We'd have to ramp up the training on equipment set up with Bud and Riley," Wayne chimed in.

The mention of Riley made Keith's eyes sparkle. "I'm all in for that. Did anyone ask Ma if it's okay to park a motorhome here?"

"A motorhome?"

"Yes. Mark has one he plans to lend us. That and a small trailer for equipment to get us started on the road," Juliet replied.

"That's amazing news. You know there's plenty of room here. Bring it on."

"Great. We'll need to practice driving it before we hit the road," Keith reminded Wayne. "Learn how to level it, and use all the bells and whistles I'm sure this baby is loaded with."

Ma handed Keith a mug of coffee to go. "I'm not sure you'll need this. Be careful and have a great night."

"Thanks, Ma. I'll see y'all tomorrow."

Cedra looked at Wayne and Juliet. "You guys ready to get to work?"

CHAPTER TWELVE

The group was seated around the living room Saturday afternoon when they heard a vehicle approach.

"I wasn't expecting anyone," Ma said. "Keith, see who it is, please."

"Oh my God," Keith called out from the front door. "Come look." Keith flew out the front door before anyone could speak.

Mark pulled up in the drive with Carrie following him in her car. Mark waved at Keith from behind the wheel of a great-looking motor home. He stepped out of the vehicle just as the others arrived. "I should have called before driving out here, but that would have spoiled the surprise. This baby just got checked out and serviced, so I thought it might be a good time to show you around."

"She's beautiful," Keith said as he ran his hand across the hood.

"Why do men always refer to vehicles as she?" Juliet asked.

"Because she's beautiful, sleek, and reliable," Wayne answered.

"You answered that perfectly," Mark replied. "Let's take a peek inside."

Mark led them around to the entry door. When it opened, a set of steps lowered to the ground.

"That's perfect for short legs," Cedra said. She took a step inside. "Wow, this is nice."

Mark and Carrie followed them inside. "Not exactly a tour bus, but it will get you started."

"This is great," Juliet said. "We call dibs on the back sleeping area."

Carrie laughed. "You might want to consider the over cab bed instead. It's farther away from the bathroom."

"Nope, stinky boys have to go outside," Cedra teased.

"It has a good exhaust fan, and there's plenty of deodorizer spray," Mark said as he opened the drawer under the sink.

"So, two here," Juliet said, pointing to a queen size bed. "Two over the cab, and where else?"

"The dining room also converts to a queen sized bed. You lower the table with this switch, add a few cushions, and boom, you have a third bed." Mark demonstrated the setup for them.

"We can cook, too," Cedra said.

"Or get Ma to freeze some home cooking that we can warm up with the stove or convection oven," Juliet suggested. "There is plenty of space in the refrigerator and freezer."

"That wouldn't be hard to do at all," Ma replied.

"Can you show us how to operate the stabilizers and slides?" Keith rubbed his hands together with excitement.

Ma looked at Carrie. "I was just about to make a pot of coffee, and I have cookies that should be cool enough to eat. Would you two join us?"

"Sounds great. We'll be in as soon as I run the boys through their paces," Mark said.

Juliet stepped down first and offered a hand of support to Ma, Carrie, and Cedra. "This is a pleasant surprise," Juliet told Carrie.

They started walking back to the house. "You shouldn't have trouble locating an RV park, and the setup is relatively simple. It will be slightly inconvenient to unhook and go to your shows, but it will be safer than hotel rooms."

"I think it will work perfectly," Juliet said as she swung the door open.

"Ma, those cookies smell delicious," Carrie said as they entered the kitchen.

"Oatmeal and chocolate chip and plain chocolate chip," Ma said. "Will you grab some plates and check the milk while I start the coffee?"

"Already on it, Ma," Cedra replied on her way to the pantry.

"That motorhome is a grand idea," Ma said as she poured water into the coffee maker.

"The band's first few gigs will be Saturday night shows. We figured they could travel on Friday, set up their equipment and do soundchecks on Saturday before the bar opens, and perform on Saturday night. They can break down Saturday night and be back on the road home on Sunday." Carrie placed napkins on the table as she talked.

"Sounds like a good introduction to live shows and road trips," Ma said.

"That's what we're hoping for. We get new requests for them almost daily," Carrie answered.

"Really?" Cedra asked with surprise.

"Yes, really. I wouldn't exaggerate about that. We could book you every weekend, but we don't want you to burn out."

"We need studio time and creating time," Juliet reminded them.

"That's exactly what Bud said, too. He's already been working with Riley on setting up the equipment and soundboards this week. If the boys follow her directions, I think you all will be fine on the road."

"You realize Keith has a major crush on her, right?"

Carrie smiled at Cedra. "I think everyone realized that when they met. You could see the sparks flying. I think the feelings are mutual."

"I think I need to meet this young lady," Ma said. She poured the first cup of coffee and handed it to Carrie. "Why don't you invite her out for Sunday dinner?"

Cedra took a cup and turned to Juliet.

"No thanks. I'm going for milk with my cookies."

Cedra took a sip of the steaming coffee. "I think that's a great idea, Ma. Why don't you suggest it to Keith? I think he'd love the idea."

"I will." Ma joined them at the table and reached for a cookie. "Eat up," she told Carrie. "Once the guys arrive, these will go quickly." She bit into a cookie. "Damn, I'm good."

Juliet nodded. "We will need a bunch of these for road trips, Ma. Would you mind cooking us some meals to freeze as well?"

"I'd be delighted," Ma said, with a sparkle in her eyes.

†

"Hey, Keith. Ma suggested you call Riley and ask her for dinner tomorrow," Cedra said as Keith reached for another cookie.

"There's only one problem with that. I don't know Riley's number." Keith shrugged.

Carrie picked up her phone. "I do have your back on this one." Carrie sent Riley's number in a text to the group. "In case you back out, someone else can call."

"I've got this." Keith grabbed another cookie and walked out on the porch.

"I guess I better plan on something special," Ma said.

"Every meal you make is fantastic, Ma," Juliet praised.

Cedra sipped her coffee. "I wouldn't argue with fried chicken, rice, gravy, and vegetables."

"That can be arranged. Will you two be joining us?" Ma looked at Mark and Carrie.

"We think it's good to let the group start doing some bonding," Mark said.

"I have a prior commitment tomorrow, too, Ma. May I get a rain check?" Carrie asked.

"You both are welcome any time." Ma freshened her coffee. "Anyone else?"

"No, I think we should be hitting the road," Mark said. "We'll see you on Monday. Thanks for the cookies and coffee, Ma."

Juliet walked them to the door. "Thanks for everything."

"You all do the hard work," Mark told her. "Just keep on making great music."

"We plan to do our best. Drive safe, and we'll see you next week."

Keith was ending his call as they walked out. "We have a guest for dinner."

"Can't wait," Juliet said and pulled the door closed.

†

Wayne and Keith went to town for pizza for supper while Ma and the ladies worked out the dinner meal for tomorrow.

After devouring the pizza and a few beers, they resumed practicing in the living room while Ma prepared an apple pie to bake.

"Let's skip 'Out and Loud' for now. I think we need the bass and drums to do it justice."

"I agree, Juliet." Wayne tapped on the table. "It needs to be loud and fast-paced for an anthem, and I don't think we want to shatter Ma's windows."

"No, I like my windows just fine," Ma called from the kitchen table.

"I guess it will be 'Breathless' and 'Hero,' then," Cedra replied. "Which first?"

"Let's go with 'Breathless.' That one involves all of us," Juliet suggested.

It took a few trials, but they were satisfied with the music. "What about your keyboards and guitars only for 'Hero?'" Wayne asked. "I think it needs to be soft."

Cedra's voice singing the lyrics made it difficult for Juliet to play her guitar. Ma noticed on more than one occasion that Juliet had stopped playing. "That is such a beautiful song," Ma told them.

"I think we'll call it a night after that one," Cedra said. "Keith needs to head off to work."

"I wish I could stay. It's always more fun playing with y'all. But I need the paycheck."

"Oh, my goodness, Ma, you have got it smelling wonderful here," Wayne said as they entered the kitchen.

"I decided to bake two pies, but they are for dinner tomorrow, so neither of you can get into them tonight," Ma warned. "There's some cookies left if you get a sweet tooth."

Cedra took a notepad and walked to the kitchen table. "Can we spend some time discussing a playlist since we've decided on the Knoxville show?"

"Aw man, y'all are killing me," Keith said.

"No worries, you'll get a look before we make any final decisions," Juliet promised.

"Twelve to fifteen songs?" Wayne asked.

Cedra nodded. "That would give us well over an hour of music. Are we good with that?"

"You've got my vote," Keith said as he walked toward the door. "See y'all in the morning."

With Ma's help, it took only an hour to create two playlists featuring their original songs and four covers. "I think that's a great job so far," Juliet said.

"We'll be ahead of the game if we can provide a couple of options to Bud on Monday. We can focus on cutting a few tracks next week and then practicing the songs on the playlists." Cedra smiled at Juliet. "I still can't believe we will be playing our first live gig so soon."

†

Juliet stretched out beside Cedra. "I am so glad Lisa Marie has decided to close on Sundays."

"We all need a break after a long week. The Pandemic has changed business, but we are still staying busy." Cedra brushed the hair from Juliet's face.

"I would have never imagined how much coffee people order early in the morning. I guess we all need a pick-me-up to get going." She caught Cedra's hand and brought it to her lips. "I enjoy working at the café too, which surprises me."

"I had the confidence you would do well. You are such a people person." Cedra kissed her lips. "You can talk with anyone with ease."

"It's just a knack I have, I guess."

"It's just one of the things I love about you."

"There are others?"

"Plenty."

"Like what?"

"The romantic side of you. Like when you leave me notes or show up with flowers or a sweet gift. How you look at me makes me feel like I am so important in your life."

"Whoa, right there. You are my life."

"See, that kind of comment makes my insides turn to butter."

Juliet rolled onto Cedra. "Butter, huh?"

"You most definitely make me melt." Cedra took Juliet's hand and placed it between her legs. "See."

"I think I need to explore this a bit further," Juliet said, teasing Cedra gently. "It does seem like you might have sprung a leak."

"I think I need you to check my pipes."

"That is an offer too good to pass on." Juliet leaned down to kiss Cedra as her fingers toyed in her wetness. "You know a good plumber can be expensive. It's probably a good thing I give you exclusive rates."

Cedra moaned as Juliet's fingers teased her opening. "I'd gladly pay double the rate for your services." She slipped her hand between Juliet's legs. "I love how your bare skin feels against my palm," she whispered between kisses. "I think I'd like to try that."

"Two silky mounds moving together might be dangerous," Juliet warned.

"I still think it would be worth the risk."

"May I do the honors when you decide?" Juliet asked.

Two fingers slid between her lips. "I would enjoy that very much."

They kissed deeply as fingers explored sensitive flesh and bodies moved together until Cedra called out Juliet's name during her release. Juliet was seconds behind her as Cedra's thumb grazed her clit to push her over the edge.

Juliet rolled onto her back, still trying to catch her breath. "Every time with you is so incredible. I love you, Cedra."

Cedra turned to face Juliet and laid her head on her shoulder. "I love you, too."

CHAPTER THIRTEEN

Monday passed quickly, and Cedra was eager to return to the studio. Dinner the previous night with Riley had gone well, and she fit in with the group. Keith was incredibly nervous, but once Riley told the group her background, Cedra could see him relax. Still, he rarely took his eyes off her during the meal and ensured Riley had the first slice of apple pie.

When they pulled into the studio, Keith had already arrived. He was talking to Riley next to his truck.

"It looks like lover boy got a head start on us today," Juliet joked as Wayne pulled to a stop.

"I'll see if he needs help carrying the instruments inside." Wayne put the truck in park and exited. "Hey, bro, you need help with the gear?"

"No, we're all set in the studio. I've got all the instruments inside, and Riley helped me set things up."

"What did you think of the Bentley Break?"

"Ma and I were glued to our seats in the kitchen. I think it was a great debut show." Keith grinned. "It made me more excited to get back in the studio."

"Let's get warming up then," Juliet said and pulled the door open.

Cedra handed Riley a piece of paper. "Will you give this to Bud while we warm up, please?"

"Sure thing." Riley left the studio, and Bud's voice came over the speaker.

"Good afternoon, and welcome back."

"Thanks, Bud. Riley is bringing you a couple of playlists we wanted to run past you. Give us a few minutes to warm up, and we'll be ready to start."

"Excellent, Juliet," Bud replied.

"Are we still starting with 'Out and Loud?'" Wayne asked.

"That's the plan, so get warmed up on the drums and bass," Juliet instructed.

Cedra placed her music on the stand and picked up her guitar. She would use the keyboard for "Hero," but the others just required her guitar. "I think I need a bathroom break before we get started."

Keith nodded. "That's probably not a bad idea."

Cedra looked up to find Riley in the booth with Bud. She smiled as they walked by. "We'll be right back."

When they returned to the studio, Juliet caught Bud's attention. "We want to run through this one with drums and bass a few times since we don't have those at Ma's."

"No problem. Let's see what you've got." Bud smiled and pulled on his headphones.

Cedra agreed that adding bass and percussion to the song gave it more of an anthem feel. After they played it a second time with full instruments, she looked at Juliet. "Ready?"

"Yeah, I am. Before we start, do you have any recommendations, Bud?"

"I'd lighten up on the bass just a bit, Keith."

Keith gave Bud a thumbs up. "I was getting a bit heavy metal there," he said with a grin to Wayne.

"Naw, man, you don't have near enough hair for that."

Keith broke out in laughter. "You got that right." Keith turned his ball cap backward on his head. "Let's kick it."

Juliet nodded and smiled at Cedra.

Bud recorded two takes of the song. He frowned and looked at Juliet. "It's a great song, but it needs something."

"Any idea?" Cedra asked.

"I wouldn't be worth my salt if I didn't have a suggestion. I think Keith needs to sing with Juliet. Add a little deeper sound to it."

"You game?" Juliet asked.

"Bring it, sis."

Bud smiled. "One more run, and then we can take a break to listen."

Sharing the lyrics with Juliet also softened Keith's bass, and Cedra looked up to see Bud smiling and Riley nodding along to the music.

"Much better," Bud called out.

"I liked it better, too," Juliet said as she reached for Cedra's hand. "What did you think?"

"As usual, Bud's a genius." Cedra entwined her fingers with Juliet. "Let's go listen."

†

They listened to all three recordings and agreed that the addition of Keith's voice added to the quality of the song. "Would you mind a few more runs at it?" Bud asked.

"We'll do however many it takes until you're pleased with the sound," Juliet said. "It's the title track of the next album and will hold special meaning for us, so whatever it takes."

Bud smiled at Riley. "Do you see why I love working with these guys?"

"I'm amazed at your sound," Riley replied.

"You haven't seen anything yet," Keith promised. "The next two are very different but great songs."

Riley smiled at Keith. "I can't wait to hear them."

"I liked both of your choices for playlists. I'd go with your first choice for your debut performance. I am so excited for you all."

"We are, too, Bud. I'm a bit nervous, but I know the nerves will disappear once we start playing," Juliet said.

"You all have so much fun playing together. Nothing else matters. It's obvious how much you love one another, and it shows in your music."

Cedra smiled and wiped a tear. "You've got that right."

"We better get playing before our eyes start to leak," Juliet teased.

"Have fun with this song," Bud encouraged.

They played through the song three more times. "I think the second track is the one," Bud said when they finished playing. "Take a break, and let's listen."

After agreeing on the perfect track, Bud looked at Cedra. "I hear you have some new songs."

"Yes, we thought we'd tackle mine next if you're up to it."

"I think we've got time for at least one more. You choose."

Cedra looked at Juliet. "'Hero?'"

Juliet nodded. "That's the easier one of the two. I think you can knock it out quickly."

"Okay, let's do this," Bud said.

Juliet accompanied Cedra's keyboards for the song. Wayne and Keith sat back to watch and listen as Cedra sang about her relationship with Hank. When Cedra played the

171

final note, she looked up to find Bud and Riley wiping their eyes.

"You could have at least given us a tissue warning," Bud complained. "Run through it one more time. I've got my tissues ready."

Juliet watched the smile grow on Bud's face as Cedra sang of her love for her father. The emotion in her words could tug at the strongest heartstrings, and Juliet knew the song would be a huge success.

Felecia and Carrie met them in the breakroom. "Did you get to listen to the Bentley Break today?"

"We all did," Wayne answered. "It sounded great."

"I had a dozen phone calls after the first episode," Carrie said. "You guys are on fire."

Felecia smiled. "I had at least twenty emails. All were very complimentary of the show. Your fans enjoyed getting to know The Bentleys."

"The videos are getting a ton of hits, too," Carrie added.

Bud looked at Riley. "Do you want to set up the two final tracks? We've cut two amazing songs today."

Riley transferred the tracks onto the player in the breakroom as everyone donned headphones. "You better give us a break before you play the second."

"Got it," Riley said, leaving the room briefly to return with a box of tissues. She hit play and watched the reaction around the table as "Out and Loud" began to play.

"I like the heck out of that. Was that your song, Juliet?" Felecia asked.

"Yes, it was with some help on the lyrics from Cedra. It was a total group effort on the music," Juliet answered.

"I guess the next one is Cedra's if we need to have a tissue ready," Carrie teased.

Cedra laughed. "I'll take that as a compliment."

"Whenever you make this old goat cry, you know it's good," Bud said. "I teared up on the second run, too."

Riley shrugged. "I bawled like a baby both times."

Carrie smiled. "This I've got to hear."

Riley pushed play on the remote, and they listened to both runs of "Hero."

"I liked them both, but the first was the best," Felecia said. "Dang it, you've got my makeup running."

"Has Hank heard this yet?" Carrie asked.

Cedra shook her head. "I wanted it to be a surprise."

Bud looked at her. "A word of wisdom if I may. Burn a copy and send it to him before the song gets released. I'd hate for him to be driving the first time he hears it."

"That is a great idea," Juliet said.

"I have an idea," Felecia said. "Why don't you perform it live during one of the broadcasts? We can give him a head's up to be listening."

"He's glued to the radio daily at one," Juliet told them.

"A warning isn't a bad idea, though, in case he's making a run into town and listening in his truck," Cedra added.

173

"I think we can stop here for today," Bud said. "Tomorrow, if you're ready, we can work on one to two more."

"We'll be ready," Keith said.

"Have a great night then," Bud said and left the room.

Keith turned to Riley. "So, what did you think?"

"You all are amazing. I can see why Bud loves working with you. You take critiques well and incorporate his suggestions without fear. A few artists we've worked with are totally bullheaded."

"Bud has yet to steer us wrong, and we appreciate his guidance. He's taught us all a lot in a short time."

"Amen to that, bro," Wayne said to Keith. "Are we ready to load up?"

†

It took three more sessions to cut the following three tracks, but they were in good shape by the end of the week.

"May I make a suggestion?" Bud said after the final recording session.

"Sure, Bud," Juliet answered.

"Let's spend a couple of days practicing the songs on your playlist next week. I want you as prepared as possible for your first paying gig."

"That's a great idea. It has been some time since we played some of the songs," Cedra replied.

"Let's plan on it then, and I'll show Riley where she can adjust the soundboard for some of the songs." He smiled at Riley. "Come prepared to take notes."

"No problem there," Riley answered.

"We can finalize our plans for traveling to Knoxville, too," Keith said. "I've already booked us at an RV camp for Friday and Saturday night. I can get things packed up, and as soon as you all get home from work, we can hit the road." Keith smiled at Riley. "Maybe you can come out early to help me."

Riley nodded. "If you pull the trailer here with your truck, we can load all the equipment."

"That's a fantastic idea," Keith agreed.

CHAPTER FOURTEEN

"You're going to wear my floor out if you don't stop pacing," Ma warned.

Keith spun on his heel and plopped down in a kitchen chair. "I swear that clock hasn't moved for at least ten minutes," he complained.

"I promise you it has. Do you have everything loaded and ready to go?"

"Hours ago, Ma."

"Why doesn't Kitchen Keith make some brownies and cookies for the trip? It will take your mind off watching the clock and help the time pass. Besides, it would be nice to have some sugary snacks."

Keith jumped up from his chair. "Brilliant as usual, Ma." He rushed to the pantry for brownie mix and then removed cookie dough from the refrigerator.

"Preheat the oven while you mix up your batter. I'll get the cookies ready to go."

Keith grabbed Ma in a hug. "Thank you." He bent down and kissed her cheek.

"What time is Riley coming out?"

"She was stopping off for ice for the cooler, and she should be here soon."

"You two seem to be getting close," Ma observed.

Keith looked at Ma. She could see the heat rising to his face. "She's a special young lady. Smart, talented, and well organized. She has the equipment trailer labeled in the order we should load and unload the equipment."

"She does appear to be a take-charge person. One who takes her responsibility seriously."

"Riley is the first apprentice Bud has taken on in years, and she doesn't want to disappoint him. Traveling with us will allow her to expand her knowledge of sound systems further and create the best sound for the venue."

"That sounds like a great experience. Hey, did you remember to hang the outfits for Saturday's performance in the wardrobe?"

"Yes, I did, Ma. There are all tucked away and wrinkle-free. I am struggling with a dilemma, though."

"What would that be?"

"The RV has a decent-sized clean water tank, that should accommodate five adults showering once we are connected to water at an RV park. It would take forever for us to get ready though."

"I have an easy fix for that. Find a truck stop close by and go in and shower there. You can add the final touches once you are back in the RV."

Keith poured the brownie batter into the pan.

"Let me put those in the oven for you while you get on the phone and find a truck stop close to where you are staying."

"Are you sure you won't sign on to be our manager? You have all the right answers, Ma."

"Nope, my advice is always free to those I love," Ma answered.

✝

"I think that's the last of the cleanup for the day," Cedra told Lisa Marie as she wiped down the counter. "I know we will only miss work on Saturday, but will things be all right while we are gone?"

"Ma has the routine down pat, and I'm pretty sure we can muddle through one day together. Don't worry about us. Hit the clock and get out of here."

"She is excited about coming in to help," Wayne said. "I think staying busy will help to keep Ma from missing us, to be honest. She's already hinted how quiet it will be around the house."

Lisa Marie smiled. "Maybe I'll suggest Ma, Patsy, and I have a girl's night. Get some pizza delivered and play some cards or rent a movie. Help keep her mind off missing you all."

"That's a wonderful idea," Juliet said. "Make sure she doesn't cheat if y'all play poker."

Lisa Marie laughed. "I know. I must watch them both for dealing from the bottom of the deck."

When Cedra returned from the time clock, Lisa Marie handed each one an envelope.

"What's this?" Juliet asked.

"Your paycheck for the week and your share of tips. It is Friday, and I took the liberty to pay you in cash this week, so you will have a bit of jingle in your pocket."

"That will save us time from stopping at the bank," Cedra agreed. "If I know Keith, he's probably wearing out Ma's floor pacing. He was already chomping at the bit to leave this morning."

"Yeah, I couldn't believe he was up with us this morning. He said he wanted to get everything loaded and ready to roll," Wayne stated.

"Travel safe and knock their socks off in Knoxville. Tell Riley I expect to see pictures and maybe some video of the show."

"Will do, Lisa Marie. We'll see you Monday," Juliet replied as she swung the door open.

"Let's get ready to hit the road," Cedra said as she reached for Juliet's hand. "We have plenty of time to make it to Knoxville before dark and scout out the venue."

Wayne climbed into the backseat behind them. "Do you think it's safe to let Keith start off driving?"

179

"There's no way you will be able to pry him from behind the wheel," Juliet joked. "I'm sure you both will have your share of driving over the next few months."

†

Keith came flying out the front door when Cedra's truck pulled to a stop. "Finally. I thought you'd never get here."

"Excited much, bro?" Wayne teased.

"I've already had to order some new wood flooring," Ma told them. "He made cookies and brownies to help pass the time and give you a nice travel snack."

"He was wearing you out too, huh, Ma?"

"I must admit, Juliet, I was feeling dizzy watching him. He's been good to go for three hours at least. Riley's arrival kept him busy for a few minutes."

"Ma came up with an excellent idea for tomorrow," Keith said. "She recommended we hit a truck stop for showers, so we don't use all the clean water showering."

"That is a smart idea," Wayne said. "Five of us trying to clean up at one time could be a bit hectic."

"I've done some research and picked out options close to the RV park and the venue," Keith informed them. "All we need to do now is load up and take off. It's only a three-hour trip, so we should hit the town with time to check out the venue."

"Can I make one last bathroom stop?" Cedra asked.

"If you must." Keith sighed and crossed his arms.

"I've got shotgun," Wayne called out.

"Fine. The rest of us will kick back for a nap or in a recliner while you two get us there in one piece," Juliet said.

Keith smiled at Wayne. "I bundled some firewood and put it in the trailer. We can have a nice campfire tonight."

Ma handed Wayne a box. "Keep Keith out of these biscuits until you warm up the chicken and dumplings tonight."

"I'll try my best. I think Keith will be distracted driving the RV."

Cedra bounced down the stairs. "All set?"

"Let's do this," Juliet answered.

"Give me a call or text to let me know when you arrive, please," Ma told Cedra. "Be safe and have a fantastic time. I look forward to seeing pictures and videos."

"I've got you covered, Ma. I have explicit instructions from Mark and Carrie," Riley answered.

Ma stood in the front yard as they pulled away for their first big road trip. "It's already deathly quiet around here," she grumbled, and walked inside after the RV disappeared.

†

"Play us some music, Mr. Navigator," Juliet called out to Wayne.

"On it." Wayne tuned the dial to a country station on the satellite radio. "Is this good?"

"Wonderful," Juliet replied. She turned to Cedra. "Once we hit I-40, it will be a straight shot for a couple of hours. Do you want to stretch out for a nap?"

"Great idea. Do you mind if we leave you with the guys?" Cedra asked Riley.

"Nope. I'll keep an eye on them, so they don't get us lost," Riley answered with a laugh.

"Don't worry. I've driven this route many times on my way home to North Carolina," Wayne assured them.

"Almost there." Keith turned on the turn signal to enter the on-ramp for the interstate.

Juliet reached for Cedra's hand as Keith turned. "Whoa, it might be safer lying down."

"Sorry. I'm still getting used to turns, but it will all return to me."

Juliet pulled the privacy curtain behind them and kicked off her boots. Cedra was also sitting on the edge of the bed, removing hers. "I hope this mattress is as comfortable as it looks."

Juliet opened the blinds on the side window and crawled into the bed. She placed extra pillows behind them and reached for Cedra, pulling her into a hug. "Now, that's much better, and we still get to watch the scenery. Not that there is a whole lot to look at right now. Mostly bare trees with some evergreens mixed in. Oh, and the random cow here and there."

"You can count all the trees and cows you want. I'm going to snuggle into you and take a power nap."

Juliet kissed the top of her head. "I probably won't be far behind you. Today was hectic."

Cedra slipped her hand beneath Juliet's shirt to place her hand on her lover's smooth, warm skin. "Ah, better than an electric blanket." She closed her eyes and, within minutes, drifted off to sleep.

Juliet was correct in her assessment of the scenery and soon found her eyes growing heavy. She listened to Cedra's slow breathing and fell asleep with a smile on her face.

†

Keith felt the strain on the engine as the incline gradually grew. "Come on, baby, we've got this," he told the vehicle.

"Just take it slow. This baby's got plenty of power, but it's not safe to try to maintain highway speed hauling a trailer. We're doing great on time," Wayne instructed.

As they crested one of the inclines, they caught their first glimpse of Knoxville. "Welcome to Rocky Top."

"I don't remember it being this big," Keith said. "It's been ages since I've been here, though."

"With the growth of the University and the tourism industry, Knoxville has begun to expand," Wayne explained.

"It's beautiful," Riley stated as she gazed out the front window. "Would you look at that bridge?"

"You'll see it up close and personal in a few minutes when we cross over. Knoxville is home to the headwaters of the Tennessee River. Two rivers, the Holston and the French Broad combine to feed the river." Wayne used his serious-sounding tour guide voice. "You can see from our vantage point the various types of watercrafts that make their home on the river, from large industrial tankers and flatbeds to paddle wheel and pontoon boats. In summer months, you might occasionally see the rooster tail spray of water from a fast-moving jet ski," Wayne announced.

"Our turn must be coming up then because our campsite is right on the river. Do we want to locate the venue first?"

"That's probably not a bad idea. We can let the rush hour traffic die down and then find the campground." Keith hit a button on the GPS to change the route to the Pub. "The food on the menu looks great, especially the pizza. Maybe we could get a couple to take to the campground and save Ma's home cooking for tomorrow night. I've got cold ones on ice."

"That works for me. We can get an idea of the stage set up, too," Wayne added. He turned to look at Riley. "Will you go wake the sleeping beauties?"

†

When the group entered the Pub, they were surprised to find the owner, Ralph, behind the bar.

"Good evening, sir," Juliet said.

He looked up from stocking the beer cooler. "Well, I'll be damned. The Bentleys have arrived. Welcome to the Pub. I'm Ralph Lewis."

Juliet was surprised he recognized them. "Thanks for the welcome. We just arrived in town and wanted to look at the stage to get some setup ideas for tomorrow. Are we still good to come in around five to get set up and a good test before the eight o'clock show?"

"You are welcome to come anytime tomorrow when we open after noon. Give me a minute, and I'll show you to the stage area."

"Can you help us place an order to go as well?" Keith asked. "We've been talking about your pizza for the last half hour."

"Do you know what you want?"

"Pepperoni and the Carnivore Special," Keith said. "Extra-large, please."

"Let me get those orders in for you," Ralph said, and walked back to the kitchen.

Cedra heard rushing footsteps and looked toward the serving window to see several of the staff looking at them. She raised her hand and sent them a wave.

Ralph walked through the door. "You have certainly riled up my wait staff and cooks," he joked.

"Would you bring them out and introduce us?" Juliet asked.

"Yes, I will, but I probably won't get a decent night's work out of them after that. They were so excited to hear you were doing a show for us." He looked at the servers and

185

waved to them. Several seconds later, the door flew open, and three women and a man stepped out. Ralph began the introductions. "Lisa, Wanda, Kathy, and Will, these are The Bentleys."

Juliet stepped forward. "I'm Juliet. This is Cedra, Keith, Wayne, and Riley. Riley is our newest team member. She's our sound tech."

"We love your music and jam to it all the time in the kitchen," Kathy told them.

Ralph nodded. "I can attest to that. I think they play 'Six Strings' at least twice every night. I can hardly wait for the full *Midnight in Nashville* to be released.

"It just so happens we have copies we will sell and autograph after tomorrow's show," Juliet said. "If that's all right with you, Ralph?"

"Perfectly fine with me, as long as you save me a copy."

"Kathy with a C or a K?" Cedra asked.

"A K, please. Oh my gosh."

"Okay, get back to work. You have two pies to go for these folks. I'm going to show them around the stage area."

"Nice to meet you," Will said, and ushered the ladies back into the kitchen.

"Follow me."

They followed Ralph to the stage area. It was a good size and had space behind the stage for storage and staging. "After you set up tomorrow, we can pull the curtain until you're ready to start the show. There's a separate stage door you can enter from tomorrow night as well."

"This looks perfect." Riley smiled at Ralph.

"I'll leave you to inspect the space, but if there's anything you need for the show, just let me know."

"We will. Thanks, Ralph," Cedra answered as he left the stage.

"Are we good with the basic arrangement we have in the studio?" Riley asked. "Cedra on keyboards and guitar there, Juliet in the middle, and Keith on the left? That leaves ample room for Wayne's drum set, guitar, and microphone."

"That's a comfortable layout for us. It leaves plenty of room for amps and other equipment, right?" Juliet asked.

Riley nodded. "Yes, I'll set up my soundboard equipment just to the right of Cedra off stage to give me a good view and perspective of the acoustics of the building." She grinned. "I can also set up a tripod for video and take candid shots during the performance." She looked at Keith and Wayne. "I have another surprise from Mark that I need your help setting up."

"What is it?" Keith pleaded.

"If I tell you now, it won't be a surprise," Riley teased.

"That is so cruel," Wayne replied. "We have to wait a whole day?"

"Yep. 'Fraid so. Boss's orders."

"You are enjoying that too much," Keith replied with a wink.

When they exited the stage to return to the bar, Ralph walked out of the kitchen.

"Here are the pies you wanted."

"They smell terrific," Keith replied.

Cedra pulled out a credit card and offered it to Ralph. Ralph shook his head. "These are on the house."

"Are you sure?"

"Consider it a welcome gift or a bribe for you all to return for another date."

"Thanks. We will see you tomorrow afternoon," Keith said and grabbed the boxes.

Juliet laughed. "We can never fill him up."

†

They checked into the campground, and while Keith set up the RV, Wayne and Juliet commandeered a picnic table. Cedra and Riley brought out plates and a cooler of drinks.

"Hey, is it too early for a campfire?" Keith asked.

"It's never too early," Wayne answered. "I'll help you with the wood."

"Hurry up, guys. You can lay and light a fire after we eat. This pizza won't stay warm forever," Juliet teased.

Wayne and Keith dropped an armload of firewood around the fire ring. "I never thought it would be Juliet to rush us to the dinner table," Wayne said.

"Yeah, that's usually my job." Keith grinned. "Who's drinking what?"

"Beer for me, bro," Wayne replied.

"I'll take one, too," Juliet and Riley both answered.

Keith looked at Cedra. "I'm sticking to a soda," she answered.

"One Mountain Dew is coming up."

Juliet moaned and swallowed. "Oh, my goodness, this tastes divine."

"You aren't kidding. You gotta try the carnivore, Wayne."

"Diving in now." Wayne chuckled and took a bite.

"It may be worth the drive just for the pizza," Juliet said. "Maybe we should get a couple for the ride home Sunday."

"We could pop it in the oven to warm it," Cedra added.

Juliet took a drink of beer. "The only problem with that is if we get it Saturday night after we perform, there may not be enough left for Sunday."

Keith nodded. "That's true, but this group has never gone hungry. If we need more food, we'll find a place to stop. I bet Ma will have a big dinner planned for our return."

"You know she will. I'd bet fried chicken," Cedra said.

"Because it's your favorite," Juliet teased.

"With rice and gravy and more fresh biscuits. Oh yeah, I can handle that," Wayne added.

"She is so sweet, and I know she loves you all," Riley stated.

"We love her, too," Keith answered. "She's been a godsend to all of us."

"I bet she'd say the same about you all. You can see it in her eyes."

†

The sun set quickly while they were feasting.

"Now, you can light a fire," Juliet teased.

"If you'll hand me those boxes, I'll drop them in the dumpster while Wayne starts a fire."

Juliet placed the paper plates and napkins inside the box. "Here you go, Keith."

He drained his beer and carried the boxes to the trash. "It's still cool out. Does anyone else want a jacket?" Cedra asked.

"I'll grab a hoodie," Juliet said.

"Me, too," Riley added.

Wayne was blowing on the fire, trying to get it started. "Naw, I'm good."

"Let me know if you need help with that. I've been told I'm great at starting fires," Juliet told him with a wink.

"I have heard that about you." Wayne chuckled. "That might not be a bad idea for a song."

"What's that?" Cedra said as she tossed a hoodie to Juliet and handed one to Riley.

"Starting fires," Wayne joked and winked at Juliet.

"We should seriously write it, Wayne," Juliet answered.

Cedra looked at Riley. "This is how many of our song ideas come to us."

190

"I love it," Riley answered. "The way you all interact. You all seem to be on the same wavelength. Some bands can't even get on the same page, and it shows."

"We are all competitive and love a good challenge, but when one of us hits a rough patch, the others jump in to pull them through," Cedra explained.

"You all didn't know each other before living at Ma's?"

"Nope, we are from four different states and had never met," Juliet answered.

Keith smiled as he sat next to Riley. "Cedra was like the magnet that pulled us together."

"Aw now, you're going to make me blush," Cedra complained.

"It's the truth. Except for Juliet, we were on the train bound to nowhere until you arrived, and then we started gelling as a group," Wayne said and bumped shoulders with Cedra. "Hell, you've even taught us how to write songs."

"You weren't writing before?" Riley asked.

Keith chuckled. "We could barely string a sentence together, but for *Midnight in Nashville*, Cedra challenged each of us to write a song for the album."

"You did a great job, too, if I might add. I am very proud of you all." Cedra smiled.

"She made us believe we could, and we ended up writing good songs together." Juliet smiled and leaned into Cedra for a kiss.

"The new song 'Out and Loud,' who wrote that?" Riley asked.

"I did. We want to play a few Gay Pride events, and not only is it a fitting anthem, but it's a great title for our next album," Juliet said.

"I agree." Riley looked at Keith and Wayne. "I must ask. Are you two concerned about playing at a gay event?"

"Absolutely not. Cedra and Juliet are like sisters to us; wherever they go, we will follow with full support. It is about damned time people don't feel a need to hide in a closet."

Wayne slapped Keith on the back. "I couldn't have answered that better myself. Country fans have grown to accept music from someone other than the good ol' boy, cowboy types. People of color and all genders have started seeing some success creating the music that stirs their souls."

"You all sound so poetic. No wonder you write such great songs," Riley praised. "It's a fresh new phase of country music that was well past due."

Cedra walked inside while the others sat around the fire. "I hope I didn't offend her," Riley said.

"Heaven's no. It would take much more than a few questions," Juliet said.

"Are you guys ready to get to work?" Cedra asked when she returned with a tray.

"Doing what?" Keith asked.

"Ma packed supplies for s'mores," Cedra answered. "Two of her long-handled cooking forks, so we've got to make sure they get back in good shape."

"I love that woman." Keith grinned as he stuffed a marshmallow on the fork. "Who's ready?"

"I will be in two seconds," Juliet said as she placed chocolate bricks onto a graham cracker.

"I'll get others set up, so keep those marshmallows coming," Cedra replied.

†

After eating their fill of s'mores, Cedra and Juliet gathered the supplies. "We will put this stuff up and call it a night. Ma sent biscuits and gravy to heat up if y'all are fine with eating it for breakfast."

"Sounds good to me, Cedra," Wayne answered. "I think I'm going to call it a night, too."

Keith looked at Riley. "Would you like to walk with me to the river?"

"Yes, that sounds great. I need to walk off some of that sugar," Riley answered.

"We'll be quiet coming in," Keith said. "Save me room up in that bunk."

"I will. But I will smack you if you start snoring," Wayne teased.

"I've already made up your bed," Cedra told Riley.

"Thanks, but I could have done that."

"No problem. We'll see y'all in the morning."

Cedra picked up the tray and followed Juliet inside. "That was a nice evening. Very relaxing."

"We've got to remember to thank Ma for the s'mores." Juliet helped Cedra store the goodies. "I am so ready to stretch out with you."

"Me, too. Tomorrow will be a long day," Cedra answered.

CHAPTER FIFTEEN

A loud sound woke Cedra with a start Saturday morning to find the bed beside her empty. She was a bit disoriented until she remembered they were in the RV. The loud sound was repeated, and she realized the sound was coming from the river. She slipped her shoes on and went in search of Juliet. Riley had made her bed, and glancing at the bunk, Cedra also found it empty. Cedra opened the door and shielded her eyes from the sun. She found her friends sitting at the picnic table, drinking coffee. "What time is it?"

"Almost eight. Take a seat, and I'll bring you some coffee," Keith said.

"Good morning. I'd say you slept well in the RV," Wayne teased. "I've never known you to sleep in."

"It was comfortable until I was blasted awake by that sound from the river."

"A tug was pushing a barge through," Juliet replied.

Cedra smiled at her. "It's probably a good thing it did, or I might have slept the morning away."

"Who are you kidding? Keith is already grumbling about being hungry."

"Hey, Juliet. I heard that. I set the oven to preheat to warm up the biscuits."

"See. My point exactly."

"Let me get some coffee into my system, and I'll warm up the gravy."

"Keith and I can handle that," Riley said. "We need to carry our share of the load, and it seems simple enough for the two of us to handle."

"That would be great. I can handle pouring the juice and setting the table," Wayne offered. "You two just relax."

"I won't argue with that," Juliet replied.

†

Keith picked up the table after the meal. "You know the campground has showers."

"No, I didn't know that," Juliet replied.

"I saw the bathrooms last night when I dumped the trash and went inside. They look relatively new and sparkling clean."

"Why don't we eat a hearty lunch before we go to the Pub to set up? Then we can come back here, relax for a while, eat supper and get dressed for the show?" Cedra suggested.

"I think that plan would work out well. Riley and I can locate a lunch spot, then Wayne and I can disconnect the RV and be ready to hit the road."

"We probably need to fuel up, too, while we're out," Wayne added.

"Is there anything, in particular, we want to eat?" Keith asked, looking up from his phone.

"Does it look like there are any decent BBQ places close by?"

"You are reading my mind, bro. I was thinking BBQ, too." Keith grinned. "They open at eleven, and it's just a few miles away."

Juliet looked at Cedra and Riley. "Good for y'all?"

"BBQ always works for me," Cedra replied.

†

"If I don't stop eating, I'm going to be useless the rest of the day," Keith said.

"We can't have that. We have the equipment to unload and get set up," Riley reminded him. "Don't worry. We can get take-out boxes, and you can polish this off while we're getting supper ready."

"It's too good to waste," Wayne replied. He reached for the check.

"Nope, this one's on Mark," Cedra replied and pulled out cash to cover the bill and tip.

197

"Fine with me. Gives us more money for pizza later." Wayne shot a look at Keith.

Keith nodded. "We can finish the rest of the cookies and brownies, too."

"Why do I get the feeling we will be going out for breakfast and eating lunch on the road tomorrow?" Juliet asked Cedra.

"You are probably one hundred percent correct. I think we can handle two meals on the road."

"Are we ready to get set up?" Keith asked.

"Let's do this," Wayne answered and held the door for the ladies.

†

Ralph met them in the parking lot of the Pub. "There's a side door to the stage. You can back the trailer up to it to make loading and unloading easier."

"Thanks, Ralph." Keith nodded and pulled around the building.

Cedra and Juliet walked with Ralph inside. "What time does the kitchen close tonight?" Juliet asked.

"At eleven. Why?"

"That pizza was so delicious last night that we wanted to get three more before we leave tonight. Originally, they were to be our lunch on the road tomorrow, but I have a sneaking feeling they won't make it through the night."

"You guys will probably work up an appetite during the show and loading the equipment. I'll make sure you have three to go by ten. Will that give you enough time after the show to load up?"

"That should be perfect," Juliet answered. "We have something for y'all too."

Cedra smiled and handed him five autographed copies of *Midnight in Nashville*. "Will you share these with your staff?"

"On one condition. That the pizzas are on the house, and you don't try to sneak in a payment," Ralph answered.

"I think we can handle that," Cedra replied as they walked toward the stage.

"Let me know if you need anything. I've already pulled the curtain."

"Thanks, Ralph." Cedra reached for Juliet's hand. "Let's get to it."

Keith and Wayne were bringing the amps and equipment in when Cedra and Juliet arrived. "Where do you need us?" Juliet asked.

"You can start bringing in the instruments and microphone stands," Keith said.

Keith and Wayne provided the muscle while Riley directed them on where to set things up on stage.

"If you assemble your drums and keyboards, Keith, Juliet, and I can work on the microphone stands." Riley pulled a roll of tape from her bag.

"What's that for?" Juliet asked.

"To make a pick holder for your microphone stands. That way, if you drop one, you grab another without missing more than a beat or two." She demonstrated how to roll the tape, so it was attached to the stand and then pressed two picks onto the surface. "There you have it."

"That's simple and brilliant," Keith replied. "I might need more than two, though."

"Place as many as you might need. I've never seen you drop one."

"Only once in the studio, but to be honest, I'm nervous about tonight," Keith admitted. "This is our first paying gig, and I don't want to screw it up."

"You all will be perfectly fine. I watched the footage from your performance at the Redbird Café and would recommend you start with introductions just like you did then. Give yourselves a minute or two to catch your breath once the curtain opens."

"That's a good idea, Riley. Even with limited seating, it will probably be a larger audience than what we're used to," Juliet said.

"Awesome. Get your instruments set up, and we can perform a quick soundcheck."

Riley made several adjustments, and the band was set up and ready for the show by two. "We'll see you at 7:30 tonight at the latest," Cedra told Ralph.

"I usually place a small cooler in the back for the entertainers. Any special requests?"

"Some bottled water would be great."

"I'll have them ice cold and waiting. Enjoy your afternoon."

"Thanks for everything, Ralph."

"Thank you, Cedra. We are excited to host your first show. I hope it will be the first of many you perform here."

†

Relaxing was impossible for the group. Juliet tried to lay down, but her mind was whirling a mile a minute. She kept tossing and turning on the bed. Cedra was making a pot of tea in the kitchen, and Juliet climbed from the bed to go to her.

"Can't sleep?"

"No. I tried, but it's just not happening. Every time I close my eyes, I start thinking about tonight."

Cedra smiled and pulled Juliet into a hug. "Everything will be fine. I would say relax, but I know that's probably not going to happen."

"How can you be so confident?"

Cedra ran her fingertips down Juliet's cheek. "We have worked hard to prepare for this. We have tremendous talent and the sexiest lead singer in Nashville."

Juliet leaned in to kiss Cedra. "One that is head over heels about the woman in her arms. I know we will do great." She looked around the RV. "Where is everyone?"

"Getting their showers done. They can't relax either." Cedra stepped back and smiled at Juliet. "I have an idea."

"I'm all ears."

"After we've eaten and cleaned up after supper, you and I can shower and dress, and then we can have a jam session."

"Without any instruments?" Juliet cocked her head at Cedra.

"We don't need them to make beautiful music. It comes from our hearts."

"How did I get so lucky?"

"We got lucky. We should be thankful that fate brought us together."

"I count my blessings every day."

The door opened, and Keith and Wayne entered. "Hey, the showers are great."

Keith grinned. "Plenty of hot water."

"So, where is Riley?" Juliet asked.

"You know you girls take more time to doll up than we do," Wayne said.

Cedra looked at them sternly. "Just don't put your shirts on yet. Ma spent a lot of time on them, and you don't need to show up with stains."

"Why don't you throw a T-shirt on and go wait on Riley?" Juliet asked Keith.

"Hey, after we get done eating, I think we should jam until it's time to dress and head to the Pub."

"Without instruments, Cedra?" Wayne asked.

"Yeah, we know the lyrics, and it will be like a warm-up." Cedra placed the pot of chicken and dumplings on the stove. "Juliet and I will shower and dress after we eat, then we can jam."

Keith pulled a T-shirt over his head. "I'll be right back."

Juliet smiled at Wayne. "Help me set the table."

"I'm on it," Wayne said.

†

"I think we're ready to head to the Pub," Cedra said.

"I'm driving," Wayne said and punched Keith's shoulder. "As nervous as you are, we'd probably end up in a ditch."

"You're still nervous?" Juliet asked.

"Just a bit," Keith admitted.

"Relax, you are going to be great. You've got a great position to look to your right and see Riley," she whispered.

"That's comforting." He grinned.

"Come on. We've got this."

When they arrived at the Pub, Riley looked at the group. "There's one last thing we need to do."

"What's that?" Cedra asked.

"We need the guys to hang this across the back of the stage." Riley motioned for Keith, and they unfolded a banner. A picture of the group and the name The Bentleys proudly adorned the banner. She smiled at them. "Just in case you forget who you are."

"That's awesome. Was that the surprise from Mark you've been hinting at?"

"One of them." Riley grinned. "You'll have to wait on the other."

"You are so cruel," Juliet said.

They watched the banner go up, and then Cedra instructed, "Grab some water, and let's hit the stage."

"Does everyone have the playlist memorized?" Juliet asked.

"It's a little late if we don't." Wayne grinned.

"Check your microphone stands. I taped a copy for each of you," Riley said. "In case you need a reminder."

"Halfway through, we'll take a break. We've got this," Juliet told them.

Ralph stepped through the curtain. "All set?"

"Yes," Cedra answered.

"As soon as the curtain opens, I'll introduce you, and you can do your thing. The crowd is excited to hear you live."

The band took up their positions and nodded to Ralph. "Let's do this," Juliet said.

Ralph signaled a staff member, who pulled the curtain across the stage. Mark and Carrie were seated at a table near the stage, smiling up at them. Mark shot them a thumbs up sign, and Carrie couldn't quit smiling.

"Ladies and gentlemen. Tonight, I am honored to bring you The Bentleys. Let's give them a warm Knoxville welcome."

Juliet stepped out to her microphone and introduced the band. Then she nodded, and they started the show with "Backwoods Boogie."

Cedra was pleased by the excitement in the room and noticed many of the patrons sang along with them. Her first song was coming up in the set, and she left the crowd speechless as they swayed in their seats.

Riley nodded to Keith and flipped a switch. Riley had pre-recorded the horn section, and Keith animatedly mimicked playing the horn, making the crowd laugh as the band played "Wine, Beer, and Whiskey," to the delight of Ralph.

✝

They had two more songs to go to before their break. Juliet felt the sweat trickle down her face from the heat of the stage lights. She was thankful Riley had reminded them to pack their sunglasses to block the intensity of the lights. Juliet sang with Cedra and glanced over at Mark and Carrie. Both were sporting smiles and singing along with their band. When they finished "Six Strings and a Dream," Juliet turned back to the crowd.

"Ladies and gentlemen, we are going to take a short break to hydrate, and we suggest you do the same."

Mark and Carrie met them off stage. "You all are doing great," Mark said, grinning wildly.

"The crowd is really enjoying the performance. I don't know whose idea it was to record the horn section, but you guys pulled it off perfectly. Your air horn worked out nicely," Carrie teased Keith.

"That was all Riley's idea," Juliet said. "We knew it would be a crowd favorite, and she came up with the idea to record the horn section for us."

"Thanks for coming to hear us," Cedra said.

"We wouldn't miss it for the world," Mark said.

"It was great to look out and see you in the audience," Juliet added.

"We wanted you to know that the studio is fully supporting your live shows," Mark said. "This being your first is a landmark for you and the beginning of a fantastic career."

"How are we doing on time?" Juliet asked Riley.

"We're a little behind schedule, but I don't think anyone will complain. Ralph is over the moon and brought fresh water and sodas for everyone."

"I forgot how hot those lights can be," Juliet said as she wiped her face with a towel.

"We're heading back to our seats, but we wanted to tell you how proud we are of you," Mark said.

"Have fun out there," Carrie reminded them.

Juliet took a drink of water. "Are we ready?"

"Let's finish this," Wayne said. "We're at 'Midnight,' right?"

"Yes." Juliet reached in her pocket for her harmonica.

She was about to lift it to her mouth when a shout came from the back of the crowd.

"Go back to Queerville. You bunch of dykes," an obviously inebriated patron shouted.

"Shut it, Billy Joe," someone called out.

"You can't tell me you like this shit," he answered.

Ralph flew over the bar like a man half his age and, with the assistance of two male patrons, escorted Billy Joe out the door.

The crowd applauded Ralph's action and then turned back to the stage. Someone else called out, "Sorry for his rudeness."

Juliet nodded and lifted the harmonica to her mouth. The haunting opening to "Midnight" settled the crowd. The next song on the list was ironically "Fire Away," which Juliet and Cedra performed flawlessly.

At the end of the set, the crowd called for an encore. The band returned to their instruments, and when Cedra nodded, they performed "Rocky Top" for the Knoxville crowd.

The group made a final bow to the crowd, and the curtain was pulled. Ralph rushed through the curtain as the group started to store their instruments in cases. "I am so sorry that happened. Please know that the crowd is buzzing with excitement, and Billy Joe is just a drunk asshole."

Juliet smiled at him. "Ralph, you do not need to apologize. As performers, we need to prepare ourselves for bad behavior. I must admit, I've never seen someone fly across a bar like that. You were awesome."

"My old ass will probably feel that tomorrow." Ralph grinned. "I really hope you will consider coming back to perform here."

"Absolutely," Keith said.

Mark arrived backstage. "You have fans waiting to buy your CDs and get your autographs. Carrie has already sold almost every copy you brought. Go, greet your fans, and we can all pitch in to get you loaded up later."

"Will and I will help too. We can at least provide some muscle. That was some show." Ralph grinned. "It may have been limited capacity, but tonight was one of the best sales nights we've had in months."

Cedra drained her water.

"Would you all like something cold to drink? Wine, beer, or whiskey?" Ralph chuckled.

"A cold beer would go down well," Wayne said.

Keith, Riley, and Juliet agreed. Ralph looked at Cedra. "Just more water for me, thanks."

"I'll bring them to the table for you."

"Let's go meet your fans," Mark said.

†

They signed autographs and took photos with fans for over an hour when they ran out of CDs to sell. When the crowd dwindled, Juliet looked at Keith and Wayne. "Let's get packed up. I don't know about you all, but I'm drained."

Will and Ralph came backstage and helped load the amps and equipment. With the extra help, it didn't take long at all.

"Thanks again. I hope you will come back soon," Ralph said.

"Hang on, and I'll get your pizzas," Will said and rushed back inside.

Cedra turned to Mark and Carrie. "Thanks for being here tonight. Will you be staying the night?"

"No, I hired a service, and they will drive us home tonight," Mark said. "Congratulations on your first show. You all sounded fantastic."

"Thank you. You all be safe going home, and we'll see you next week."

Mark grinned. "I think we need to plan more shows and another person to sell some swag and CDs for you all. We could have sold three times the CDs if we would have had them tonight."

†

When Wayne pulled the RV into their campsite, he and Keith changed clothes and got them hooked up and leveled for the evening. Riley, Juliet, and Cedra had also changed and were getting prepared for the pizza.

"I must admit, this smells good, and I am hungry after tonight's show." Juliet picked up the boxes and carried them out to the picnic table.

Keith had lit the fire he had laid earlier, and the flames illuminated the night. He and Wayne were already sipping on a beer when Juliet arrived.

"Man, I think I could eat one of those by myself," Keith stated. "Ma's chicken and dumplings are long gone."

Cedra and Riley brought out more drinks, plates, and napkins. Cedra sat next to Juliet and raised her bottle to toast. "To the first of many successful shows. Cheers, my friends."

A chorus of "cheers" was spoken around the table as they tapped their bottles together.

"That was a blast tonight. I don't think it's a night I will soon forget," Wayne said.

Cedra nodded. "I am very proud of how we performed, and it was great to see Mark and Carrie in the audience. It gave me a boost of confidence knowing they were there."

"Even a drunk Billy Joe couldn't take away from the reception we received from the crowd," Juliet said.

"I wanted to rush out there and kick his ass," Keith said with a growl in his voice.

"We can never do that," Juliet warned. "Billy Joe was only the first. There will be others that don't appreciate our music or that Cedra and I are partners. Besides, Ralph did a great job of dealing with him."

"Yeah, he did. It's not just hecklers that we have to remain vigilant for. The mass shootings in Las Vegas and down in Texas are also worrisome. Granted, they were large outdoor shows, but we should always keep our eyes on the crowd," Wayne shared.

"It's a shame our society has devolved to this," Riley offered. "I think it was a much-needed wake-up call to sponsors to provide much tighter security at the big events."

Keith nodded. "Security is much easier to control at indoor venues such as theaters or indoor arenas. They are better prepared with metal detectors and tighter security."

"Let's not dwell on the negative, but enjoy the success of our first live show," Juliet said. "It was awesome to look into the crowd and see Mark and Carrie there."

Cedra nodded. "They seemed impressed with the show and the number of sales that occurred. We need to find someone who can travel with us to handle the sales."

"I think I know someone," Riley said. "My roommate is a nurse. She works three twelve-hour shifts in the middle of the week. She's off every weekend, and she loves your music. I bet she would jump at the chance to tour with us."

"A roommate, huh?" Keith asked.

"Melissa, or Mel, and I have known each other since high school and have shared an apartment since we graduated," Riley answered.

"Maybe we can have dinner at our place next weekend, and you can introduce us to her," Juliet suggested.

"I think it's warm enough to pull the grill out, Wayne, and show these ladies our mad skills with steak."

"That sounds like a plan, bro," Wayne answered and grabbed another slice of pizza.

†

It was nearing two in the morning when the fire began to die down. "I think I am relaxed enough to get some sleep," Juliet replied. "I hope nobody wakes at the crack of dawn in the morning."

"I don't think you have to worry about that. We should all sleep in, and we can stop for an early lunch on the road," Wayne suggested. "If we leave here by eleven, we can still stop to eat and make it home by late afternoon."

"Sounds good to me. I'll bag up these last three slices unless anyone else wants them," Cedra offered.

"I am finally stuffed," Keith said. "I'll wait and take the boxes and trash to the dumpster."

"I need to hit the bathroom, so I'll walk with you," Wayne replied. "Time to lose some beer."

"We'll see you all later," Juliet said and reached for Cedra's hand. "I'm so proud of us."

"Amen, sister." Keith grinned.

Cedra and Juliet undressed and slipped beneath the cool sheets. Cedra turned to face Juliet. "We did good tonight, huh?"

"I don't think we could have asked for a better debut show. Everything went well. We didn't forget lyrics or music, and Keith didn't drop a pick," Juliet teased.

"Riley is a great addition to our crew. She had everything well organized for us and planned for any mishaps. I'm happy we didn't experience any, though."

"Me, too. I don't know about you, but I am completely drained and will sleep like a rock tonight."

"As long as I'm near you, I always sleep well."

Cedra smiled and kissed her lover. "I love you."

"I love you, too. Goodnight."

CHAPTER SIXTEEN

After everyone had a nice hot shower Sunday morning, they broke down the campsite and hit the road. Keith started the drive and looked at Wayne. "Do you think you can find us someplace to eat soon? I'm starving."

"I'm all over it," Wayne said and pulled out his phone.

Cedra, Riley, and Juliet were kicked back in recliners when Cedra's phone pinged with a text message. Cedra was the first to check her phone. "From Carrie. Check out this article in the Knoxville paper." Cedra clicked on the embedded link and started reading the article. It was a review of the band's performance at the Pub and was filled with high praise for the show.

"That's wonderful news to hear," Juliet said.

Another ping from Carrie. *I expect my phone and emails will blow up tomorrow, if not sooner. Safe travels.*

Thanks, Boss, Cedra answered. She forwarded the text message to Hank and Ma. "I think I'll send it to Lisa Marie, too."

"Send it to all of us," Juliet said. "I'll send it to Lisa Marie because I bet your phone is about to ring."

A few seconds later, Cedra's phone rang, making them all laugh. "Hey, Dad," Cedra answered and placed him on speaker.

"Am I on the speakerphone?"

"Yes, you are. We are driving back from Knoxville."

"That was a great review in the paper. It sounds like you knocked their socks off. I am so proud of all of you."

"Thanks, Dad."

"We had a blast, Hank. I wish you could have been there," Wayne said.

"Let me know how your schedule shakes out, and I'll try to make a couple of shows."

"Will do, Dad. We're proud of ourselves, too."

"I just wanted to call to congratulate you all, tell you I love y'all, and to be safe driving."

"Captain Keith is behind the wheel," Keith hollered out.

"I hope you fed him before you got on the road," Hank teased.

"That's our next mission," Wayne answered. "There's a country café that is open off the next exit."

"Have a great meal then, and I am so proud of you all. Call me later."

"Will do, Dad. I love you, too."

"Lisa Marie texted back her congratulations," Juliet said after Cedra ended her call. "Do you want me to call Ma and tell her we are on our way?"

"That would be great." Cedra tucked away her phone.

Riley scrolled through her photographs while Juliet and the others chatted with Ma. As Cedra had projected, Ma was cooking fried chicken for their return.

"We won't eat that for lunch then," Juliet told her. "Not that it could compare to yours anyhow."

"How did it go for you at the café yesterday?" Cedra asked.

"Not bad for a first day. Lisa Marie, Patsy, and I had pizza and played cards last night. It was a fun night."

"That's great to hear. When we get back on the road, we will text you our estimated time to make it home. It won't be late."

"Sounds great. Have a great meal, and I'll see you all soon. Riley, you are staying for dinner, right?"

"Are you kidding me? I wouldn't dream of missing your legendary fried chicken," Riley answered.

They could hear Ma chuckling and imagined the smile on her face. "See you soon, Ma," Juliet said and ended the call.

"I got some great candid shots of you all. I want to start by adding some of these and maybe a video clip on your website. Maybe make a file for each location that you perform. What do you think?"

"That sounds like a wonderful plan," Juliet said. "We brought a laptop, so maybe we can entertain ourselves by sprucing up our website on the way home."

"Deal," Riley answered and continued scrolling through the photos until the RV exited the interstate.

†

Keith tossed Wayne the keys after they exited the café. "You're going to have to drive, bro. I've eaten myself into a food coma," Keith teased. "I've got to take a nap after a meal like that."

"Not a problem," Wayne said and unlocked the doors for everyone. "It's a straight shot from here to Nashville. Go nap so you can help me unload later."

Cedra, Juliet, and Riley sat around the dining room table with the laptop in front of them. Riley looked at Cedra after loading the memory card. "Will you write down the numbers of the photos we want to add to the website?"

"Sure, no problem." Cedra dug out a notepad and pen.

"We definitely need to add this one," Juliet said, pointing to a picture of the band with Ralph and his serving crew in front of the Pub bar.

"Why don't we start each file with a picture of the band with the owner and staff of the venue? A testament to the confidence they shared in inviting us to play?" Cedra suggested.

"I think that is a fantastic idea," Riley stated.

†

The work on the website continued until they turned off the interstate. "I think we've got a great start on the website," Riley said as she shut down the laptop. "I'm going to wake Keith."

"I'm up," Keith answered. He sat dangling his feet over the edge of the bunk. "Man, I needed that nap."

"You don't have to work tonight, do you?" Riley asked.

"Nope. I'm off until tomorrow night."

"We all start back tomorrow," Juliet said.

"Do you think it will be hard to get back into the swing of things?" Riley asked.

Cedra smiled. "We made great memories last night, but we need to get back to reality until we can make this happen full time. Lisa Marie has been great to all of us. She keeps us receiving a paycheck. She's flexible with us when we need off to record and has offered us the use of the stage whenever we need it."

"I will probably spend the first two hours back tomorrow catching Bud and Felecia up on the trip," Riley said. "Bud has already warned me he wants a full report of every song in the performance."

Cedra looked at Juliet. "I think we will take a few days to get some writing done before we hit the studio again. We've got a few songs we could get ready to record, but I'd rather we focus on some new songs."

"Keith's latest is nearly ready, and I've got some new ideas, too." Juliet nodded toward Wayne. "He's got new music in his head. I can tell by how he bobs his head that he's creating something."

"I don't think there's any rush. You can practice both sets of songs until your next performance date in two weeks, and maybe that will help the lyrics to flow," Riley said.

"Athens is next, right?" Wayne asked.

Juliet returned the laptop to the case. "Yeah, another Saturday night show. We need to decide which playlist to use or come up with another one. What do y'all think?"

"I think we should change out a few songs," Cedra said. "We need to add 'The Devil Went Down to Georgia' for Athens."

"Not a bad idea. Maybe pick up some Thomas Rhett covers," Juliet said.

"Those would probably go over well in Georgia," Riley agreed. "I will continue working on the website and get some swag ordered. I can also suggest Mel being hired as our sales manager during shows. If that is okay with you all?"

"We all agree that you've been a great addition to our team. I think I can speak for all of us that if you think Mel will be great, we are totally on board with the idea. We still want to meet her for dinner next weekend." Juliet smiled at Riley.

Keith rubbed his hands together. "I have steaks to buy."

"It will be a lot of fun. It seems like ages since we've cooked out," Wayne added.

"I can taste your mouth-watering steak already," Riley said.

"No pressure there." Cedra looked at Juliet. "We can toss a salad, make some corn, and other veggies."

"Why don't you leave dessert to Mel and me?" Riley offered.

"Now you're singing my tune." Keith grinned. "Something sweet and lots of it."

†

"Home sweet home," Wayne said as he pulled into Ma's driveway. "Why don't you ladies go inside and check on Ma while Keith and I begin unloading?"

"Will you place my bags in my car?" Riley asked Keith as she handed him the keys.

"Your wish is my command." Keith bowed.

"You are such a goof," Juliet said as she carried her guitar inside past him.

Cedra pulled the door open. "We're home, Ma."

"Welcome home." Ma wiped her hands on her apron and took them into a hug. "I missed y'all."

"We missed you, too. You would have enjoyed the show," Juliet said.

"I'm sure I would have. You'll have to tell me all about it over dinner. It will be ready in another fifteen minutes or so."

"Do you need any help with anything?" Riley asked.

"You can set the table and pour some tea while the others get their bags settled," Ma responded with a smile.

"On it, Ma," Riley responded as Cedra and Juliet carried the first bags upstairs.

"Hey, boys," Ma said when Keith and Wayne finished unloading.

"It's good to see you, Ma," Wayne replied.

"Smells delicious in here." Keith dropped down into a chair. "I know I ate myself into a food coma this morning, but the aromas in here are making me hungry."

"Ma, we may have to drive to Knoxville soon so you can try the pizza at the Pub. It was the best I think I've ever had," Wayne told her as he poured a cup of coffee.

Keith nodded in agreement. "It would be worth the drive for sure."

"Maybe you and I can take a drive while the others are at work," Ma suggested.

"As long as we can eat a few slices along the way. I can't imagine surviving a three-hour drive smelling the pizza on an empty stomach. They have one called 'The Carnivore' that has about two pounds of meat on it."

Ma raised an eyebrow in disbelief.

"It was really loaded," Wayne stated. "I think there may be a slice or two in the RV's fridge."

"It will be lucky to survive the night," Keith answered.

"When should we plan to return the trailer?" Wayne asked.

"I'll take it back to the studio tomorrow," Keith said. "It's easier if I just pull it with my truck."

Ma placed a platter of fried chicken on the table. Cedra dug into the fried okra while the chicken was passed around the table.

"Pass your plates for the gravy," Ma instructed.

"My mouth has been watering all day thinking about this meal," Juliet said and bit into a piece of crunchy fried chicken. "The pizza was great, but this meal is to die for."

"The chicken and dumplings hit the spot before the show last night," Cedra added.

"So, tell me about the show. The review you all received was outstanding."

"It was so much fun, and we were surprised when the curtain opened. Mark and Carrie were in the audience," Cedra stated.

Juliet passed her plate to Ma for gravy. "Riley's idea to record the horn section worked out perfect, and the crowd got a kick out of Keith's air horn performance."

"I don't think we could have asked for a better live performance debut. All the CDs were sold, and we will add a person to the crew to handle sales. Mark and Carrie want to add more swag items, like T-shirts, posters, and other items for sale." Cedra smiled at Ma. "We'll have to show you the photos and video Riley shot. We've already uploaded a couple of dozen on the website during our ride home."

"I am so glad y'all had a wonderful time."

Cedra and Juliet helped Ma clean the kitchen while Keith walked Riley out to her car. Juliet couldn't help but sneak a peek out the front window to see Keith lean in and kiss her, then open her door. He smiled and waved as she pulled away, and Juliet rushed back to the sink.

"Were you spying on them?" Cedra teased.

"I just wanted to see if he would kiss her goodbye. They seemed to get close on our little road trip."

Ma smiled. "Maybe fate will see fit to bring Melissa and Wayne together."

"Stranger things have happened," Cedra said. "I know he still pines over his high school sweetheart. It would be great if someone new caught his attention."

"Only time will tell," Ma said. "If it's meant to be, it will happen."

†

The next few weeks seemed to fly by, and they were preparing for the trip to Athens, Georgia. Mel would be joining them to handle sales during and after the show. She was a cute, red-headed young woman. Mel and Wayne hit it off the night of the cookout and spoke several times afterward. When Keith drove to the studio on Thursday, Riley surprised him when she brought out a dolly filled with boxes.

"What's this?"

"These are the copies of *Six Strings* and *Midnight Mel* will be selling. This is just the first load. I have another stack of T-shirts and other swag to bring out."

Keith picked up the first box to carry it into the trailer. "Keep it coming. If we keep adding more, we'll need a bigger trailer," he joked.

"Just wait until the hats, coffee cups, shot glasses, and beer mugs arrive. Or the key chains, bottle openers, and koozies."

"That's a lot of products. Mark must really believe in us to dish out this kind of money for promotional goods."

"Can you seriously still have doubts?" Riley teased.

Keith wiped the sweat from his forehead. "This still doesn't seem real. I keep pinching myself to make sure I'm not dreaming."

"The Bentleys are the real deal. I don't know how long you will be able to perform a one-night showing."

"Is there really that much interest in our shows?"

Riley smiled. "Ralph has already requested we come back for a two-night performance."

"It may be time we sat down as a group to discuss schedules again. I might need to give notice to the Ryman if we will be traveling more often. The same for the guys working at the Redbird for Lisa Marie. I know it's not a conversation they are eager to have with her, but we must strike while the iron is hot."

Keith closed and locked the trailer door after loading the last of the boxes. "Will you ask Carrie to send Cedra or

Juliet a list of potential dates and venues tonight? I don't know why we can't discuss them on the drive to Athens."

"I sure will," Riley said and leaned over to kiss Keith. "Mel and I will come out tomorrow morning. Do you already have reservations at a campground for us?"

"I sure do. I'll load up some firewood and other supplies when I get home, so we can get on the road tomorrow as early as possible. It's a five-hour drive to Athens, so we can make it before nightfall if everyone is on time tomorrow."

"See you in the morning." Riley spun on her heel and returned to the studio.

†

"Are you all excited about your next road trip?" Lisa Marie asked Cedra during a break at the café.

"Yes. Now that we know more about what to expect, I think we will be better prepared."

"Snag me one of those T-shirts before they all sell out."

"I will, Lisa Marie."

"I think we need to consider hiring some replacements soon. I don't want to appear like I'm rushing you all off, but your popularity is growing, and you will be doing a bunch of travel. You won't be able to keep up this pace long term and still have time to create and refresh."

"I will discuss it with the group tonight. Why don't you start an ad to see what kind of replacements you can hire, and we will help you with the training. You know we would never leave you high and dry."

Lisa Marie nodded. "I know you wouldn't, but I don't want to hold you all up from playing some great gigs because it's too far to travel in a day. It's not fair to you."

"We will work this out," Cedra promised.

†

The Athens show went off without a hitch, and the miles and venues multiplied until the end of spring. Lisa Marie was able to hire their replacements, and with Wayne's and Cedra's help, they were trained and ready to take over full-time. Lisa Marie asked them to stay longer than usual on their last day of work.

"I know it's not a proper going away party, but I wanted to have a little get-together to express my appreciation for all you have done for the café."

Platters of bacon cheeseburgers and French fries were passed around the table. Ma, Keith, Riley, Mel, and Carrie joined them for the celebration.

"You can bet we will come for a visit every time we are in town," Keith said and bit into a burger.

"Don't forget to email me and let me know how things are going on the road. I know I can check in on the website, but I'd love to hear from you," Lisa Marie told Cedra and Juliet. "Are you excited about your first big road trip next week?"

"Yes, we are," Juliet answered. "Mel managed to switch around her work schedules so she could travel with us."

"I don't know how much longer that will work out as your shows continue to expand, but I want you all to know I'll be there in spirit with you. It's been so much fun, so far."

"Did you ever dream you would be going to College Station, Texas?"

"Heck no, we had to look it up on the internet," Wayne said. "We play there Friday night and Saturday before traveling to Norman, Oklahoma, the following week for two shows."

"Did I also overhear you are doing a big outdoor show at the Spirit of the Suwannee Music Park in Florida?"

"Yes. It looks like a fantastic venue. An entire weekend at a campground with two live stages. We will play two shows on Saturday and Sunday. Stone and Sarah will be joining us for the weekend. Dad, too," Cedra answered.

"That sounds like a fun trip. Hopefully, I can see a live performance when you return to Nashville."

Juliet reached for a handful of fries, saying, "We'd like that. We've got a good routine down and have been able to do some writing while on the road. We will spend some time in the studio after the Norman trip. Bud is chomping at the bit to record some new songs to finish *Out and Loud* before the summer ends."

"I think Carrie is working on a show at the Lynchburg Music Fest. Jack Daniels is courting us for sponsorship and has sent us lots of wonderful clothing and gifts," Keith said.

"I could make that one easily," Lisa Marie said. She looked over at Ma. "Ready for a road trip? We could get a hotel and spend the night after the show."

"I'm game," Ma said. "I could always help out with sales, too."

Mel smiled at Cedra. "You know Ma would be perfect for the dates I can't attend. You could get her a hotel room; that way, you will have a private space to shower and get dressed."

Juliet nodded and grinned at Cedra. "We had already discussed that. What do you think, Ma?"

"Oh, I'd be delighted," Ma answered. "I'd hate for you to go to the expense of a hotel room, though."

"It would actually make it much easier for us to get ready," Cedra replied. "The guys are fine showering anywhere, but it takes a bit more for us to get ready." She looked at Keith and Wayne. "They could drop us off at the hotel and then pick us up for the show."

"Keep me posted on dates," Lisa Marie said as the group packed up to leave. "She handed Cedra, Wayne, and Juliet envelopes as she hugged them goodbye. "Stay in touch," she told Cedra.

"We will," Cedra promised.

CHAPTER SEVENTEEN

"Turn on the television," Keith called out from the driver's seat.

Juliet reached for the remote and clicked the power button. "What's going on?"

"They had a gunman at a concert last night in Texas. The security team detected him early and prevented him from firing off any shots," Keith answered. "At least that's what I just heard on the radio."

They gathered around the table in the RV to watch the news broadcast on the event. The ticker tape at the bottom of the screen provided the documentary of the event. A twenty-year-old college student wearing an American Flag headband was arrested in Houston the previous night with three semi-automatic weapons in his possession at a local festival park. The scene on the screen showed armed security guards wrestling the young man to the ground and placing handcuffs on him. The reporter finally came on screen.

"The young man whose identity is yet to be released was arrested for possessing concealed firearms with intent to cause mayhem. The alleged perpetrator claims the music at the rap concert was immoral and incited violence against white people."

His mug shot flashed on the television. "It is undetermined if the gunman was acting alone or with potential accomplices. Authorities ask anyone who knows this young man to call them with the information. Two people suffered minor injuries when the panicked crowd rushed out of the park. No other updates are currently available."

"This is insane," Wayne responded. "People shouldn't fear for their lives while attending a concert."

"No, but it's happening much too frequently," Ma said from her recliner. "It makes me worry for your safety. I know this is your first big outdoor show, but there is no way security can check all the vehicles thoroughly that will be coming into the park."

"We just need to have faith that the promoter will have adequate security on hand to prevent anything from happening," Juliet said. "We can't be held hostage by what ifs."

"This is a group decision. Do any of you wish to cancel our performance?" Cedra asked.

"Hell, no," Keith said. "I agree with Juliet."

"Me, too," Wayne answered.

Cedra looked at Riley and Ma. "We just need to remain vigilant in watching the crowds for potential problems," Riley said. "No one would criticize the band for not performing, but it sends a reinforcing message to the crazies who would consider such an act if performers start canceling shows."

"I think Mark and Carrie need to be cognizant of promoters' measures to keep everyone safe. Promise me that if you ever feel unsafe at a venue, you won't hesitate to pull the plug," Ma requested.

"I don't think anyone of us has a problem with that, Ma," Juliet assured her.

Keith pulled off the interstate into the entrance of the hotel where Ma would be staying.

"We will get checked in at the park and drop the trailer. You can get checked into your room, and we'll be back for dinner if you'd like." Juliet smiled at Ma.

"I can just grab something from the hotel restaurant," Ma said. "Honestly, I'm ready to have my feet on solid ground and a comfortable bed to rest on."

Wayne jumped out and rushed to get a luggage cart. "I'll get Ma's bags and you gal's clothes for the shows if you'll get Ma checked in."

"I've got this. Let's go, Ma," Juliet said. She and Cedra accompanied Ma to the front desk.

Once Ma was settled into her room, Cedra hugged her. "After we get the equipment set up and complete a sound check tomorrow, we will come back to get you. They have breakfast downstairs, and we will scout out food vendors tonight at the park."

"If there isn't anything good, we will grab a bite to eat in town. We can set up the vendor table and get you stocked with plenty of time for you to get settled," Juliet said.

"You sure you're okay here, Ma?" Wayne asked.

"You are more than welcome to stay in the RV with us," Juliet said.

"Thanks, but this nice king-sized bed will suit me just fine. Don't worry about me. I will see you all tomorrow."

Wayne kissed her on the cheek. "Good night, Ma."

"See you soon," Cedra replied and closed the door behind them.

†

Keith pulled into the park and was directed to the office. James Conner and his staff welcomed them to the park and provided a map of where the stages were located and the camping site they had been assigned. "Would it be okay to park our equipment trailer next to the stage?" Wayne asked. "We won't need to set up until tomorrow morning."

James nodded. "Absolutely. There will be round-the-clock security set up at both stages and across the park starting tonight as people start to arrive. No need to worry about your equipment. It will be under constant monitoring once you set up tomorrow, between shows, and overnight. We want this to be a pleasant experience for everyone."

Cedra and Juliet shared a look. "I know this may sound odd, but are you confident of the security at this outdoor venue?"

"Are you referring to what just happened in Texas?"

"Yes, sir, we are," Juliet replied.

"Besides our normal security crew, we have off-duty deputies from the Sheriff's Department who will be working the crowds. In addition, there is a State Police Training Academy five minutes down the road, so we will have seventy-five trainees across three shifts, for some real-life experience, as their Commander calls it."

"That makes us feel much better," Cedra replied. "Thank you."

"We have a large crowd eager and excited to hear you play. Me included," James said, and handed each of them a business card. "We have several tables set up for sales at your stage, and if you need help getting anything set up, just call me at this number."

"Thank you. Let's go get the RV set up, guys," Juliet said, and they left the office.

Keith handed Wayne the map. "Okay, Mr. Navigator, get us to the stage."

"Recalculating," Wayne sounded off with a laugh as he looked at the map. He smiled at Keith. "Take the first left, up ahead."

"Damn, something smells good," Keith said after climbing out of the RV.

"Why don't you and Wayne drop the trailer and do some scouting while we check out the stage," Cedra suggested.

"No problem," Wayne said. "Let's get to it, bro, so we can find out what that smell is."

†

"This stage is huge," Juliet said as she spun around in the middle. "No bumping elbows in here."

"Not at all," Cedra replied.

"You guys will rock this stage," Riley said. "I must warn you that Keith may be dancing all over this stage. Ever since we let him ham it up with the air horn, he's been itching to dance."

"Can he dance?" Juliet asked.

Riley smiled. "Oh yeah, he's got some moves."

"Maybe we should cut him loose to have some fun then," Cedra replied.

"We have room, and I've got a surprise for all of you."

"I love your surprises. What is it this week?" Juliet asked.

"Mark bought headsets for you all. He thought you could move around more freely without being tied to a microphone stand. Hence, Keith's dance moves." Riley chuckled.

"Did Keith know about that?" Juliet asked.

Riley shrugged. "He might have seen them when we loaded up."

"This should be fun," Cedra said. "It will add a layer of entertainment to the performance."

"That it will." Riley looked at the steps leading up to the stage. "Fans love it when they are brought on stage to dance or sing with the group."

Cedra looked at Juliet and cocked her head. "Do you remember our first autograph?"

"The young girl at the Country Music Hall of Fame?"

"Do you remember how excited she was to meet us?"

"Yes. I get where you're going with this. If we can inspire anyone, we should at least give it a try. You win." Juliet held up her hands in surrender.

Cedra pulled Juliet into a hug and kissed her. "Sometimes you can be so easy."

"That's not always a bad thing," Juliet answered.

Keith and Wayne arrived carrying bags of food. "That delicious smell was a food truck selling BBQ sandwiches. We couldn't resist any longer," Wayne said.

"You have your choice of pulled pork or brisket, chips, and soda," Keith said as he opened a bag and started handing out sandwiches.

The group sat on the stage steps, eating while watching a steady stream of campers fill the campground.

Keith smiled. "This place is going to be packed."

"Have you heard anything from Hank or Stone yet?" Juliet asked Cedra.

"Hank sent a text that he was at the hotel, and he and Ma were going out to dinner," Cedra replied. "I think that's your answer about Stone." She pointed at three people approaching.

"Bro," Keith said and reached out his hand. "It's good to see you."

"Sarah and Destiny, too. You sure are growing up," Cedra said to Stone's daughter. "I hope you're ready to start beating the boys off with a stick."

"Goodness, Cedra, don't rush her. She already thinks she's grown," Stone said. "You all look great."

"You, too," Juliet said. "This is Riley. She's Bud's apprentice in the studio, and she travels to shows with us to help set up equipment and run the soundboard."

Stone smiled. "Bud's assistant? He must be going soft."

"Apprentice, not assistant," Riley corrected him. "He's still as tough as ever, but he's a great teacher."

"Damn, that smells good," Stone said.

"There's a food truck just down the path with incredible BBQ sandwiches," Keith said.

"Mind if we join y'all then?" Sarah asked. "We're starving."

"I was just about to go for a round of seconds," Keith said. "Follow me."

Keith, Wayne, and Stone left the stage. "Grab a seat," Juliet said.

"I've got an idea," Riley said. "Since there is security on site, why don't we see if we can set up tonight and complete our sound check? Maybe jam a bit and give the campers a taste of the show. Ask Stone if he wants to join in?"

"He would love that," Sarah said. "He brought his guitar and fiddle, just in case."

"I'll call James," Cedra said and pulled out her phone. She ended the call and nodded. "James loves the idea."

"It will give y'all a chance to try out the new headsets, too," Riley said.

The boys returned with more food. "Here we go," Wayne said and passed out sandwiches and drinks.

"Riley had a wonderful idea. We'll set up tonight, perform a soundcheck, and jam for a little while to give the early campers a bit of a show."

"That sounds great. Wayne can get the RV settled in and then come back to help us set up," Keith answered.

Cedra looked at Stone. "Will you jam with us a bit tonight?"

Stone almost dropped his sandwich. "I'd love to." He smiled. "I brought some instruments just in case."

"Eat up then and let's get busy," Juliet said.

†

The group had gotten proficient with the setup routine. Riley instructed them on how to use the headphones, and after the soundcheck, they invited Stone to join them on stage. Campers had begun drifting in.

"Is it okay for us to watch?" a new arrival asked.

"Absolutely," Cedra said and waved them forward.

"So, what's on the playlist?" Stone asked.

"Do you remember 'Backwoods Boogie?'" Keith asked.

"I sure do. I've been keeping up with your new stuff, too," Stone said. "'Midnight in Nashville' turned out great. It's Destiny's favorite. I think we listened to it five times driving here."

Quite the crowd had gathered after they finished jamming. When the group started casing up their instruments, the crowd applauded.

"Thank you," Juliet called out to them. "We'll see you tomorrow."

"This was just like old times on Ma's porch," Stone said with watery eyes.

"Ma and Hank will be out tomorrow," Cedra said. "They are in town in a hotel."

"I can't wait to see them," Sarah replied. "Stone talks about them often."

Stone was helping Wayne with the instruments. "Are you getting any writing done?"

Stone shook his head. "There's just no time or energy left at the end of the day. This trip is the first time off I've been able to take since I've been home."

"We're glad you came to spend it with us. We miss you, man."

"I miss you all, but staying home was the right decision. I swear Destiny grows an inch a week."

After returning to the group, Juliet called Stone to the side. "Would you mind if I brought Destiny up on stage when we play 'Midnight?'"

"She'd love that. She might not sleep for a week, but she'll never forget the experience."

"It's about halfway through our first set. I'll find her in the crowd and ask her to join us."

"Thanks, Juliet. She's already asked if she can buy some posters and get your autograph to hang in her room. I think she's your number one fan."

"Ma and Hank will work the sales table tomorrow, so we'll ensure she gets whatever she wants."

"We are cooking breakfast tomorrow if y'all would like to join us," Sarah said.

"That sounds great. We can go to the hotel for showers and prepare for the early show after we're done," Cedra replied. "Setting up tonight was a plus."

"We can help Ma and Hank get set up," Stone offered.

"They would love that," Juliet said.

"I think there's a pizza truck set up," Keith said. "Would you like to join us for a late dinner and a few beers around the fire?"

Stone looked at Sarah, who nodded. "That sounds perfect." He grinned at Juliet. "Speaking of which, will you be singing that?"

"It's part of the second show covers," Juliet answered.

"Let's go see a man, or woman, about some pizza," Wayne said to Keith and Stone. "We'll see you in a bit. Man, you should have been with us in Knoxville. The Pub we played at had the best pizza I've ever eaten. It was so good, we had it twice." Keith laughed.

Destiny slipped her tiny hand into Juliet's. "Do you like s'mores?" she asked.

"I love s'mores," Juliet answered. "Do you want to make some after we eat?"

"That would be awesome," Destiny said and turned back to Sarah. "Coming, Mom?"

"Right behind you," Sarah replied. "I think Juliet has a new best friend."

"I've got to admit, they are cute together," Cedra replied.

†

Destiny barely made it through the s'mores before falling asleep in Stone's arms. "I guess it's time for this little one to go to bed. Thanks for the pizza and beer."

"We'll see you for breakfast in the morning, right?" Sarah asked.

Cedra nodded. "You most certainly will. What time?"

"Is eight too early? I know Destiny will be up with the sunrise. Every day she gets up with Stone."

"Aww, that is so sweet." Juliet brushed Destiny's hair out of her face.

"Eight will be perfect," Cedra answered.

"We'll see you tomorrow then." Stone stood and carefully repositioned Destiny.

"Goodnight," Juliet whispered.

Cedra jumped when a log shifted in the fire pit as the flames died down. "I think we should all get some rest. Tomorrow will be a big day."

"Yes, it will," Keith said. "I'll dowse the fire if y'all want to head inside."

†

Cedra and Juliet curled up in the bed. "Stone sure looks happy. I can't get over how much Destiny has grown. She really looks up to you," she told Juliet.

"She's adorable."

"You interacted well with her. I think you'd make a good mom someday."

"I don't know about that, but I could be a darned good aunt." Juliet smiled and kissed Cedra.

"When Keith and Wayne get married and start having babies, we will do our best to spoil them. I love you."

"Love you too, Baby Girl. Are you excited to see your dad?"

"Yes, I'm surprised he and Ma didn't drive out tonight."

"I think Ma had all the riding she could handle for one day. She has a busy day tomorrow, too. Making sure we are all looking good and then selling our products. Did you see all those boxes of items?"

"I think Mark didn't want us to run out of anything," Cedra replied with a chuckle.

"Have I told you lately how happy you make me?"

Cedra snuggled in closer to Juliet. "You might have mentioned something this morning, but a girl never gets tired of hearing it from the woman she loves."

Juliet's hand caressed Cedra's back. "I don't think I could ever tell you how much I love you enough. You are my world." She felt the warmth and dampness of Cedra's tears on her shirt. Juliet lifted Cedra's face and brushed away her tears. "I didn't mean to make you cry."

"I didn't mean to cry. I get overwhelmed with the beautiful things you say to me sometimes."

"I mean every word of it."

Cedra smiled. "I know you do. I feel the same way."

"Are you excited about tomorrow?"

"Yes, everyone is back that was with us at the beginning. Everyone except Lisa Marie."

"I know. I wish she could have been here for our first outdoor performance."

"Me, too, but she still has a business to run. It's not easy for her to leave."

Juliet kissed the top of her head. "I'm confident she will make the Lynchburg show."

They rested in silence until Cedra's breathing slowed, and Juliet smiled, listening to the sound of Cedra sleeping as she gazed out the RV window.

CHAPTER EIGHTEEN

Cedra pitched in to help Sarah cook breakfast as they served a mound of pancakes, bacon, and eggs. "This looks terrific," Keith said as they pulled a picnic table over to Stone's truck.

"Eat up, and if we need more, I'll gladly cook it," Sarah said.

Destiny settled in next to Juliet and smiled up at her. "I love mommy's pancakes. She puts chocolate chips and special love into mine."

Juliet looked at the smile on Sarah's face. "I'm sure she does. They taste delicious." She put a bite of pancake in her mouth.

"This reminds me of one of Ma's feasts," Stone said.

"Some things never change. Ma still feeds us incredibly well." Keith patted his stomach.

"I see you still burn off every calorie. Are you still a sugar hound?" Stone asked.

"Ha! Don't get between Keith and anything sweet," Riley teased.

"That didn't take you long to learn," Stone said with a smile.

Riley laughed. "The first time I carried a box of cookies into the breakroom at the studio, I thought I was in the middle of a stampede."

"Hey, now." Keith pouted.

Juliet slapped him on the back. "You know she's totally right."

"Yeah. Yeah." Keith stuffed a piece of bacon into his mouth.

"What time are you heading to the hotel to prepare for the show?" Stone asked.

Wayne looked at Juliet. "Ten-thirty?"

"Yeah, Hank said we could use his room to shower," Keith replied.

"That will make things go faster," Cedra said.

Stone looked at Wayne. "James offered us a golf cart if you two want to explore the park with me."

"Sounds great." Wayne nodded.

"I'm in," Keith agreed. "That will be fun."

"You guys go ahead. We'll pick up here and relax," Sarah said.

243

†

Ma fussed over Keith and Wayne. "Someone could use a haircut," she teased Keith. When Keith hung his head, Ma smiled. "Regardless, you both are handsome."

Keith perked up immediately and hugged Ma. "Thank you."

"I must agree with her assessment. You're both looking great," Hank said as he picked up a light jacket. "We'd better get rolling and check on the girls."

"Y'all go ahead and wait for us in the lobby, and I'll check on the girls." Ma picked up her coat.

When she walked back into her room, Ma stopped in her tracks. Lisa Marie was sitting on the bed, tying off Juliet's braid. "Lisa Marie," she cried out. "I didn't know you were coming."

"We didn't either," Juliet said. "We heard a knock on the door, expecting one of the guys, and opened it to find Lisa Marie."

Lisa Marie shrugged. "I couldn't stand the thought of missing your performance. So, I closed the café for today and hit the road."

Cedra hugged her neck. "I'm so glad you've joined us. We have everyone together again, and I couldn't be happier."

Juliet looked at her watch. "We need to get rolling."

"What time are your shows?"

"The first is at one and then again at eight," Cedra answered.

"Do you have everything set up already?" Lisa Marie asked.

Juliet reached for Cedra's hand. "We set up last night and had a jam session. It was a lot of fun, especially playing with Stone again."

Lisa Marie opened the door. "That's right. I forgot he was planning to come."

Ma ushered them toward the door. "Come along. The guys are waiting for us in the lobby."

✝

After a final soundcheck, The Bentleys were ready to go. The bandstand had filled quickly, and with the additional help, the sales booths were stocked and prepared for business.

"Would you mind if I stay to help you and Hank?" Lisa Marie asked.

"We could use the extra help until the show gets started."

"Thanks, Ma."

"No, thank you. That first rush was something else," Ma answered, fanning herself.

The band stepped onto the stage, and Juliet began the routine by introducing the members. Keith was excited about starting the show, and the crowd sang along to "The Devil Went Down to Georgia" with him as he played his fiddle. The addition of the headsets proved invaluable, especially on that song.

The crowd was enjoying the show. Juliet scanned the front rows and smiled when she found Stone, Sarah, and Destiny. She nodded to Stone. "For this next number, I wondered if Miss Destiny Watson would join us on stage?"

Cedra smiled at the surprise on Destiny's face when she heard her name called. Riley brought a stool on stage and placed it next to Juliet. Juliet covered her microphone with her hand when Destiny climbed onto the stool. "Are you ready to help me sing 'Midnight?'"

Destiny nodded her head and smiled up at Juliet. Juliet pulled out her harmonica and played the opening to "Midnight." When she reached the chorus, she leaned down so Destiny could help her sing. Her tiny little voice was barely heard over the music, but the smile on her face was beaming. When the song ended, Juliet reached a hand to Destiny to help her off the stool. "Will you give Destiny a big round of applause, ladies and gentlemen?" The crowd applauded, and Destiny and Juliet bowed together. Destiny pulled Juliet's hand until she bent down and then planted a kiss on Juliet's cheek. A chorus of "Aw" was heard throughout the crowd as Destiny rushed back to her seat.

"We are going to take a quick break, but we will be right back."

The band walked off the stage and grabbed cold bottles of water. Riley smiled at Cedra. "I think you've got some competition for Juliet's heart," she teased. "That was a fantastic performance. I bet Destiny's face will hurt tomorrow from all the smiling."

"She did a great job," Juliet replied. "Plus, it was a lot of fun." She looked at Keith. "Do you want to bring some fans on stage when we play 'Backwoods Boogie,' and you can show them how it's done?"

"Seriously?" Keith asked.

Juliet and Cedra nodded. "It's the third song on the set after our break. Why don't you pick out your dancers, and we'll bring them up so you can show them your moves?"

"Is four too many, Juliet?" he asked.

"No, I think that will be just fine. You can leave your guitar and have the entire front of the stage. We'll play while you sing and dance," Juliet suggested.

"You are so on," Keith said.

"Let's get busy and knock out the rest of this set," Cedra suggested.

She and Juliet covered "Fire Away" as the crowd sang along with them. Cedra glanced at the sales table and saw three smiling faces.

When the song ended, Keith looked over at Riley and gave her a nod. "She started the music, and Keith started playing his air horn to begin "Wine, Beer, and Whiskey." The crowd loved it and gave them a big round of applause. Keith removed his guitar and walked toward the front of the stage.

"Does anyone know our song 'Backwoods Boogie?'" he asked.

"Heck yeah," someone called out.

"But does anyone know how to do the Boogie?" he asked. The crowd was silent. "I need help from these four people," Keith said as he pointed out the kids to bring up on stage.

The kids squealed with excitement as they left their seats to rush up on stage. Keith covered his microphone to huddle up and speak with them.

"Okay, I will sing the song and begin the dance when we start playing. You can follow my steps or add your own. Just have fun. Ready?"

Keith turned to his bandmates and smiled. He was so in his element with the kids, and they started to play when he nodded. Riley stepped away from her soundboard and began shooting a video of the performance. Keith sang the song with the others and danced at the front of the stage, two kids on either side of him. The three older ones caught on to his moves quickly, but the youngest girl of about seven entertained the crowd with her own moves. At the song's end, Keith moved in front of each child, bent down to hug them, and asked them to call out their names on his headset. Then they all held hands and took a bow. Keith helped them back down the steps to rejoin their families, then he bounced back on stage. Keith picked up his guitar as Wayne began to sing his version of "Ol Red" for the crowd.

"Six Strings" came up next, and then Juliet and Cedra sang "The Wedding Song" to close out the set.

Juliet walked to the front of the stage. "We hope you will enjoy the rest of the entertainment today and join us again tonight at eight. Before we close, I'd like to thank Ma Bentley, Hank Tyler, and Lisa Marie for handling our sales table. If you haven't visited with them yet, feel free. After a quick drink, we'll arrive to sign anything you want and take some photos."

†

For over an hour, they greeted fans, signed autographs, and took pictures. Juliet was surprised by the number of products sold after the first show. Hopefully, much more would sell after the following three shows to limit the boxes they would load for the trip home.

"What's next?" Ma asked.

Keith looked at Wayne. "We have several hours before the next show. Are you all up for more BBQ?"

"That sounds delicious," Ma said. "Do me a favor and take off your good shirts. I don't want BBQ sauce on them."

Wayne smiled. "Yes, Ma. Let's go, guys. I'm starving."

Hank helped Lisa Marie cover the tables with blankets, and Ma grabbed the cash box and iPad before following the others to the RV. The picnic tables were still set up from the previous night, so Hank and Lisa Marie took a seat while Ma stored the equipment.

Wayne, Keith, and Stone volunteered to hit the food truck while the others relaxed.

"Grab a beer or a cold drink, and we'll be back as soon as we can," Keith said.

†

249

"That was a fantastic show," Hank said as they settled around the tables. "I love the new stuff you have incorporated into the show."

Ma grinned. "Keith was in his glory with those kids."

"I know someone who hasn't stopped smiling and will have stories to tell all her friends," Sarah said as she nodded toward Destiny.

"You did a fantastic job," Juliet praised the young girl.

"It was a lot of fun," Destiny replied. "I sing with Daddy, but it was so much different on stage with you."

"It was great to have you join us," Cedra replied.

"I got videos of both events," Riley said. "I'll send you a copy," she told Sarah.

"I'll make a backup. I'm certain one will be worn out quickly."

When the guys returned, they were carrying two boxes of food. Hank shook his head. "Did you leave any for the rest of the crowd?"

"We did, and guess what else we found?" Wayne asked. "We found a vendor selling street corn, so we got everyone an ear with various seasoning packs."

"Yummy," Destiny yelled out. "I love corn."

They could hear the music from the other band chosen to perform that weekend as they ate.

"I may be biased, but they don't sound half as good as y'all did," Lisa Marie commented.

"I think they are a local group, just getting started," Keith replied.

"Are you going to kick back and relax for a bit?" Hank asked. "Ma, Lisa Marie, and I are going to take a stroll and check out some other vendors."

"Scout out something for dinner," Keith said.

"Always planning for your next meal." Ma chuckled. "We thought we'd bring some biscuits from a local restaurant for breakfast in the morning if that's okay."

"That sounds perfect," Wayne said. "Will you let us give you some money?"

"Nope, we've got this," Lisa Marie answered. "We'll stop for milk and juice."

"We've got several gallons left, so that can be our contribution," Stone offered.

Juliet turned to Cedra. "Do you want to stretch out for a while?"

Cedra looked at Hank. "Will you wake us when you get back?"

"Only if you feel like losing some money," Hank teased. "Ma brought her cards, so we thought we'd play a few hands while y'all rest up."

"Okay then. Don't let us sleep past six." Cedra leaned over and kissed his cheek. "Remember to watch Ma for dealing from the bottom of the deck.

"I remember," Hank teased.

"We are so happy y'all could join us this weekend. We'll see you in a bit."

"I think I'll stretch out, too," Wayne said.

251

Keith shrugged. "You all know I can't sleep. I'm too pumped up and would keep y'all awake. If Riley's up for it, I thought we'd ride down that trail we were on this morning. The river is so beautiful."

"That sounds wonderful." Riley stood and reached for Keith's hand.

†

The second show was going great. The crowd was into the music, and they had just played a song after the break when all hell broke loose. Juliet was about to begin the next song when they heard loud, rapid-fire explosions near the stage. Juliet rushed to cover Cedra while the guys ducked down. The crowd dropped to the ground, with several people crying and screaming. Seconds later that felt like an eternity, the sounds stopped. Juliet looked up to find two huge men dragging two young boys from around a fire pit. Before they could resume the show, James entered the bandstand and walked on stage. The crowd was deathly silent.

"I am very sorry about the incident that just occurred. Two young boys thought it would be fun to toss a few packs of firecrackers into a firepit. Given the recent events, this was not a wise decision. The boys have been detained, and the families have been asked to leave the park."

He turned back to look at the band. "Is everyone okay?"

"Yes, we're fine," Juliet said.

"I am so sorry about the disruption of your show."

"James, there was nothing you could have done to prevent that. Boys will be boys," Cedra answered.

"I know they are young, and I'm certain the two state police that detained them will give them a stern lecture about the seriousness of what just occurred. The two families have camped here for years and sent their apologies. Those two young men won't sit comfortably for a few days."

Juliet turned back to the crowd. "Sorry, folks. That was not exactly the type of fireworks we were hoping for. Just two young boys who made a poor decision. We hope everyone is okay and ready for the show to continue."

A few people left, but most of the crowd returned to their seats. The band played the remainder of the show without incident and greeted their fans afterward. When Hank and Stone returned carrying boxes filled with food, they closed the sales booth and returned to the RV.

"Well, that was quite the scare," Lisa Marie said.

"Some stupid kids tossed firecrackers into a fire pit," Keith said.

Wayne shook his head. "I don't think they will make that mistake again. Did you see those guys chase them down and tackle them?" he asked Keith.

"Yeah, they were quite impressive, but I wouldn't be surprised if the kids peed their pants."

Hank and Stone placed large boxes of fried chicken, baked beans, and biscuits on the table, along with paper plates.

"I hope everyone's hungry," Stone said. "I know it's not Ma's, but I bet we can enjoy it just the same."

Destiny ate a drumstick before falling asleep in Stone's arms. "She's had an eventful day."

"We all have," Juliet said.

"I think we'll head back to the hotel," Lisa Marie said. "Breakfast at nine?"

"That sounds good. Will one of you text us to let us know you made it back in safely?" Cedra requested.

"I can do that," Hank said with pride. "I'm finally getting this phone figured out."

"We'll see you all tomorrow, too," Stone said before carrying Destiny back to their campsite.

†

Cedra leaned over and kissed Juliet awake the following morning. "Good morning."

Juliet kissed her back. "You seem eager to start the day."

"I had a thought last night I want to share with you and get your opinion."

"I'm all ears," Juliet replied as she propped up on pillows.

"I'd like to sing 'Hero' live for Dad. I know it's not released yet, and we'll use it on the new album, but I think this is a great opportunity to share the song with him in person."

Juliet reached for Cedra's hand. "I think it's a wonderful idea. Not only will you share it with Hank, but

254

you'll give the crowd a taste of what's to come. Let's discuss it with the guys and decide where it would be a good fit."

Cedra smiled. "We can do that after breakfast. Speaking of which, Lisa Marie's truck just pulled up. Stone, Sarah, and Destiny have already arrived and are chatting with Wayne."

"Keith won't be far behind once he smells food," Juliet teased. "I guess we need to get moving too."

†

After a leisurely breakfast, Lisa Marie tossed Wayne her truck keys. "We've decided to stay behind, and reorganize and stock the sales tables while y'all get ready for the show."

"Hank and I have already scouted out a nice local restaurant for an early dinner before your second show," Ma added.

"That sounds terrific," Cedra replied.

"Get a move on then," Hank said. "Our room keys are in the console."

"Let's grab our hygiene kits and hit the road then," Juliet said. "Maybe we can have another short jam session to warm up again. That seemed to work well yesterday." She looked at Cedra. "Sit tight, and I'll grab ours."

"I'm sorry we haven't had much time together this weekend," Cedra told Hank.

"Are you kidding? I'm having a blast, and it's good to see Stone and his family. Not to mention Ma and Lisa Marie. I couldn't be prouder of you guys."

"It's been a great weekend so far. Do you think you'll make it up for the Lynchburg show?"

"I wouldn't miss it for the world. It's quite something that Jack Daniel's is sponsoring the band."

"It was quite a shock when we heard the news. They have sent us some cool stuff to wear, too. We'll all wear new shirts for the second show today to get some photos on the website."

Juliet returned. "Ready to roll?"

"See you soon, Dad. I love you."

"I love you too, Baby Girl."

Cedra took Juliet's hand and walked to Lisa Marie's truck.

After they had left the park, Cedra spoke up. "I'm glad we have a few minutes to ourselves. I want to ask you all something. I'd like to sing 'Hero' for Dad, so he can hear it live for the first time."

"That's a great idea. Hank will love that song," Wayne said.

"Why don't you perform it after the third song in the set? I think it would fit well with those songs," Riley suggested.

"Thanks, guys," Cedra replied and leaned her head on Juliet's shoulder.

†

The first performance went perfectly. After the third song, Cedra addressed the crowd while the band took their seats.

"I have someone very special to me in attendance today, and I want to share a new song with you that will be on our next album. We've never performed it live, but I want him to hear it straight from me." Cedra looked over at the sales booth. "Dad, will you stand up?" Hank stood and waved at the crowd, who applauded him. "This one is for you, Dad. It's called 'Hero.'"

Cedra could see Hank wiping his tears as she sang straight from her heart. She also saw many people become emotional and wrap their loved ones in their arms during the song. When she finished singing, Cedra stood. "I love you, Dad, and I wouldn't be here today if it weren't for you."

Hank couldn't wait for the crowd to finish applauding before he stormed onto the stage and hugged Cedra. "That was beautiful." He kissed her forehead. "Your mom would be very proud of you as well."

"Thanks, Dad. I love you."

Hank waved to the crowd as he took the steps back to the sales booth. Cedra watched as Ma and Lisa Marie hugged him. She turned toward her bandmates and nodded. Juliet, Keith, and Wayne returned to their instruments, and the group finished the show.

†

"That was a pleasant surprise," Hank said after placing their food orders. "I had no idea that was coming. I could have used a tissue warning, though," he teased.

"I'll remember that next time. It was a spontaneous decision this morning. Originally, it was meant to be a surprise on the new album, but I felt I needed to sing it to you first."

"I'm so glad you did, Baby Girl, but you better stop before my eyes start leaking again. It's a beautiful song."

†

Monday morning, the crew was busy loading the equipment when Ma and Lisa Marie arrived. Hank was just a few minutes behind. "I can't believe the weekend went so quickly," Lisa Marie said. "Would you have a problem with Ma riding back with me? I can travel much faster than the RV, which will give Ma time to prepare a late supper for you."

"Ma is more than welcome to ride home with you, but we can stop for supper along the way," Juliet said.

"Nonsense, it's time for you to enjoy some home cooking," Ma answered.

Juliet threw her hands up in surrender. "We will never dream of passing up on your cooking."

"I'm glad that's settled." Ma nodded toward Hank and Cedra. "It's never easy for either of them."

"No, but he'll be up next month for the Lynchburg show," Juliet said. "Y'all come to say goodbye so you can hit the road."

The three of them walked over to the group. Keith and Wayne were wrestling with the last dolly of boxes. "I can't get over how much you sold," Riley said when she looked up to see Ma.

"Less to carry back home." Ma smiled. "I am going to ride with Lisa Marie. Will you stay for supper once y'all get back?"

"You can count on it," Riley answered.

"I'm going to ride part of the way with Dad," Cedra told Ma. "It will allow us to catch up on the drive."

Ma shot a glance at Juliet, who was wearing a broad smile. "I think that's a great idea." Ma turned to the boys. "I'm going to make a big dish of lasagna for supper, so don't spoil your appetites."

"You should know better, Ma. I'm hungry again twenty minutes after I eat," Keith claimed.

"We'll see you at home. Drive carefully."

"You too, Ma. We'll see you tonight," Wayne said.

Hank walked them to the truck and hugged them before they drove away. Keith was placing the lock on the trailer. "I think we're all set to go."

Cedra kissed Juliet. "I'll see you in a few hours."

"Have fun with your dad. I may settle in for a nap."

"You all set, Baby Girl?"

"Right behind you, Dad."

"I'll be right behind you, so be careful," Hank told Keith. "Are you good on fuel?"

"Yes, sir, we are good to go."

†

Cedra rode with Hank until they reached their cut-off. "I will see you soon, Dad. Love you."

"I love you, too. Text me when you make it home, please."

"I will if you do the same."

"Be careful, and I'll see you soon."

Hank waited until she climbed inside the RV, and they pulled away. He fueled his truck and started for home.

Cedra walked to the back when Juliet wasn't in front with the rest of the crew and climbed onto the bed with Juliet. Juliet slept on her side, so Cedra wrapped her body around her as the RV returned to the road.

CHAPTER NINETEEN

Since they weren't working full-time jobs, The Bentleys were able to finish the album and record several more sessions for the Bentley Break. On the way back from the studio one evening, Juliet turned to Cedra.

"Since we have a short break before the next show, I was wondering if you'd go on a road trip with me?"

"I'd love to. It seems like forever since we've had time together. What did you have in mind?"

"I've rented a small cabin on a creek in Blue Ridge, Georgia. I want to show you how beautiful it is there."

"Does this include a visit to your family?" Cedra asked.

"That part I haven't decided on yet," Juliet admitted. "I'm still torn."

"So, when do we leave?"

"On Friday," Juliet answered.

"That only gives me one day to pack."

"You won't need to take a lot." Juliet grinned.

"That sounds perfect."

†

Juliet had rolled down the windows in Cedra's truck as they drove. It had turned into a beautiful day, but the air had grown cooler as they went through the mountains. "I'm glad we packed our coats," Juliet said. "The nights are still cool, and I want to take advantage of the fire pit by the creek."

"That sounds very romantic." Cedra smiled.

"There is also a fireplace in the cabin. I'm sure we'll get some use out of it too."

"I can't get over how beautiful and green everything is." Cedra spotted a roadside picnic table and slowed down. "Are you hungry?"

"I could eat."

"Ma packed egg salad sandwiches, chips, and drinks for us," Cedra replied. "This looks like a good spot." She parked the truck close to the table, which provided them a view of a fast-moving creek. They could see two fishermen out in the water just upstream.

"Great choice," Juliet said as she placed a small cooler on the table.

Cedra carried a bag with chips and a loaf of bread. "How are we on time?"

"We should arrive just in time to stop at the rental office to pick up the keys and a map to the cabin."

"I never did ask when you came up with this idea."

"I searched while you were riding back with Hank a few weeks ago."

"You managed to keep it a secret all this time?"

"It wasn't easy," Juliet commented.

They finished eating, and Cedra snapped some photos. She set up a tripod and placed Juliet with the creek in the background. She set the timer and raced over to stand beside her.

Juliet laughed as the camera took five shots in quick succession. "Wow. Let's go look."

They returned to the picnic table to review the pictures. "These came out pretty well."

"I'd like to have some of these blown up," Juliet said.

"I think I can handle that. Are you ready to hit the road?"

"Sure," Juliet answered and picked up their trash. "Let's roll."

†

"Turn here," Juliet said and pointed to a drive.

Trees covered the driveway, and when they ended, the view showed a beautiful log cabin next to a swift running creek.

"This is beautiful." Cedra looked over at Juliet, who wore a broad smile.

"I thought you might like this."

Cedra pulled up beside the cabin. "I can't wait to see the inside."

Juliet held up the keys. "Go ahead, and I'll grab our bags."

Cedra took the keys and rushed up the steps to unlock the door. She swung the door wide, and the first thing she noticed was the large stone fireplace. She walked through the cabin to the large master bedroom and bath. A deep clawfoot tub was the highlight of the bathroom. Cedra smiled at the thought of sharing a luxurious bath with Juliet. She turned and walked back through the cabin until she reached a sliding door leading to a vast deck that went beyond the bank of the creek. Cedra was leaning against the railing, looking at the stream, when she felt Juliet's arms around her waist.

"What do you think?"

"This place is gorgeous, and it's so peaceful."

"I did good, huh?"

"You did an excellent job of picking this spot. It hit me that this is the first overnight trip we've shared alone."

"I know. We should have done this sooner, but life's been so busy. We have this place for the next three days, so let's make the most of them. I brought food for supper and breakfast, but we'll need to hit a grocery store tomorrow."

"That's not a problem. What can I help with for supper?"

"You can toss a salad and set the table later. Let's just enjoy the rest of the afternoon."

"I don't have any problem with that. It's so relaxing. We could fish right off this deck," Cedra replied.

"Sorry, but I didn't pack any fishing gear this trip."

"Maybe next time we visit."

Juliet nuzzled into Cedra's neck. "I love the way you think. I need to grab the cooler and a few bags from the back of the truck. Will you join me for a drink down at the creek? That swing looks inviting."

"Did you bring beer?"

"I brought a six-pack."

"I'll have one of those with you. I think I can stand the taste again." Cedra grinned.

"Grab us a couple from the cooler."

"Do you need my help?"

"No, ma'am. I've got this."

Cedra pulled two bottles from the cooler before Juliet carried the ice chest inside. She walked over to the swing and took a seat. It was chillier by the water, so she walked back to the truck for a light jacket.

Juliet joined her on the swing and draped an arm over Cedra's shoulders. "To a great weekend," she said, tapping her bottle to Cedra's.

"Cheers," Cedra answered. "This is nice. The only sound is the trickle of water in the creek and birds singing. No traffic or construction noise."

†

The sun disappeared, and the temperature dropped quickly. "Are you hungry?"

"Yes, but I'm not starving. Are you ready to return to the cabin?"

"After grabbing my coat from the truck. It's cooling off."

They walked into the kitchen together. "I'm going out to light the fire for these," Juliet said as she lifted the lid to reveal two excellent steaks that had been marinating.

"Do you want me to go ahead and toss a salad and get it chilling?"

"If you don't mind. I've got corn, onion, and potatoes to cook on the grill."

"That sounds delicious," Cedra said. She plucked a bottle of water from the refrigerator. "Do you want another beer?"

"I think I can handle one more."

Juliet took the beer Cedra offered, walked out to check the grill, and started the fire. She returned inside to light the fire in the fireplace. "We need to take the chill off. I'll carry in more firewood, too."

"Sounds great." Cedra was busy at the sink rinsing and chopping ingredients for the salad. "Would you like a pitcher of tea?"

"That would be good. I thought about bringing a bottle of wine but decided against it since neither of us enjoys the taste."

"Sweet tea suits me just fine."

Juliet oiled and wrapped the potatoes for the grill, then sliced an onion that she placed in an aluminum pie pan with some butter. "I'll get these started and put the steaks on in a little while."

Cedra finished tossing the salad and placed it in the refrigerator to chill before putting a pot of water for tea on the stove. When Juliet came back inside, Cedra reached for her hand and led her to the fireplace. "Come get warmed by the fire."

"It is getting chilly out there," Juliet said. She sat on the hearth next to Cedra. "I didn't think it would still be this cool."

"Gives us more reasons to snuggle," Cedra said and wrapped her arms around Juliet.

"You never need a reason or excuse to snuggle with me."

"This does feel good on my back."

"Yes, it does. After eating, we should toss some pillows and a few blankets in front of the fireplace."

"I agree. I'm not complaining, but have you noticed there's no television or phone in the cabin?"

"I didn't think we wanted the disruption of either."

"You're right. It's nice to have some peace and quiet."

Juliet kissed Cedra. "I'm going to check the veggies, and if they are close enough, I'll put the steaks on."

†

"Who knew you could cook a meal like that?" Cedra teased. "That was a fantastic dinner."

"I'll agree with that. I'll clean up the kitchen if you want to change into something comfy."

"Let's do it together so it will get done quicker. Then we can make a pallet to lay on in front of the fire."

Juliet kissed Cedra and then carried the dishes to the kitchen while Cedra stored the leftovers. They rinsed the dishes and placed them in the dishwasher before walking to the bedroom to change clothes. Juliet chuckled when they undressed.

"What?"

"Who are we kidding? We don't need clothes."

"You are right. We don't," Cedra replied as she reached for Juliet. She turned off the lights as they entered the living room. The fire shed enough light for them to pull back one of the blankets before stretching out. Cedra leaned back against a pile of pillows. "This is comfortable."

"Yes, it is." Juliet was propped on her elbow and leaned down to kiss her. Her fingers trailed down Cedra's face across her chest. She noticed Cedra's nipples were erect. "Are you cold?" she asked as her hand cupped Cedra's breast.

"No, I'm just anticipating your touch and warm mouth."

Juliet smiled. "Very nice answer." Her tongue parted Cedra's lips as her fingers rolled a nipple between them. She sensed Cedra's need and kissed down to her right breast, sucking her nipple deep inside her mouth.

"Oh, yes, just like that," Cedra whispered. She gasped when Juliet opened her mouth to suck her breast.

Her hand glided between Cedra's legs to find her wet with excitement. She parted her folds and penetrated Cedra with two fingers, slowly entering and withdrawing them as Cedra's hips arched up to meet them. The pile of pillows Cedra's head was propped on was too tempting for Juliet to pass up. She slowly removed her fingers and moved her body to straddle Cedra's face with her hips.

"Yes," Cedra whispered as her hands pressed Juliet's hips down toward her waiting mouth.

Juliet's tongue replaced her fingers as she explored Cedra's wetness while Cedra caressed the bare skin between Juliet's thighs. The excitement between them was elevated, and it didn't take long for them to release an explosive orgasm. Juliet moved to sit beside Cedra.

"I'll be right back."

Cedra's eyes shone with excitement when Juliet returned carrying the Feeldoe. She watched as her lover inserted one end into her body and then positioned the tip of the toy at her entrance. Juliet's fingers guided the toy inside Cedra and turned on the vibration, handing the remote to Cedra to control the intensity.

Juliet pressed her hips into Cedra until she felt her body against her bare skin. She looked up to find Cedra biting her bottom lip. "Too much?"

"No, not at all." Cedra turned the vibration up a notch. "Love me."

Juliet began a slow rhythm, and their mouths joined in a long, deep kiss. She took her time pleasuring Cedra and elevating her own level of excitement. The vibration of Cedra's moans in her mouth made it difficult for Juliet to hold back. Cedra's hands urged deeper thrusts, and Juliet could no longer hold back. "Damn, I'm coming," she called out when she broke the kiss.

"Almost there," Cedra groaned as she thrust her hips to meet Juliet's. "Oh, yes," she cried out when her climax arrived. "Don't stop yet," she pleaded with Juliet. Cedra could feel her muscles quivering around the toy as it stretched them wide.

Juliet was nearing exhaustion when Cedra nodded and held her body still. She turned off the vibration and caressed Juliet's back. "That was fucking fantastic," Cedra whispered to Juliet. "Come lay beside me."

Juliet removed the toy and stretched out beside Cedra. She was about to speak when the room lit up, and the boom of thunder rattled the windows. The rain pelted down on the tin roof. Cedra snuggled into Juliet. "I didn't hear it begin to rain, but it sounds nice."

"I think we were both focused on something besides rain." Juliet grinned. She reached down and pulled the blanket to cover them. "I love you."

"Yes, you do, and I love you, too," Cedra replied.

The storm passed quickly, and a gentle rain continued as they fell asleep in one another's arms.

CHAPTER TWENTY

Cedra slept later than she had in months. Only her aching bladder could rouse her from her comfortable position snuggled into Juliet's warm body. She slowly turned away from Juliet and was about to stand when she heard Juliet's voice.

"Hurry back. I snuck out an hour ago."

"I must have been sleeping deep. I didn't feel you leave."

Cedra returned and snuggled under the blanket with Juliet. "That's much better."

"Come here. You're cold," Juliet said.

"It's a bit nippy outside that blanket and your warm arms."

"I'll gladly be your heater. Do you want to eat breakfast and then hit the grocery store?"

"We could do that." Cedra's hand rested on Juliet's stomach. "Have you given any more thought to visiting your family?"

Juliet turned to look at Cedra's face. "Do you really want to meet them?"

"Only if and when you're ready," Cedra said.

Juliet nodded but didn't say anything for several minutes. "I brought eggs, cheese, and ham cubes. Will you make us an omelet? I'll make the toast and drinks."

"Yes, I will. Let me grab our robes and slippers," Cedra answered. She leaned into a kiss and then walked to the bedroom. She slipped on her robe and shoes before returning. Juliet was folding the blankets and placing the pillows on the couch. "Last night was beautiful, but tonight I think we should try out the big bed."

"I won't complain," Juliet replied. She slipped into her robe and shoes. "I'd like to try out that tub, too."

Cedra smiled. "Did you bring a good razor?"

"Yes, I did. Do you need to borrow it?"

"I was thinking. Maybe you could shave me, so I can experience how it feels."

"I would be delighted," Juliet answered. "I'll go get the supplies ready while you start breakfast."

†

Juliet was smiling when she entered the bedroom. She was surprised by Cedra's request but also very excited for her to experience the sensation. It would be a new experience, too, having a lover who was clean-shaven. She checked the batteries in a small shaver and put a new blade in her razor. Juliet searched her bag and found a small bottle of baby oil to prevent razor burn. Her heartbeat was racing as she walked into the kitchen to find Cedra toiling at the stove. Juliet slipped her arms around Cedra and kissed the back of her neck.

"That looks good."

"I'm making a large one we can split if that's okay."

"That's great. I'll start some toast."

"The coffee should be ready, too," Cedra replied.

"I'll pour us a cup and pull down some plates."

"I've already dropped some toast. It won't take much longer."

Juliet pulled the toasted bread out when it popped up and dropped two more slices. She placed a piece on each plate as Cedra cut the omelet in half. She scooped up the concoction and plated the meal before carrying the plates to the table. The second round of toast popped up, and Juliet placed it on a napkin to bring it to the table.

"This is delicious," Juliet said after taking a bite. "You will have to teach me how to make these."

"I can do that." Cedra smiled at her lover's praise.

†

Juliet placed the rinsed dishes in the dishwasher and turned to Cedra. "Are you ready?"

Cedra nodded. "Yes, I am."

"Let's start in the shower then. It has a small bench you can sit on."

Juliet slipped the robe off Cedra's body, then her own. Cedra sat on the bench and watched Juliet as she knelt before her and rested back on her feet. "Last chance to change your mind."

"No, I'm sure," Cedra replied.

Juliet placed a small towel between them and spread Cedra's legs. She used the small shaver to trim Cedra as closely as possible. Her hand shook as she gently opened Cedra's lips to trim the edge. This was such a sensual experience for both. Juliet could feel moisture building inside her, and her fingertips were coated in Cedra's wetness. When she finished trimming, she filled a small bowl with warm water and used the handheld nozzle to rinse the loose hair from Cedra. Then Juliet lathered Cedra and carefully shaved Cedra's sensitive skin until she was entirely smooth. When she rinsed again, she coated Cedra's skin with baby oil.

"Tell me how it feels."

†

Cedra watched the intense concentration on Juliet's face as she trimmed her and then began to shave her clean. The gentle touch of Juliet's fingers was incredibly sensual, and Cedra felt intensely aroused. She could feel her body responding to Juliet's careful ministrations. When Juliet finished and coated her with baby oil, she investigated Cedra's face.

"Beautiful," Juliet said. She ran her thumb softly up the edge of her entrance.

Cedra reached down to feel her soft skin. "This feels so amazing." Her fingers caressed the smooth skin, and she felt her clit swell with excitement. She felt her body shudder. "Really amazing," she said and closed her eyes.

"Go ahead," she heard Juliet softly urge.

Cedra's fingers slipped into her wetness. "Oh, my goodness." The velvety moisture and the smoothness of her skin felt incredible.

"Go ahead and make it feel wonderful," Juliet whispered.

Cedra had never masturbated in front of anyone before, but the intense pleasure she was bringing herself was terrific, and it didn't take long to feel an orgasm crashing down on her. "Holy shit," she said when her body stopped quivering.

†

Juliet smiled at Cedra before leaving the shower to start drawing a bath. She dropped some bubble bath into the water and the room filled with the scent of vanilla. Juliet placed two thick towels within reach of the tub and walked over to Cedra. "Are you ready to have a nice soak?"

"Yes." Cedra walked toward the tub.

"Let me climb in first, and then you can join me." Juliet turned off the flow of the water. She stepped into the tub. "It's a bit warm, but it feels good." Juliet sat down and reached for Cedra's hand. "Would you care to join me, my love?"

Cedra climbed into the tub and nestled between Juliet's spread legs. She leaned her head back on Juliet's chest and closed her eyes. "This feels great."

Fragrant bubbles swirled around them as Juliet wrapped Cedra in her arms. "It is heavenly."

Cedra covered Juliet's hands with her own, and they relaxed in the tub until the water started to cool. "What do you say we shower and go into town to shop, then spend the rest of the day lazing around here until it's time to cook?"

"I am in total agreement with that. Let's pick up some ingredients for simple meals that won't take long to prepare."

"Some deli meat for sandwiches and some creamer for coffee," Cedra replied.

"I so totally forgot about the creamer," Juliet apologized.

"Maybe I can treat you to dinner in town tomorrow night?"

"There are several nice restaurants we could try out." Juliet nodded. "I like that idea."

"Let's get a move on then."

†

Juliet drove since she was familiar with the town. Cedra noticed Juliet had slowed down as she passed a small church. The house next to it had several cars parked in the drive. Juliet didn't make any comment and sped past the house. She gave Cedra a tour of the small town, and they picked out a restaurant for dinner the following night. They pulled into the lot of a grocery store and purchased their supplies.

"I'm kind of hungry," Juliet said. "Would you mind if we hit a drive-thru and grab some burgers and fries to take back with us?"

"Not at all," Cedra replied. "What about that one?"

Juliet nodded and pulled into the lane. "I'm thinking a double cheeseburger. What about you?"

"That does sound tasty."

Juliet placed their order at the speaker and pulled around the building. She stopped at the window to pay for her order and pick up their meals.

"Well, I declare if it isn't Juliet Tucker," the young woman working the window said when they arrived. "I hear you guys on the radio all the time. You sound great. Is that Cedra with you?"

Cedra leaned over and smiled at the young woman. "Hello."

"This is Phyllis Barnes. Phyllis, this is Cedra Tyler. Phyllis is one of my cousins. How have you been?"

"Doing all right, but not near as famous as you. Are you here to visit the family?"

"No, we're just stopping over for a relaxing weekend," Juliet answered and handed her the payment.

"We'll that's a shame. Maybe The Bentleys could come down for a show sometime," Phyllis said.

"Maybe so," Juliet answered and handed Cedra the bag.

The car behind them honked. "It was good to see you," Juliet said and pulled away.

"You, too," Phyllis called, hanging out of the drive-thru window to wave.

"That was a surprise," Cedra said.

"I had no idea Phyllis worked there," Juliet said. "This probably wasn't the best location I could have selected."

"The cabin or the burger place?"

"Both."

"That's nonsense. I love the cabin, and these burgers smell pretty darn good."

"They used to be. I ate them often in my high school years. Phyllis is not known for discretion, though, and she will probably let my family know we're in town."

"Is that really so terrible?" Cedra asked.

Juliet turned on her blinker and drove onto the lot at the small church. She looked over at Cedra. "This is my dad's church, and the house is their home."

Cedra looked at the Southern Baptist Church, and the brick house next to it, then looked back at Juliet. "Your dad is a preacher?"

"And my mother plays the organ and is the choir director," Juliet replied. "They are staunch Southern Baptists. All hellfire and brimstone."

"That explains a good deal about their reaction to our lifestyle," Cedra replied.

"I'm in no hurry to subject you to their old fashion values. I should have known better than to rent a cabin here."

"There's no need to second guess yourself. The cabin has been great, and if you don't want to visit with family, that's not an issue for me."

Juliet put the truck in gear. "Good. I just don't want to spoil our trip with their criticism. I'm not lucky enough to have a dad like Hank."

"Well, I hope you know he considers you his second daughter." Cedra reached over and covered Juliet's hand. "Let's go devour these burgers."

†

After storing their groceries and eating the burgers, Cedra and Juliet decided to spend the afternoon by the water. It was so peaceful, and the sound of the water relaxed Cedra to the point of falling asleep in Juliet's arms. When the sun began to fade, and the temperature dropped, Juliet woke Cedra, and they returned inside. Juliet started a fire in the fireplace and brought in extra wood while Cedra cooked them a spaghetti dinner.

Juliet checked her phone to find two voicemails. The first was from Keith, who was just calling to check in on them. "I think Keith misses us," Juliet teased. When the following message began to play, Juliet's smile faded. Her dad's voice was on the recording, and he said that Phyllis had told them she was in town. He wanted to invite them to church the following day and Sunday dinner on the grounds.

"No fucking way," Juliet said with a growl in her voice.

"What's wrong?" Cedra asked and rushed to her.

"Dad invited us to church and to have Sunday dinner on the grounds at the church."

Cedra took Juliet in her arms. "Just forget you even got the message. I don't need to meet your family. I've got you, and that's the only Tucker I need in my life."

"You know just what to say. Thank you. I love you so much, and I don't want them to say anything hurtful to you. They can say whatever they want to me, but I will not tolerate anyone bullying you."

"I have learned how to deal with bullies, but I will honor your request. Maybe at some other point in our life, we can meet them together, but now is not the time. We've been working hard for months and deserve our time together. We will not allow anyone to ruin it for us."

†

Sunday passed all too quickly for them. Cedra stripped the bed, piled the linens and towels, and emptied the dishwasher while Juliet loaded their bags and the cooler in the truck. They looked around the cabin to ensure they hadn't left anything behind. Juliet pulled Cedra into her arms in front of the fireplace.

"Thank you for sharing this time with me and creating memories we will cherish for years." She softly kissed Cedra.

"We will definitely revisit this place," Cedra promised. "We shared many firsts in this cabin, which will always be special to us."

Juliet sighed. "Let's drop off the keys, and then we can start for home."

"Home is wherever I am with you."

"Stop it, or you're going to make my eyes leak," Juliet warned.

Cedra took Juliet's hand, and they locked the cabin behind them.

CHAPTER TWENTY-ONE

The Bentleys were invited to tour the Jack Daniel's distillery, and afterward the head of promotions for the company met them.

"It's so great to finally meet you," Laura Phillips said as she offered her hand to Juliet. "I am a huge fan, and we are happy to be able to sponsor the band. I hope you enjoyed the tour and were able to sample a few of our products. If you follow me, I have a few things for you."

Juliet looked at Cedra and shrugged. "No idea," she whispered.

Laura led them into a conference room with a large table. In front of four chairs were a box and a denim jacket. There were names written beside each one.

"I know it's a bit warm for these jackets right now, but we teamed up with Wrangler to provide these for you."

Juliet was first to pick up a jacket and examine it. On the back panel, there was the logo for Tennessee Fire and The Bentleys embroidered across the shoulder panel. The coat was beautiful, and when she turned it around, her name was embroidered on the left. "This is beautiful. Thank you."

"You are all welcome, and in the box is a gift set with the whiskey assigned to your jackets, and a set of etched lowball and shot glasses to match. We hope one day to have a special Bentley Blend."

Keith was tickled to have the Gentleman Jack brand, Cedra had the Single Barrel, and Wayne proudly held up his Old No. 7. "I think this says, I'm a classic."

"We are excited about the show tomorrow night and hope it will be the first of many performances you grace us with," Laura told them. "I've included one of my business cards in the boxes, and I hope you will reach out if there is anything you need."

"Thank you so much for the beautiful gifts," Cedra replied. "I'm positive the coats will see much use in the coming years, and we will celebrate our performances with some of the whiskey."

"Don't be surprised if you hear some of your brands in future lyrics," Keith said. "This may prove to be a perfect inspiration."

Laura smiled. "We would love any mention of the JD brand in your music. I'll let you get settled in, and I will see you tomorrow night. I have the pleasure of introducing you at the concert, and I'm looking forward to the show."

They collected their gifts and followed Laura to the front door.

"Have a great evening, and I'll see you tomorrow."

"Thanks for everything," Cedra replied and followed her friends to the RV.

"That was totally unexpected," Keith said as he modeled his coat.

"Do we have time to drop the trailer off before we meet the others for dinner?" Juliet asked.

"Yes, we're doing great on time. Ma and Lisa Marie will meet us at the restaurant, and Riley and Mel may already be at the campground," Wayne answered. "The last text I got from Mel when we arrived at the distillery was that they were about a half hour out."

Wayne pulled up next to the bandstand, and he and Keith worked quickly to secure the trailer. A metal roof covered the entire stage, so at least it would be shaded when they set up the equipment tomorrow.

Keith's smile broadened, and they turned to see Riley and Mel walking toward them.

"This place is amazing," Juliet stated as she walked the stage.

"It's definitely a boogie-sized stage." Riley chuckled.

"Keith can do all the dancing he wants out here," Cedra said. "I know we've practiced it a few times, but I think it's time to play Chris Stapleton's 'Tennessee Whiskey' for the show tomorrow night."

Out and Loud

"That's a great idea. I think it will go over well with 'Wine, Beer, and Whiskey,'" Juliet agreed.

"This should be a great party crowd tomorrow. Laura said many of the distillery employees would also be here. Maybe we could dedicate the song to them for all their hard work." Cedra smiled and waited on a reaction from her friends.

"I think that will be perfect. We just need to decide where to plug it into the show," Keith said. "Man, I hope we can do some boogie dancing on this stage."

"Have you been practicing your moves?" Mel teased.

"Yeah, I have. I think I've got them down pat."

Riley's face lit with excitement. "That gives me an idea. Why don't we record you performing the 'Backwoods Boogie' and ask Felecia to add it to the streaming videos?"

"Hey, that's not a bad idea at all," Juliet said. "You better pick some good dancers tomorrow," she told Keith and punched him in the shoulder.

"That will be so much fun. We will need to ensure we have consent to use the video." Riley looked at Keith. "Maybe that should be a condition for anyone joining you on stage."

"We can announce that we are looking for six volunteers to join you on stage before the break and then ask them to join us backstage during the break to sign the releases," Juliet added.

"They will need to be over eighteen, too," Mel suggested.

"I love how our shows continue to evolve," Cedra said. "Each big show, we add a little more to the entertainment aspect of the performance. It appears to work well, so we need to continue dreaming up fresh ideas."

"The ideas seem to drop in out of the blue," Riley stated.

"Let's hope they keep dropping in then," Wayne said.

"Can I make a suggestion?" Keith said.

"Sure, go for it," Juliet answered.

"Let's go eat. I'm starved." Keith grinned.

†

They settled in at the campground after dinner once Ma and Lisa Marie were settled at the hotel. Keith kicked back in a recliner. "I think we should try out one of our gifts."

"What gift?" Riley asked.

"You didn't show her?" Juliet was surprised.

"Show me what?"

"When we went on the distillery tour, the manager Laura gave us gifts," Juliet said as she pulled out her coat and showed it to Mel and Riley. "We also got gift boxes with each of our flavors, and etched glasses."

"And I think we need to break open my bottle of Gentleman Jack," Keith suggested. "Grab us some cokes, Bro, and I'll get to pouring."

"Make mine light, please," Cedra requested. "I want to taste it, but the memory of New Year's Eve is still too fresh."

Mel cocked her head. "What happened on New Year's?"

"My dad and the boys made us a low-country boil, complete with a keg of beer. Keith did an excellent job making sure everyone's glass stayed full. I didn't realize how much I had drunk until it was too late," Cedra answered. "The next day wasn't a fun one. That was my first and last hangover."

Mel let out a soft laugh. "I can relate to that. Hangovers are no fun at all."

Keith prepared drinks and passed them around. "Here's your coke with a splash of Jack," he said when he handed Cedra her glass.

Wayne lifted his glass. "To our newest sponsor and their great generosity."

A chorus of "cheers" filled the RV. "Laura even mentioned The Bentleys having our own special blend one day," Keith said.

"Is anyone up for some time around the fire pit?" Wayne asked.

"Fire it up," Juliet said and took Cedra's hand.

✝

The Lynchburg show was a tremendous success, and they were on the way back to Nashville on Sunday when Juliet's phone rang.

"Carrie," she said, and answered the call. She listened for several minutes and ended the call with a fist pump. "Yes!"

"What's the good news?" Keith asked.

"We just got signed for the Gay Pride event in Ashville. It's not the biggest, but it is a great place for us to start." She smiled at Cedra. "It's in three weeks, so we'll need to start rehearsing a playlist for a Saturday night show."

"That will work out perfectly with the release of 'Out and Loud' as a single next week," Cedra responded. "I think we should debut 'Kiss You Breathless,' there too."

"I don't think Mark or Carrie will have a problem with that," Riley stated. "They love the sound of the new album. The event might also give us an opportunity for more video footage."

Juliet smiled. "It's a two-hour set, so we have a lot of planning ahead of us."

"This is going to be so much fun," Wayne said. "My family has been dying to see one of our shows."

"You think they will come to a Gay Pride event to see us?" Cedra asked.

"They will jump at the chance. I have a cousin that just came out to the family, so I'm sure he will be a driving force. They have welcomed his new partner into the family with open arms, and they are excited to meet the three of y'all."

Cedra didn't miss the flinch of pain on Juliet's face when Wayne discussed how his family welcomed a gay child into the family. She knew it sent a painful reminder of how negatively her family had reacted to her news. She reached over and covered Juliet's hand.

"This is so exciting."

"Yes, it is. We will give the crowd a show they will never forget," Juliet promised.

CHAPTER TWENTY-TWO

"I sure hope this rain blows through quickly," Keith said as they crossed into North Carolina.

"The weatherman said it was supposed to be a great weekend. You know they are never wrong," Wayne joked.

Juliet pointed through the windshield. "I see blue skies ahead, so maybe that's a good sign."

Wayne looked over at Keith. "You know we must try out some Carolina BBQ while we're here."

"I don't know if I'm ready for the mustard-based sauce." Keith wrinkled his nose. "Don't they know BBQ is red or, at best, a deep orange?"

Wayne laughed. "I'll have you whistling a different tune after supper tonight."

Cedra smiled. The guys had argued for weeks about which state had the best BBQ.

"I guess we'll find out soon, but you can't declare a winner until you've had BBQ from Alabama," Cedra said.

"Georgia, too," Juliet said.

"This is going to be fun. And tasty," Cedra said.

†

"I have to admit that was pretty good," Keith admitted. "I'm not sure I'd say as great as Kentucky BBQ, but not bad."

"One good thing is you won't go to bed hungry." Juliet punched him in the arm.

"I'm glad the rain finally pushed through. Are you ready to set up the RV?" Wayne asked.

"Absolutely, bro," Keith said.

"I can't get over how fast the night disappeared," Juliet said.

Mel smiled. "Don't forget we changed time zones. So, it's an hour ahead of our time."

"I had forgotten all about that. Thanks for the reminder. It would have been embarrassing to be late for our show," Cedra said.

"After we set up and do our sound check tomorrow, I'd like to check out the event," Juliet said. "We have plenty of time before the show."

"I've never been to a pride event," Cedra said.

"Even more, the reason to stay and have some fun." Juliet looked at the guys.

"I told my folks I'd meet them for dinner," Wayne said.

"I'll stick with you, sister." Keith smiled.

"We will, too," Mel said, and Riley nodded in agreement.

Juliet smiled at Cedra. "Why don't we call it a night?"

"Biscuits and gravy in the morning?" Cedra asked.

"Sounds good to me," Keith said. "Is it morning yet?"

"Good grief. There are cookies on the counter," Riley informed him.

"We'll see you in the morning," Juliet said, reaching for Cedra's hand.

†

Saturday morning was sunny and a bit cooler than they had expected.

"If this weather stays cool, we may get to try out our new coats," Juliet said as they stepped outside at the bandstand area.

"Brr, you aren't kidding," Cedra replied. "I think I'll grab my coat, just in case."

Keith grinned at Wayne. "We'll get warm moving all this equipment, bro."

"Let's get to it," Keith said.

After setting up, they conducted a quick soundcheck.

Wayne handed the keys to Keith. "I'm going to call for an Uber so you guys can take the RV back to the campground."

"Are you sure about that?" Juliet said.

"Yeah, I'll be back to change by six."

"Have a great time," Cedra said.

"You, too. Keep this one out of trouble." Wayne slapped Keith on the back.

"No pressure there," Riley teased as she slipped an arm inside Keith's.

Keith locked the RV, and they walked toward the park's center. Men and women of all shapes, sizes, colors, and ages wandered through the booths. Juliet took Cedra's hand in hers.

Juliet lifted Cedra's hand to her mouth and kissed it. "This feels right," she said.

"Yes, it does. I've never seen so many of our kind of people in one place before."

Juliet smiled. "This is a small event compared to some of the others. I like the setting for this one best, though."

"It is beautiful with all the trees and flowers," Cedra said.

"Oh, hell yeah," Keith called out. "Funnel cakes."

"I swear you must have a hollow leg or two," Riley teased. "Go, get one for me and Mel to split, too, please."

"Cedra and Juliet?" he asked.

Cedra nodded. "Yes, please."

Juliet wiped the powdered sugar from Cedra's lips and kissed them softly. "I knew you were sweet, but even more so today." She took her hand, and they walked to the next booth. Juliet noticed Cedra admiring a silver bracelet. Juliet nodded to the vendor. She picked up the bracelet and handed it to Juliet. "Let's see how this looks." She placed the bracelet around Cedra's left wrist. "It fits like it was made for you."

The vendor winked at Cedra and handed her an identical bracelet. "They are a matched pair just like the two of you."

Cedra placed the bracelet on Juliet's arm and smiled at the vendor. "We'll take them." She handed her a credit card.

"Let's barter instead."

Cedra looked confused.

"I'm looking forward to your show tonight. I'll trade you these bracelets for a couple of CDs and T-shirts for my wife and me."

"Are you sure?" Juliet asked.

"Positive. We love your music and what you are doing for our community. We saw you in Lynchburg and enjoyed the show."

"What size shirts?" Juliet asked.

"A medium and a large," the woman answered. "I'm Beth, and my wife is Cindy. She went in search of some coffee for us. It's odd that the weather is this cool. It must have been the rain that moved through last night."

"Could you call her and ask her to bring two more?" Juliet asked.

"Sure, that won't be a problem."

"Will you stay and browse a few minutes? I'll be right back," she told Cedra.

"Yes, that's not a problem. I'll wait right here."

"I'll hurry," Juliet said and kissed her cheek.

"Love you," Cedra said.

"I love you more." Juliet grinned. She turned and jogged away.

"You two are adorable together."

"Juliet is the best thing that's ever happened in my life. Right from the start, I knew she was something special."

"That is so sweet."

"Oh, my God," a woman spoke as she walked up. "Are you seriously Cedra Tyler?" the woman asked.

Beth smiled at Cedra. "This is my wife, Cindy."

"I had no idea why you wanted the extra coffees," Cindy said as she placed the drinks on a table. She held her hand out to Cedra. "It is such a pleasure to meet you."

"Likewise," Cedra answered. "We are in the process of bartering with your wife for a set of matching bracelets."

"We?"

"Juliet will be right back."

"I'm sorry to be totally fangirling right now, but we love you guys," Cindy said with a blush rising.

"Come have a seat with us and enjoy your coffee," Beth said.

"Thanks," Cedra answered and walked around the table to take a seat.

"I brought several kinds of sweetener and creams," Cindy said. She opened a small bag to empty the contents on the table.

"This is perfect," Cedra said and picked up French vanilla creamer for her and Juliet.

They were sipping coffee and chatting when Juliet returned with an armful of goodies. "Sorry, I couldn't find a bag." She placed the stack on a table. "Hello," she said to Cindy.

Beth's eyes grew wide at the delivery Juliet made. "This looks like more than we discussed."

"Well. It's CDs, a poster, and a couple of T-shirts. It's cool today, so I brought a short and long-sleeved one for each of you." Juliet smiled. "I still think we got the better end of the deal."

"It's a great trade," Beth said as she held up the long-sleeved shirt. "I know what I'm wearing later today."

"This is incredible," Cindy stammered.

Cedra handed Juliet the coffee. "Thanks. That smells delicious."

"It tastes good, too," Cedra said.

"Do you travel to many of the Pride events?" Juliet asked.

Beth nodded. "As many as we can. Cindy is a schoolteacher, so she has the summer months off. I work on jewelry year-round, so we have plenty of items to offer for sale."

"She also has a lucrative online store. Beth is incredibly talented," Cindy praised.

"We can tell." Juliet raised her arm to show off the bracelet. "These were perfect for us."

"Where do you call home?" Cedra asked.

"Florence, Alabama," Beth answered. "We've got a small farm. A few acres, a nice workshop for me, and a garden plot for Cindy. We grow vegetables, and what we can't eat or can, we sell at the local Farmer's Market."

"That's like my candy store in Nashville," Juliet said. "We usually spend hours shopping there during the season."

"Someone loves all the free samples. It's kind of like grazing through the market," Cedra teased.

When they finished the coffee, they swapped business cards. "We may decide to play a few more pride events, so we may see you down the road. Give us a call if you're going to be in the Nashville area."

"Likewise, if you're near Florence, give us a holler," Beth said.

"Thank you for the bracelets," Cedra replied.

"Thank you for all the goodies," Cindy answered. "We look forward to the show tonight."

"Speaking of which, we'd better get a move on if we're going to check out any other vendors," Juliet told Cedra. "It was great to meet you. See you later."

Juliet slipped her hand inside Cedra's as they walked through the park. As they passed another food vendor section, Keith hollered out.

"There you are. I thought we'd lost you," he said, waving a giant turkey leg in the air.

"I'm not surprised to find you camped out in the food section," Juliet teased. "We're going to finish walking through the park and then head back to the RV."

"We'll meet you there," Riley replied. "We can head back to the campground and get ready for the show."

†

The crowd roared to life when Juliet sang "Out and Loud." They were on their feet, dancing and singing along with her. After they had taken their break, Cedra turned to the audience. "I know this is a bit premature since our album *Out and Loud* hasn't been released yet, but we all want to share another song off the album with you. It's called 'Kiss You Breathless.'"

Juliet started to play, and the rest of the band joined in. Juliet locked eyes with Cedra as they sang the first verse and then turned to the audience. Smiles beamed back at her as they wove their magic through their words. She watched couples as they kissed or draped an arm across their lover's shoulder as they listened to the song. This was the perfect place to debut the song.

Juliet pulled out her harmonica and began to play the beginning of "Midnight in Nashville" when several loud booms filled the air.

That was not fireworks, Juliet thought as the crowd fell to the ground and people began screaming. *Those were gunshots.* Juliet raced across the stage and lunged forward to protect Cedra with her body. She lost her footing and struck her arm, then her head, on the keyboards. Juliet felt intense pain in her left arm, and the warm trickle of blood ran down her cheek. Her heart was pounding as she looked at Cedra and then at Keith and Wayne. The boys were crouched down, and Cedra stared back at her.

Cedra reached for Juliet's face. "You're hurt," she cried out.

"I'll be okay," Juliet promised.

Keith and Wayne rushed over to them and saw the blood running down Juliet's face. Keith grabbed a bandana in his back pocket and wrapped it around Juliet's forehead to stop blood flow with pressure.

"Is everyone else, okay?" Riley asked as she rushed onto the stage.

Cedra nodded. Her heart pounded in her chest, but she was not harmed. Juliet was holding her left arm against her body. Cedra feared it was broken.

When the crowd's screaming died, Juliet walked back on stage. Hundreds of scared eyes stared back at her. "I am sorry for the interruption, but I'm happy everyone is okay."

"But you're hurt," someone yelled from the crowd.

"I will be fine. We will close the show out early, but I want to end it with this song. It says it all, for you and us."

The band played "Out and Loud" again as a finale to the show. Riley had called for an ambulance, and the EMTs were waiting backstage when the song was over. Blood had soaked through the bandana, and her arm was throbbing, but Juliet still wore her smile.

"I'm riding to the hospital with her," Cedra announced.

"We will pack up here. Call us when you can to let us know which hospital," Wayne said.

"She will be taken to Mission Hospital. She will probably need some stitches and treatment for a broken arm." The female EMT smiled. "She's going to be just fine, so relax. She's in good hands."

"Will you not use the sirens?" Juliet asked. "I think the crowd has had enough trauma for one night."

"What happened here tonight?" Wayne asked.

The male EMT looked at Wayne. "A truckload of skinheads thought it would be fun to drive through the park and fire off an assault rifle. Luckily, they shot in the air, so no one was shot, but there were injuries in the panicked crowd."

"We had several ambulances staged nearby in case there was trouble, and we were lucky enough to catch your call. We love your music," the woman said.

"Thanks," Juliet said. She refused to lie on a stretcher and climbed the ambulance steps with assistance.

Cedra scrambled up the steps, and the door was closed behind them. She looked back through the window at Keith's shocked face and reached for Juliet's hand as she sat beside her.

"Let's get a better pressure wrap on that head of yours," Sheila, the EMT said. "The splint will keep your arm secure but try not to move it too much. I can't believe you went back on stage and sang a song."

"I had to. We had to. We needed to send a message to fans that we are strong and will continue to be our authentic selves for all of us," Juliet said. "It probably wasn't my greatest performance of the song, but it felt like the strongest I ever have sung for a crowd."

"Listen. I know you wanted to be strong back at the park, but we will be in big trouble if you're not secured on a gurney when we reach the hospital. Protocols, you know."

"All right, but can I at least sit up?"

"Yes, you can," Sheila answered. "Is she always this stubborn?"

"Oh, yeah," Cedra remarked. "I love every stubborn bone in her body."

"Even the broken ones?" Juliet asked.

Cedra looked at the air splint on Juliet's arm. "Even the broken ones." She looked at Sheila. "She was trying to protect me from the gunshots. She shielded me with her body to make sure I was safe."

Juliet laughed and immediately regretted her actions when she grimaced in pain. "In the future, remind me to move the keyboard first."

"I hope there will never be another incident, but I know you will be there to protect me at all costs."

"Yes, I will." Juliet allowed Sheila to position her on the gurney in a seated position as Cedra held her hand.

†

Three hours later, Cedra walked out to find the rest of the crew in the waiting area.

"How's Juliet?" Keith asked.

"She's going to be okay. She got three stitches above her eye but no signs of a concussion. X-rays revealed a broken left arm. They will keep her in an air splint for now, and she will need to be iced for the next few days until the swelling subsides. Once the swelling decreases, she will be in a cast for six to eight weeks. I'll need to get her an appointment with an orthopedic doctor when we get home."

Riley saw the exhaustion in Cedra's face. "How are you?"

"Relieved now that I know she will be okay."

"We got everything packed up in record time, and the RV is outside," Wayne said. "Carrie called to check on everyone and has us three rooms reserved at a hotel just down the street for the next two nights."

Cedra looked at Mel. "Will that interfere with your work schedule at the hospital?"

Mel shook her head. "I already swapped my shift on Monday for one later in the week."

"Great. I feel more comfortable knowing we have someone with medical experience." Cedra looked at the rest of the group. "Is everyone okay?"

"Yeah, just a little frazzled by the events tonight," Keith said. "It galls me how stupid people behave sometimes."

"I know, but the outcomes could have been much worse."

"The cops were on the job tonight. They had the men trapped and in custody within four blocks of the park. I hope they put them under the jail," Wayne said with anger in his voice. "It was all so senseless."

"I agree. Juliet will be released in just a few minutes. Can you bring the RV around?"

"I'm on it," Keith said.

"I can't believe I'm saying this, but I'm hungry," Cedra said.

"We'll hit a drive-thru on the way to the hotel. I doubt anything is open for deliveries," Wayne replied.

Cedra nodded. "See what you can find on our route, please. I'm going to check on Juliet. When I left the room, she was arguing with the nurse about riding in a wheelchair."

"Good luck with that," Riley teased.

"Will they release her with enough pain medication for a day or two?" Mel asked.

"That's what we are waiting on. For them to be delivered from the pharmacy. I don't think it will be much longer."

Cedra returned to the room, and Juliet smiled at her with a goofy smile. The pain medications had kicked in, and she felt loopy. "I'm all set." She held up a bag. "Are you ready to break me out?"

"I think we'll take the easy route. Keith has pulled the RV around, and we have hotel rooms for the next two nights, courtesy of Carrie."

The nurse handed Cedra discharge orders and instructions for icing for the next 24 hours. "She may not feel much tonight. We gave her a good dose of the pain medications, but when those wear off, it will be a different story."

"Thank you. One of our friends is a nurse, so I'm sure she will be a great help."

"I'm sorry this happened, but it was a pleasure to meet you both."

"Thanks. Ready to roll?" Cedra asked Juliet.

"Yes. Giddy up," Juliet slurred.

†

Once they were loaded in the RV, Wayne turned to Cedra. There's an all-night place next door, so while you all get settled in, Keith and Riley will make a food run."

"Is two people enough to carry back everything Keith will order?" Cedra teased.

"If not, we'll make two trips," Riley answered.

†

They were lucky to get three adjoining rooms. With Keith's and Riley's help, Cedra was able to get Juliet onto the bed.

"All you need to do is knock on either door. We'll come to help," Riley said.

"That's comforting to know," Cedra replied.

"Wayne can bring in the rest of the bags. I'll get an ice pack set up if you'll get Juliet ready for bed," Mel instructed. "Keith and Riley are making the food run."

Cedra found a large sleepshirt in Juliet's bag to slip over her head and removed her shirt and bra. Juliet's boots and jeans came off easier than Cedra expected. "There, can you sit up in the bed? I'll grab some extra pillows to prop your arm with."

Juliet sat with her back to the headboard, and Cedra raided closets to get extra pillows. She pulled the bed linens up to her waist as they waited for Mel to return. Wayne dropped off another bag for Cedra.

"What else can I do?" he asked.

"Grab a bath and hand towel from the bathroom. Mel will need those when she puts the ice pack on."

"Got it," Wayne said.

Mel knocked on the door adjoining the rooms, and Wayne let her in. "Sorry, finding the ice machine took a few minutes." She looked at Juliet. "She's propped up nicely, and I see you've got a towel underneath her arm. Good job."

Wayne handed her the hand towel to wrap the ice pack with.

Mel took the towel. "We'll start with fifteen minutes, but if it feels like too much, let me know."

"I will," Juliet said. Her speech wasn't slurred like before. "It hurts like a mother."

"We can't give you more pain medicine for an hour, but the ice should help. You need to eat something, too," Mel instructed. "Pain meds on an empty stomach is not a pleasant thing." She wrapped the ice pack on Juliet's arm gently.

Keith and Riley returned carrying a box and bags of food just as Mel removed the ice pack.

"That was perfect timing," Cedra replied. "Thanks for getting food. I'm starved."

"We tried to get a little bit of everything," Riley said as she set food on the desk. "We got some finger foods, too."

"Cheese sticks and chicken fingers?" Juliet asked with a lopsided grin.

"Of course. With honey mustard dipping sauce," Keith answered.

"You are so awesome," Cedra said. "Which do you want first?"

"Both," Juliet answered. "What do we have to drink? Any cold beers left?"

"That's where I draw the line. No beer." Mel shook her head.

Juliet sighed. "Party pooper."

Cedra used the tray for the ice bucket for Juliet's food. "Soda or water?"

"Water, I guess."

Cedra bit into a juicy bacon cheeseburger and let a moan escape. She watched the frown form on Juliet's face. She leaned over to her and offered her a bite. "Trade you a bite for a cheese stick."

Juliet took a bite of the burger. "Damn, that's good."

Keith chuckled. "It just so happens that we bought extras." He handed a burger to Cedra.

"Take it slow on that burger," Mel warned.

Cedra offered her a bite. "You heard the boss."

Juliet smiled. "I love that you are feeding me." She closed her eyes as Cedra wiped a dab of ketchup from the corner of her mouth.

"For as long as you need me," Cedra promised.

"It's getting mushy in here. Is it okay if I drop by to ice again in an hour from now?" Mel asked. "I think one more will be good for tonight. We can start back up in the morning."

"I can't promise I will still be awake," Juliet replied after swallowing.

"That's okay. Sleep when you can. I'll be gentle and try not to wake you."

Cedra smiled. "Thanks for everything, Mel."

"I'm happy to help. I just wish it wasn't necessary."

"We'll head out to let you get some rest. You, too," Wayne told Cedra.

Cedra looked at Juliet, who was beginning to nod off. She woke her long enough to stretch out on the bed and prop her arm on the pile of pillows. "Thanks."

"I'll see you in a bit. If she wakes up when I come to ice, we'll give her more pain meds if she needs them," Mel assured Cedra.

CHAPTER TWENTY-THREE

Juliet was allowed to leave the bed the next day only to use the restroom. Cedra doted on her all day while the others played tourist. After breakfast in bed, Cedra snuggled into Juliet as they watched a movie.

Cedra called Ma to let her know they would be another day before returning home, and called to make a doctor's appointment for Juliet. Keith and the gang brought several large pizzas back for dinner.

"Not as good as the pizza at the Pub in Knoxville, but still pretty tasty," Keith admitted.

"We'll get us packed up early in the morning," Wayne said. "I think we're all ready to be home."

"I'll second that," Juliet said. "I've enjoyed the extra special attention from Cedra and Mel, but I'm ready to be back at Ma's. In our own bed, eating Ma's cooking. Just home."

"Careful. That would make a great country song," Wayne said.

"That's another thing. I can't play for a couple of weeks, but I can still write and sing. I don't want us to have to cancel shows because of this," Juliet said as she lifted her arm.

"You have a doctor's appointment Wednesday. You'll get a cast for a few weeks if everything looks good."

"We don't have another date for two weeks until the Auburn show, so you'll have plenty of time to recuperate. We can pick up the slack with guitar, and maybe you'll be able to play harmonica with a cast. The show will go on," Keith teased.

"How are you feeling tonight?" Mel asked.

"Good. I haven't taken any pain medication all day."

"That's great news. It looks like the ice is helping, too," Mel replied.

"Keith and I will get us loaded after we eat a good breakfast in the lobby. I hear they have biscuits and gravy planned for tomorrow."

Cedra placed a hand on his arm. "That sounds like a perfect plan, Wayne. I'll have us packed early once we are up and moving around."

"Thank you all for taking such good care of me," Juliet said.

"We must take good care of our sexy lead vocalist," Keith teased. "I'll see you all in the morning.

"Goodnight, everyone," Cedra said as they headed to their rooms.

†

Cedra drove Juliet to her appointment on Wednesday. She received an excellent report from the doctor and was sent to the casting lab to have a cast applied. Cedra's phone rang just as they were leaving the exam room. She looked at the phone and then at Juliet.

"Go, I can handle this part on my own."

"I'll wait for you in the lobby," Cedra said and walked away to answer the call from Carrie. "Hey, Carrie. Yes, Juliet got a good report from the doctor. The bone is in perfect alignment, and the swelling is down enough to allow her arm to be cast."

Cedra took a seat and listened as Carrie informed her that she had received a call from the Asheville police about pressing charges. Carrie told her that if Juliet wanted, they could add assault with a deadly weapon to the four men in the truck. They would all face prison for the other charges, but assault would add a few more years to their sentence.

"Juliet and I have already discussed it, and she suggested they not add the additional charges."

Carrie remained silent for several long seconds. "If you're sure that's what she wants, I'll let them know."

"I will ask her again when she finishes getting her cast, and we'll give you a call." Cedra ended the call and waited for Juliet. She smiled when the door opened, and

Juliet walked through sporting a rainbow-colored cast. "That is so you." Cedra reached for her hand, and they walked out into a glorious fall morning.

"So, what did Carrie want?"

"She wanted to know if you wanted to press charges against the men for assault with a deadly weapon."

Juliet looked at Cedra with tears in her eyes. "They caused a lot of harm and terror with their behavior. I get angry when I think about it. But, on the other hand, they were stupid drunk men, two of them with kids, that made deplorable decisions. They will do time for the other charges, so I can't see adding to the anguish of their families. Some people might not agree, but I think it's the right thing to do."

Cedra lifted Juliet's hand to her lips and kissed it. "I agree with you one hundred percent. At first, I hoped they would be tossed in jail forever for hurting you, but I hate to think of their families suffering because of that."

"We need to move on and hope that our actions might inspire change and acceptance by more people. We love whom we love, and that should be all that matters."

Cedra handed Juliet the phone. "Call Carrie to confirm your decision and let her know we are still on for the Auburn show."

Juliet nodded. "You know this experience has inspired some new song lyrics, and I hope you will help me create a few."

Cedra looked at Juliet. "I love writing with you, and our songwriting together has only just begun."

"I love you," Juliet declared.

"I love you more," Cedra answered and started her truck for the drive home.

ABOUT THE AUTHOR

Ali Spooner

Ali Spooner lives in beautiful northwest Florida with several fur babies. Ali's writing began as a hobby, and with the assistance of the Affinity Rainbow Publishing team has advanced her love of storytelling to a new level.

Ali's characters are primarily everyday people, from cowgirls to psychics. Ali also has created a few supernatural characters in her paranormal series. Several of her twenty-plus books have been Amazon-rated number one choices and always include a happily ever after. Ali's hobbies include photography, reading, travel, college sports, and spending time with family and friends.

OTHER AFFINITY BOOKS

<u>Undercover Love</u> by Annette Mori
When the domestic terrorist cell Emma Schmidt has infiltrated summons her to an abandoned warehouse for a loyalty test, Emma immediately recognizes the battered woman. Emma must act fast to protect her cover and save the woman, Jimena Aguilar, she's never forgotten.
Emma and Jimena team up on a dangerous mission to take down the terrorist cell and save the life of the popular California governor.
Will this lead them back to the closeness they once shared or have the years in between hardened their hearts to love.

<u>Changing Times</u> by Jen Silver
Thirty years on from when we first met Dani Barker and Camila Callaghan in *Changing Perspectives*, they're enjoying marriage and semi-retirement in a luxury flat near London.
Dani's niece, Holly, runs their mixed media business, now

gaining a foothold in the highly competitive online games market. Holly's older sibling, Luc, influences people to take action on climate issues with their website, Gaia One: One Earth, One Chance.

Romance has been in short supply for both Holly and Luc. Immersed in her work, Holly's dating life is non-existent. For Luc, family prejudices stand in the way of a relationship with the love of their life.

Can Holly and Luc succeed in making the changes necessary to achieve their own happy ever afters?

Midnight in Nashville by Ali Spooner
The Bentleys have successfully finished cutting their first album, *Six Strings and a Dream.* When the Covid-19 epidemic hits, tours and live performances are cancelled as the world goes into lockdown. With the closing of the restaurant, employment for the band members has been severely impacted. The group comes together to make life work at Ma Bentley's Boarding House. They take advantage of their down time and use of the studio to record more songs. Cedra has challenged each of her bandmates to create a song for their next album. Juliet's song, "Midnight in Nashville," is chosen as the title track. Join the group as they venture into new marketing avenues and create their first music video for the title track.

Compound Interest by Annette Mori
The kick-ass women in The Organization are back and they have their sights set on a few new recruits. Not everyone is

jumping for joy at the choices, considering subterfuge is front and center in the games the new recruits have been playing.

Dani is supposed to get her happily ever after, but she's not sure what's real anymore including Candy's feelings for her. When a new enemy takes Candy captive, Dani vows to uncover the truth by insisting on going on the mission to save her. Candy is not what she seems, and that presents a new set of complications for Dani and her feelings.

The Organization continues to have challenges when those damn book magicians and book witches keep popping back in to warn them of new catastrophes on the horizon. She doesn't have time for their warnings, until their enemies intersect once again to keep them working together.

From award-winning author, Annette Mori, find out what happens in this final chapter of the combined *Asset Management/Book Addict* series.

Six Strings and a Dream by Ali Spooner
Cedra Tyler's dream of becoming a songwriter in Nashville was put on hold due to her mother's failing health. When the time came for Cedra to start her journey, she left her home in south Alabama with a heavy heart.

Arriving at Ma Bentley's boarding house, meeting her housemates, also fledgling musicians, she feels the warmth she was missing since leaving home.

Her housemates realize Cedra's talent as a song writer and begin to gel as a group. The pain and loss she had experienced added a layer of emotion and longing in her lyrics unusual for someone of her age.

They form a band, The Bentleys, named after Ma who is much more than a landlord to them all. Cedra falls for bandmate Juliet, and that inspires her creativity even more. Will The Bentleys achieve their dream of making it big in Music City? Has Cedra found her forever in the arms of Juliet?

Trouble in Paradise-Trophy Wives Club book 4 – Ali Spooner & Annette Mori

The gang from the Trophy Wives Club is back. This time they're taking their fun to a new and exciting location. The club's future is looking bright, and as a thank you, Lindy rewards the crew with an all-expenses paid trip to paradise over the holidays. Soon after arriving on the island, an attractive stranger catches the eye of more than one person in their tight-knit group, but Lindy is especially intrigued. Could Angel Dubois, the owner of an all-woman financial planning company be the answer to Lindy's crushing feelings of loneliness? Along with fun in the sun, the gang navigates treacherous waters to ring in the New Year.

Georgetown Glen by Annette Mori

Lucy Manetti is positively euphoric over her recent purchase of an old ghost town. Unfortunately, she failed to consult with her wife, Bea, before buying the abandoned village. Predictably, Bea is not as enamored with transforming the ghost town into a sapphic retirement community, but Bea's love for her wife trumps her displeasure over Lucy's impulsiveness. The mature couple hires Fiona, an expert at restoring old houses, and Saville, a certified electrician, to bring the ghost town back to its glory days.

According to the adorable real estate agent who recommended the pair, Fiona and Saville have *history*. Lucy detects a spark between the two young women and decides, against the advice of her wife, to play matchmaker, bringing her beautiful niece into the mix. As the ragtag team begins their work on the old saloon, they discover a lot more than they bargained for, including ghosts, long-buried secrets, an abused golden retriever, and maybe even love.

Affinity
Rainbow Publications

eBooks, Print, Free eBooks

Visit our website for more publications available online.

https://affinityebooks.com/

Published by Affinity Rainbow Publications
A Division of Affinity eBook Press NZ LTD
Canterbury, New Zealand

Registered Company 2517228